Annie on a Bun

A.L. Duncan

About the Author

A.L. Duncan is an American storyteller who writes literature of various genres for the women-loving-women and sapphic communities. Her main character will always be a woman who loves women. A 2015 Golden Crown Literary Finalist for Debut Author, a 2015 Rainbow Awards Runner-Up for *Secrets of Angels*, and a 2017 Rainbow Awards Honorable Mention for her Short Story/Poetry Anthology. She considers herself a poet and artist who just happens to write stories. Her writing weaves tales of common themes of personal struggles and triumphs mixed, at times, with ancient myths or modern spiritualties. She lives in Cincinnati, Ohio with her partner of sixteen years.

Annie on a Bun

A.L. Duncan

BELLA BOOKS
2022

Bella Books, Inc.
P.O. Box 10543
Tallahassee, FL 32302

Printed in the United States of America on acid-free paper.

First Edition - 2022

Editor: Ellie Nalle
Cover Designer: Heather Honeywell
Cover Art Work by ALESIA

ISBN: 978-1-64247-395-7

Acknowledgment

I have a host of folks I must thank for this wonderfully fun book to have come together as it did. Besides Annie, I must thank Tim, Scott, Bones, Pork and Beans, and Potato. Friends, family, and four-legged companions are our best assets in making a life lived so valued. Every day we have can never be replaced. I am thankful. My heart is full of love for you all. And to Karen, for all that you are in my life, you are the biggest gift.

Dedication

A big shout out to Annie. Thank you for your name, kindness, warm heart, and interest in making humanity a little sweeter with your smile.

CHAPTER ONE

Every other day, Annie would walk or swim with her elderly landlady's dogs. The sprite Chihuahua mix, Saqi, made the perfect companion to the rescued beagle-bird dog mix named Bones. Bones always seemed to enjoy giving her rusty joints a stretch. Such time with them both gave Annie an excuse to start her day out with a smile. Today was a pool day. Saqi paddled around in an inner tube chasing his ball while Annie joined Bones in a chase for several tennis balls that had splashed into the water. A wide-eyed game for them both, as Annie attempted to grab a ball with her teeth too.

Before visiting her father, Annie decided it was always a good idea to mentally prepare herself. Today, she walked through the downtown to the city's carousel. There, she drank a coffee by the river and watched the barges go by while listening to the faint pipe organs of the spinning carousel. She drove her tiny, yellow, electric Smart Fortwo across town as clouds bore down, torturing the streets with endless sheets of rain.

"Why does it always rain on my day off, dammit?"

While stopped at an intersection, Annie blared the volume on the song, "Bad to the Bone" and met the smug smirk of a man in a towering SUV. He clearly was not appreciating her choice of vehicle. She pulled away, flipped him the finger, and continued headbanging.

When visiting her ailing father, Annie would drive to the local suburban farmer's market and pick up his favorite handmade rosemary and olive oil bread and a handful of local fresh fruit. On this occasion, she picked up some strawberries. She also added in a bonus bag of black licorice. It wouldn't hurt to butter him up a bit. She never knew where she stood with her father. He was either warm and pleasant or bitterly cold and contemptible. In the car, Annie scanned through chapters of a book on dementia for caretakers at more stoplights on the way.

It was closer to lunch by the time she got there, but her father always made breakfast. It was his favorite meal. She stepped in from the garage and received his usual gruff greeting, along with his Dobermann's bombardment of hysterical jumping, tackling, and rambunctious joy at her presence.

"Sit down. Breakfast is ready." Her father placed a plate of scrambled eggs and potatoes on the table in front of her. "Gunny, go lay down."

Gunny leapt at Annie's bag in an attempt to disarm her. Missing her as she twisted and sidestepped, he hurled himself into the living room empty-mouthed. His expression was hardly one of defeat. She knew not to feel cocky just yet. She laid the market bag on the counter and handed Gunny a big bone. He was so excited.

"Lucky for you, I happened to stop at the pet store," she said.

Her father poured himself a drink. "He'll bury it. I'll find it in a day or two stuck inside the cushions."

"Yes. But I've seen his eyes when he finds it and hands it to you. So proud of himself."

Her dad scoffed a laugh.

Annie placed the fruit in his fridge. "I found your favorite licorice. Thought you might enjoy it over a ball game or something."

"The Reds lost yesterday. They're on a bye today."

"Well, you can enjoy it later watching the Pirates get stomped on by someone."

"You getting fat again?" he asked, poking at her belly.

"No. It's probably the shirt."

The dutiful charge of being a good daughter always put Annie in a less-than-obedient mood to honor thy father and mother. With a churning gut and mixed feelings, Annie sucked in her sore feelings and took a seat at the table.

He offered her a demeaning snuff, his go-to reply to most things.

She'd tired of trying to convince her dad she was doing well in her life, happy with most days. On other days she still noticed the scars on her forearms and chest, abuse from a previous lover who had an affinity for kitchen knives. Then, there were moments she wished she had more time to enjoy those brief glimpses of ease, of satisfaction, of being in her element. Moments with her dad certainly put a crimp in things—the instinct to always be Daddy's little girl had gotten harder as she'd grown older and his derailing criticisms became harsher. She was used to changing the subject.

Annie poked at her eggs. "How was your lunch with Scott yesterday?"

"Your brother never showed up. Never called." Her father stabbed at a piece of meat. "I called him later and he gave me some damn excuse about being caught up with fixing something in his house."

"You're kidding me."

"He doesn't give a shit. Nobody gives a shit."

Annie scoffed. "Hello. I'm here."

Her dad set his fork down and applauded her before returning to his eggs.

That did it. Annie felt her being unhinge. "You know, I could leave."

"I don't care."

"I don't have to be here. I came because I wanted to. I actually wanted to spend a little time with you. If you're asking for a pity party, you'll have to do it alone. I don't party anymore. It's bad for my complexion. I break out over soap opera melodrama and end up looking like four-day-old Chinese takeout. I can't help you when you're like this. And it's not right that you should take it out on me."

Silence.

Annie was shaking. She hated talking back to her dad. It had taken years to find her voice and even longer to feel confident enough to use it. She picked at her food and sipped the organic orange juice he always bought just for her visits.

Small boxes of pens, letters, bills, and junk spilled over each other, with only enough space for the two of them to eat. His house was a mess of clutter she was never allowed to touch or toss. In fact, he never threw anything away that he considered useful or repairable. And in his mind, he could repair or use just about anything.

"How's your breakfast?" he asked.

"Good."

"Yeah?"

"Mm-hmm. It's…really good. I like the green peppers with the potatoes."

Annie slipped into her car seat, closed the door, and moaned with relief as she leaned her head against the steering wheel. The drops of rain on the windshield soothed her tension and hid her face from her dad's figure at the door. She returned his wave before heading out.

* * *

The supermarket was always a mix of education and disinterest. Exotic and ugly fruit. Wilted lettuce, wrinkly poblanos, overripe avocados, and underripe bananas. New labels for GMO-free snacks dried with inorganic seasoning. Energy tea bottles with a hidden one-percent alcohol content.

"Oh, I wouldn't drink that," Annie said as she watched a pregnant mother of a frantic, screaming toddler pull one of the bottles off the shelf. "In your condition, I mean. Did you know it has alcohol in it?"

The mother barely acknowledged her. "Do you want your milk?" she cooed quietly to her little boy. "Do you?" A silver cross dangled from her neck as she bent over into the cart and pulled an airline bottle of brandy out of her purse. She masterfully opened the kid's bottle with one hand as she twisted the top off the brandy with her teeth, pouring it into his milk with her other hand. The top was replaced, the bottle shook, and it all took less than a minute.

"Helps him sleep," she insisted to Annie. "Doesn't it, sweetie? We all want to sleep later, don't we, hmm?" The woman snatched up three more bottles of the energy tea before disappearing down the aisle of baby food.

"Walk away, Annie," she told herself. "You are not going to 12-Step an infant."

Once Annie had gotten home, the clouds cleared, allowing the June day to be drenched with plenty of sunshine. Annie placed a handful of daisies she bought from the grocery store in a ball jar and stuck it on her kitchen table. Pork and Beans leapt up to the open window and purred for her to stroke their heads, and joined Annie for a big sniff at the fresh air. She decided to distract herself with some good old-fashioned chores to escape the feeling of angst, which always settled in after a visit with her dad.

With her earbuds in, she mowed the yard with much palooza, wiggling to all her favorites. Afterward, she relaxed in her inflatable kiddie pool with a glass of Tang, enjoying the quiet of her small backyard, limbs dangling over the top the puffy plastic.

She felt a shadow loom over her. Something had cut off the warm sun from her face. She opened her eyes to spy the goofy smile of her landlady.

"Oh. Hi, Mrs. Winkle."

"Hello, dear."

Annie raised her sunglasses to get a better squint at the woman filled with halos from blocking the sun. "Is everything all right?"

"I'm so sorry to bother you."

"You're not bothering me."

"It's such a beautiful day, isn't it?"

"Yes, it is." Annie started to roll out of her kiddie pool, and soon understood why toddlers looked so awkward standing up from those limp rubber tubes. It's a perfectly natural position to have your butt up in the air as you attempt to find your feet after hitting the grass. Mrs. Winkle handed her a towel.

"Thank you."

"I'm so glad the sun came out and warmed things up. Oh, I used to sunbathe all the time."

Annie dried herself off with a towel. "I bet you had a beautiful tan."

"Oh, yes. My grandmother was an Indian through and through."

"Was she, now?"

"She wasn't very good at catching a foul ball. But she loved sitting in the stadium when the team was playing the Pirates. Got the best tans in the northeast seats."

"I see. You do know the Indians changed their name, right?"

"Yes. What a shame to choose a name like the Radicals."

Annie shook her head. "The Guardians. They're the Guardians."

"What kind of name is that?" Mrs. Winkle wrinkled her nose. "What's to guard in Cleveland, for God's sake? Lake water? Akron? They would have done better with a name like the Rebels."

"Mrs. Winkle?"

"Hmm."

Annie placed hands on her hips. "Was there something you needed to ask me?"

"Oh. Yes. If it's no trouble."

"No, no trouble at all."

"Good. It'll just take a minute."

Annie followed Mrs. Winkle back inside the house. "How's your grandson?" Annie queried. "Have you heard from him?"

"Did I tell you he moved to Minnesota to live closer to his girlfriend?"

"No."

"He decided to change his name." Mrs. Winkle pet a vining mandevilla on her way past. Its blooms were bright red and warmed by the sun. "Isn't this gorgeous?"

"What does he call himself?"

"Who?"

Annie ruffled her forehead. "Uh. Your grandson. You were saying he changed his name. What does he call himself?"

"Why does he need to call himself?"

Mrs. Winkle occupied the first floor of Annie's rental, a two-story rowhouse. She kept her patio and sliding glass doors impeccably clean, as if they were brand new. The kitchen and small dining table was also kept tidy. Usually. A bag of flour had fallen over, powdering the table and the tiled floor as both her dogs sat perfectly still in the middle of it.

Annie bleated, "Oh, my."

"Yes, well. You see, I thought I would make some egg noodles for tonight's supper." Mrs. Winkle picked up the torn flour bag. "But the bag got away from me."

The flour had spread far and wide, even outside of the room, with paw prints marking a trail of chaos in all directions.

"I tend to have this acid reflux reaction to excitement nowadays. Then I get gas. Don't get old."

"Well, I'd prefer it to the alternative." Annie bent down and the two dogs raced to her, getting white powder all over her damp skin and bathing suit. "I'll get this cleaned up for you." She laughed at the licks on her face. "Okay. Stop. Stop."

"If you have the time, could you take my trash out too? It's trash day tomorrow, you know."

Annie's phone dinged. A calendar reminder that she had a doctor's appointment in an hour. Her heart vaulted and breath halted. "Oh, no. I forgot about my physical." Her blood rushed. "Um—you know, Mrs. Winkle, never mind. I can do it."

"Are you sure?"

Annie waved aside her concern. "Yeah. I'll do it."

Mrs. Winkle stood beside Annie as she opened the garage door. Piles of black trash bags fell out before her.

Mrs. Winkle gave a sly wink. "Found a burst of energy. Thought I should clean out a little. Oh. If you have the time, could you also wipe down Saqi and Bones for me?"

Annie made quick work of sweeping and mopping the kitchen, then washed the dogs in her kiddie pool. Rinsing Saqi, the Chihuahua, with a hose was hell. It was a challenge not to shoot him away with the jet of water. She would retract him into position like an old typewriter after every shot, and he stood dutifully with every slide. He did seem to enjoy running away afterward, dashing about the yard and rubbing himself all over the grass when she gave him the word to go. Bones intended to take up more time than Annie wanted to give her, and she couldn't help getting herself wet too in the process because making a game of it was so much fun, and ole Bones seemed to enjoy the massage.

The only problem occurred when Annie attempted to haul out the trash bags. One felt like it weighed over sixty pounds. Tugging and pulling and pushing and gasping, she lost her grip and fell into another bag that burst, sending Styrofoam into the air like a poof of confetti, covering her still-damp body like a snow mummy. Thank goodness the neighbors weren't watching. Maybe they were. At this point, she no longer cared. She spotted a woman across the street she once met at a LBGTQ festival. She had been seeing her everywhere lately. Reluctant to make eye contact, Annie felt her pupils dilate in reply to a happy hand wave. After the last bag was dropped at the curb, Annie made a dash upstairs to her apartment. Within minutes, she was zipping down the narrow, winding street in her Fortwo.

* * *

Annie sat on the examination table with a tech taking her blood pressure as she spit out a Styrofoam pellet and combed another few out of her hair. The tech grinned at the distraction.

"I hate those things," the tech murmured.

"Big box companies must get a kick out of selling something to old people just in case they want to send themselves to China in all that free packing material nobody else wants."

"Your pulse is really high today. Too much coffee?"

"Too much excitement. Good thing I don't get gas. Inside joke."

The tech dismissed herself. "The doctor will be in shortly. I hope your day calms down a bit."

"So do I."

Annie's doctor was the old-school type. A slightly built fifty-something fella with a graying beard and hitched suspenders that made him look like he should be in a silent film. His mustache curled in a smile as he shook her hand. His voice always reminded Annie of Bob Ross, the artist she watched on PBS as a kid. She'd sit alongside her mom, who'd converted the dining room table to an art studio, and watch Bob's reruns. Painting was therapeutic, her mother would insist.

"You've been quite active lately?" the doctor asked.

"Of late. Really late. Yeah."

"Keeping busy?"

"Even when I don't try."

"Good. Well, your numbers are excellent. Across the board."

"Really?"

"Yep. Whatever you're doing. Keep doing it. Still sober?"

"Seven years."

He shook her hand. "Good job."

"Thanks." Her cheeks warmed. She did feel proud of that milestone.

He unclipped the papers from his board and handed them to her. "Beware the seven-year itch."

Annie scrunched her face. "That's for marriage, isn't it?"

"Murphy's Law. It's for everything. What they don't tell you is that it happens every year, every month, every day. The key is to make sure you're really enjoying your life."

"Well, I have moments. Small, incremental moments. Not the whole day, of course. Some days. Now and again. On occasion."

"And how do you think about yourself in those moments?"

Annie puffed out her cheeks. "I don't. That's the distraction."

"And what do you do when you're not distracted?"

"I sleep."

"Are you depressed?"

"No." Annie had to let that question sink in for a moment. "I don't think so. I enjoy my life today. I'm a productive part of society. It's very freeing to know that."

He nodded. "What are you doing for you?"

"What do you mean?"

He opened the door. "Just think about it." His mustache curled into an uplifted wooly worm.

"Well, if all my numbers are good, everything's right, then what am I doing wrong?"

"You can be doing everything right, everything the world needs you to do. But, if you're not happy in the process of just living, all the rest means nothing. Obligations and good deeds aren't always enough. It's different than following the spirit intent of something. I have to ask myself why it is I really want this thing or this situation to work in my favor. If it's for the sole purpose I believe it will make me feel good, then it is the wrong intent. Be happy first."

Annie slouched. "But what if I'm anxious?"

"Anxiety is the body's response of what we are thinking. We are what we think about. Doing things that make you feel good can keep you healthy and happy."

"Happy little trees, huh?"

"Happy little trees. Happy little clouds. Happy little me."

CHAPTER TWO

Annie's brother, Scott, was a lounge pianist at a local coffee house and jazz club in the hip neighborhood of Walnut Hills. He could play Beatles to Billy Joel and every conceivable German and French obscurity in between. His favorite, though, was Scott Joplin. When he finished tickling the ivories he got a tiny hand clap from a ninety-year-old who seemed to be the only patron paying attention.

"Thank you. Thank you very much," Scott acknowledged with a wave.

The lunch crowd started to dwindle. Annie slid a plate before him. "Egg salad sandwich?"

He reached for one half as she ate the other. "How's your day going?" he asked.

"The usual," she answered with mouth full. "Dad's a grump. The dogs are needy, but precious. Mrs. Winkle is a dear, no matter what. And the doc says my numbers are terrific."

"And?"

"And, I'm bored." She sipped at her root beer.

"Bored? Your day's only half over. What are you going to do the rest of the day?"

"I don't know. I don't have a talent like yours to while the hours away."

"I thought you were going to take up knitting?"

Annie frowned. "I discovered the needles worked better as chopsticks in my chow mein."

"They're great back scratchers. Hey, I actually sold my first woodworking project on eBay."

"Oh my God, Scott! That's great, hon."

"I know. And I've had more requests for rocking horses. I've just got to find a better gig than this to afford the exotic woods."

A drunk man fell against the piano before he slid and staggered away. "Why don't you two get outta my way?" he slurred.

"You could always pick up the pieces of free piano wood after I rile him up a little more," Annie puffed.

"You forgot your keys, Frank," Scott said to the man.

Frank turned around. "What?"

"Your keys." Scott pointed to the table nearby.

Annie watched as Frank threw a lazy wave to Scott, swiped up his keys and shimmied his way to the door. "He's not driving, is he?"

"Those are house keys. He lives upstairs. He owns this joint."

"Crap almighty," Annie blurted. "Guess I'd better not rile him up."

Scott's eyes diverted as he sipped on his lemonade. "Are you dating anyone?"

"Me? Are you serious? You know me better than that. I'm insane, not stupid."

Scott wiped his hands and began to play a soft tune. "I just asked because there's a blonde checking you out from the corner table over there. Very low-key on the profile."

Annie glanced up and met the woman's smile and wave. She recognized the curly shoulder-length hair, and glasses.

"Oh, no."

"You know her?"

Annie turned her back to the piano and held her head down. She pulled her glasses off and cleaned the lenses with Scott's T-shirt. "Cindy Russo. She's been following me for weeks. Hanging around the coffee shop, the bookstore. I spotted her this morning when I took out Mrs. Winkle's trash."

"What was she doing?"

"I think she was taking a picture of me wearing Mrs. Winkle's collection of Styrofoam pellets."

"Early Halloween costume tryouts?"

Annie yowled in her root beer. "The motion-capture suits. The...the green onesies with white darts on them. What a great idea, Scott."

"Yeah, not really. I wore that once a couple years ago. The girl I was interested in at the time was dressed as a Pixar lamp."

"Oh, I bet she was cute too."

"She was wearing that cone around her head." Scott gestured with fingers stretched wide around his face. "It was her dog's, so it was awkward. She didn't see me. Tripped over my foot and knocked us both down the stairs in front of the courthouse. The only thing that stopped us was the Channel 5 newswoman."

"Vanessa Young? The blonde? She's a hottie."

Scott smooshed the corner of his lip. "It was either Vanessa's microphone, long blond hair, or the battery box in my girlfriend's headpiece that short-circuited the lit bulbs on my onesie like a Charlie Brown Christmas tree. We blew out the entire block of street lights after it threw her cameraman across the street."

"Geez'o. You never told me that."

Scott began to play a soft 1920's twinkle on the keys. "Well, enough time has passed I think I've healed from it."

She swooned over him and attempted to place a hand on his shoulder.

"Don't touch me. Memory pain still comes up once in a while."

"Right."

* * *

Annie decided to ignore her stalker, but when she drove away, she spotted Cindy in the rearview mirror, sitting behind her car at a light. Cindy was driving the quintessential hot-girl car, a four door Jeep Wrangler. The baby-blue machine was given to her by her parents two months ago on her birthday. Annie heard through Varsha at the bookstore the only reason she wanted it was to impress Annie. The only thing it did for Annie was turn her gut into knots as the lipstick kiss-shaped headlight covers inched closer.

"Oh, for crap's sake. Doesn't she know this is such a turn-off for anybody?"

She seethed under her breath and slammed the gas pedal at the green light, ready to destroy what few cylinders she had in her tiny car to escape. Once she got inside the grocery store, she noticed Cindy standing ahead of her, her back turned, examining a shelf full of batteries.

How the hell did she get in here so fast? Annie thought. She broke out in a sweat and turned down another aisle, glancing over her shoulder as she walked. She flung a tub of oatmeal in her cart and swiped up a box of cereal to hide behind. After a moment, she gazed around the aisle. No Cindy. Annie turned around and pushed her cart around the corner, taking quiet steps.

Guy with beanie. Woman with cranky kid. Older worker scratching his ass and stocking green beans on a middle-of-aisle display. No Cindy.

Good. This is good. Annie breathed a little lighter and headed over to the deli meats. She passed by a cling-wrapped salmon with one grotesque, white eye and picked it up, wondering if her cats might like it for dinner. *Maybe she was just in here for batteries. People buy batteries. I buy batteries. We're good. It's all good.*

"Hi," Cindy said.

"Aaahh!" Annie jumped back two feet, then took a deep breath and pressed the raised hairs on the back of her neck back down. "You really have to cut that out, Cindy."

"I'm sorry."

"No—don't be sorry for being you." Annie held her chest. "You just have to work on your social skills."

"I can be someone else for you."

"What? No. Don't do that. Don't ever do that. You've got to work on some things. Like appropriate behaviors."

"You want to go out?"

Annie scowled. "No. I already told you that the last time you came to the bookstore. You're not my type."

"I can be whatever type you want."

"Stop that. Don't say that."

"Why not?"

Annie paused. "Look. I don't want to go out with you. I'm very happy being single. Okay?"

"Okay. I guess."

"And this—this—me, you, me thing—this has to stop. This is not cool. You're freakin' me out here. Understand there's a good way to hang with someone and a bad way to hang with someone. Some people might find this sort of thing strangely attractive. Some people think this one-eyed salmon is attractive." Annie held up her cats' dinner, waving it in front of Cindy's face.

"There's more to it than hiding around corners and changing yourself to get someone's attention," she said. "Sneaking around houses, taking pictures of people without their permission, and following them like bad breath is totally unacceptable. You can find a nice girlfriend somewhere. Just don't expect it to be me. Nothing personal, I just like what I like. And for the moment, I like just being me."

Annie stopped herself. She turned to where Cindy had stood. She had vanished. The only other person around was a man hunched over his braunschweiger, staring blankly at her.

"Bologna. It's overrated," Annie said to the man. "Always asking for attention, you know? Big celebrity. Braunschweiger. Braunschweiger is where it's at, man. Totally authentic and likeable. Doesn't ask for much. Right? Right." Annie tossed a log of braunschweiger in her cart and whisked her cart away.

* * *

Chronic aloneness seemed preferable to peopling, thought Annie. A dear friend, a couple family members, and few acquaintances she deemed enough to juggle in her life. Any more personalities felt more akin to walking a tightrope, with hiccups, and holding onto someone's fifty-gallon fish tank full of precious tiny lives.

The only supreme relief of her day was when she entered the door of her apartment. The world could not create enough acceptance and love than was witnessed from her two tabby cats, Pork and Beans, when they'd greet her.

Annie hit her knees on the floor, plunked the groceries down and slid into the warmth of purrs, tails, and headbutts.

"Yes. Yes. Yes, babies. I missed you too."

Beans was the big talker, and had to express to Annie all sorts of things he missed.

"Really? Is that right? Did your brother ignore you again?"

By his appeals, Annie was certain there was always more to the story.

"Okay, fellas. Come on." She stood with bags in her hands and led them to the kitchen. Pork and Beans waited patiently beside their bowls as she unloaded the bags on the counter. The crack of opening a can of tuna delighted their eyes and wiggled their tails. It was typical that Beans should wish to instruct her how best to place the spoonful in his bowl, with Pork looking at him with irritation.

The first piece out of the grocery bag was the braunschweiger. She held it limply and felt a wave of disdain.

"I don't even like braunschweiger anymore."

A piece of paper was stuck to the bag of French-style green beans. She peeled it off to read, "Making peace with my today will improve my future." She snuffed and flipped the paper around. It was her grocery receipt. The motion of balling it up in her fist and tossing the wad into the trash didn't give her the satisfaction she anticipated. Taps of rain appeared on the window above the sink.

Annie slumped. "No way. Really? That's just great. Now, what am I supposed to do?"

Nothing Annie began invited her interest. She stood before the television with remote in her hand, waiting for the inspiration to turn it on. The dot matrix printer soothed her momentarily, as she sat watching the beam of light move back and forth. Laying with her back to the floor, she blew at a small white goose feather pulled from her pillow, and watched it come back down. Up and down, until Pork flew overtop her, snatching it away. After waking herself up in a deep sleep snore on the couch, Annie realized even flipping through the pages of an interior design magazine bored her with little contentment. Although, she was dreaming of someday having her own home. An article's title lifted off the page before her that read, *Dull life? Maybe it's your home.*

A fluff-ball toy smacked one of the framed paintings next to her. Annie walked over to the painting, squared it back on the wall, and bent down to the fluff ball. Something tingled her brain. She lifted herself back up and stood there staring at the painting, with Pork and Beans on either side of her feet. That painting was old. She recalled stepping into her grandmother's house and admiring it on the wall above an end table, with a glass bowl of hard candy Annie would always dip into. Only out of nostalgia had she accepted the painting. The warm fuzzies had since equaled the analogy of glancing into an empty bowl of popcorn, with a few unpopped kernels to remind her of how good it was.

"Sorry, Gran."

Annie lifted the picture off the wall and tucked it into the attic, a hole above the hallway, with several other pictures and framed family photos of bad hair and poor fashion choices of decades gone by. Furniture was moved and floors swept. Even the trim, doorways, and ceiling fans were dusted; a rare and underappreciated task, as Pork and Beans related to her through a series of sneezes.

Back in the attic, Annie remembered she had tossed a couple of canvases up there after attempting to paint landscapes when she was in a funk. They were quite ugly. It was a wonder why she still held onto them.

With Pork watching the birds outside her wide desk window, and Beans curled up next to her paints, Annie proceeded to paint over the canvases and start anew. Abstract was freeing. She had forgotten how fun it was and how clever she could be with the colors, using all sorts of kitchen utensils in creating textures and patterns.

The living room spaces on the walls were finally bright and beautiful, filling the room with something new and expressive. Including, of course, a bit of bright yellow on Beans's tail.

Annie crossed her arms and sighed thankfully as she stood in pride before her paintings. It had been a long time since she allowed herself to be in a good emotional space.

CHAPTER THREE

The following day, Annie sat behind the desk at Yodel's Bookstore calculating expenses when her boss Tim Tiddle walked in. She handed him a business card.

"A woman from the Woodland Cemetery foundation visited and was asking for information on how to best place her brochures here."

Mr. Tiddle twisted his face all around in his typical ill humor. "Oh, ha-ha." He crumbled the card and dropped it on the desk. "My accountant will be here in an hour to pick up the documents for last quarter. Please make certain he has everything, Miss Freckle."

"Yes, sir," Annie replied. When he had turned his back, she muttered, "He won't have much to calculate."

Mr. Tiddle peeked from around a bookshelf. "I heard that."

"The web thickens," Annie's coworker Varsha chirped.

"The plot. The plot thickens." Annie walked around the desk and handed Varsha a price gun and started pulling books out of a box. "Wouldn't it be nice if we made this area into a bar?"

"You mean like beer and books or something?" Varsha said as she rifled through a magazine full of porn.

Annie reached over and snatched the magazine out of Varsha's hand. "No, silly. We don't need people reading our books upside down. And the patrons don't need to see us reading this stuff." She slapped it against Varsha's chest. "I mean a coffee bar. If Mr. Tiddle would just invest his money in meaningful enterprises instead of blowing it on blackjack at the casino, his accounts would be smoother this month."

Varsha sneaked a peek at the centerfold before tucking the magazine under a book. "Invest? Tiddle? He's too busy as it is adjusting his finances by whatever article the Chicanery Chronicles publish. Another great recession is gonna happen right after Ho Hos are dropped from production."

Annie gripped her heart. "No more Ho Hos?" A daft stare from Varsha convinced Annie she was kidding. "Oh. You almost had me there." She watched as Varsha unwrapped a candy cane and stuck it in her mouth.

"Is that from last Christmas?"

"Yep."

"Isn't that stale by now?"

"Oh, yeah." Varsha crunched on the candy. "I'm used to eating stale candy, chips, pretzels. Most of my childhood food was hand-me-downs from my cousins."

Annie drew her eyebrows together. "Really? That's pretty sad. Your mom couldn't buy you fresh snacks?"

"Oh, it wasn't my mom. My cousins would always get way too much in their stockings and never eat it. So, my Aunt Silla would put it all in a grocery bag and give it to me for my birthday." Varsha slouched and scratched at the shaved neon green strip of color above her ear. "I kind of like it now, I guess. You get used to stuff, you know? Even stuff that's not good for you. Something about endorphins. I read that somewhere."

Annie watched as Mr. Tiddle grumbled over his sorted mail. "I can relate. And it's definitely easy to blow money you don't have. Especially when you've got a gambling problem."

"It's a nightmare," Varsha said. "We met up at a casino a while back. I'd set aside some cash, and I burned it all in thirty minutes. But he went back to the ATM, like, five times. Kept losing at the slot machine with the unicorn, and he just wouldn't give up."

Annie envisioned Mr. Tiddle beating on the slot machine in heated disgust at the animated unicorn as it jumped around the screen. "Nah. I just can't picture that one."

Varsha shook her head. "I don't even think it's about the money. He just goes because this hot guy he's interested in gambles. Some hotshot dude from Mexico City who visits here every once in a while."

Annie sat back at her desk. "Oh—that one guy with the Elton John shoes?"

"That's the one."

"Hey, he had a really cool pair of psychedelic oxfords I would have loved to add to my own collection." Annie lovingly rubbed a smudge off her camel-brown oxford shoe.

Varsha made a chirping sound to get Annie's attention and nodded to the brunette by the classics. "Welcome to Yodel's Bookstore," she called out to the woman. "Now she's like a smooth piece of jazz, isn't she?"

"More like a crap shooter with titty rings."

"I wouldn't mind if she had titty rings." Varsha nibbled on a multigrain cracker from Annie's lunch. "Any prospects for you?"

Annie stopped herself from being mildly offended as Varsha reached into her bag for another. "There's progress in my fire. I'm enjoying my little embers not being fanned right now. Maybe in the next lifetime. Say, how's it going with Whatsername?"

Varsha made a face to a pack of pickles and tossed them aside. "Tracy. Her name was Tracy."

"Hey." Annie grabbed for her lunch bag. "Lay off my lunch, and put my pickles back. Tell me about this Tracy person. Sorry she's a *was*."

Varsha dismissed the sympathy with a shrug. "Your run-of-the-mill chick who thought a few nights in bed meant we were gonna U-Haul it."

"I wouldn't have thought she was a fast mover with all the times she made you wait on her ass."

"Yeah, well. You would think that ass was worth every penny when you saw it in black leather pants." Varsha bit her lower lip and shimmied. "No worries. I've got my eye on another fuel burner."

"Better watch it, Varsha. That kind of life will age you quick."

"Race cars are meant to be leased, not owned."

"I've had my Italian race car days. It almost killed me with toxicity and tacos."

Varsha began pulling books out of a box. "I think I remember you dating an Italian girl…Hey, wasn't she the one who wanted you to buy her a clit piercing or something?"

"Yep. Tore in half. There went my seventy-five bucks."

"Yowzah." Varsha bent over the desk and gawked at a passing figure in short shorts. "Still, living conservatively sucks, Annie. Once in a while, you've got to blow those petrified preserves out with some black leather and a few buttery nipple shots, you know."

Annie snuffed back the shadowed recall of her crack addict days. "I've done enough blowing. I'm safer this way. And so are the people around me. Look—you're still my friend."

Varsha opened her arms and wiggled her fingers. "Proof's in the pudding, darlin'."

Cindy entered the bookstore.

Varsha turned to Annie. "She still stalking you?"

"If I plead guilty to a misdemeanor, will you be a witness?"

"Now, don't do anything stupid."

"I just want her to stop breathing around me."

Varsha clicked her tongue. "Glad I missed that shot."

"Dodged that bullet. The phrase is dodged that bullet. But yeah, she's not your type."

"What do you mean? I drink all blood types." Varsha snatched Annie's wince with her teeth as if it floated between them.

Varsha turned to Cindy's approach. "Hi, Cindy."

"Hi, Varsha. Annie."

"Hi, Cindy." Annie acted busy behind a pile of paperwork.

Cindy asked, "What are you two up to today? Anything new?"

"Varsha is standing," Annie said. "She works incredibly hard to make it look easy."

Varsha scrunched her nose and slipped away.

A sharp-dressed woman *ding-dangled* the little doorbell as she entered, stealing Annie's attention. A snug skirt fit around the woman's thighs like they were daring someone to lift it so her shapely legs could be freed to curl around someone else's.

Annie met her at the counter and attempted to hide her awe. "Hi. Can I help you?"

"I'm probably way too early. I'm here for Mr. Tiddle."

"Mr. Tiddle."

"Yes. I'm Mr. Dally's assistant. The accountant?"

"Oh, yes." Annie pulled out a file from the desk drawer. "Actually, I have all your paperwork right here."

"Excellent." The woman smiled and stuffed the folder into her briefcase.

"Mr. Tiddle is here if there's anything you need to discuss with him. He's right in the back."

"Oh, that won't be necessary. If Mr. Dally needs anything, he'll call. Thanks. Have a great day."

Annie watched her turn and leave. "You too."

Varsha returned to ogle the woman's figure as she departed down the sidewalk. "I'm sure there's no dilly left to Mr. Dally if that's who's working for him. Did you see that ass?"

"Lovely legs, I have to say," Annie admitted.

Varsha inhaled a hissing breath, imitating Hannibal Lecter. "She's got a revolution going on in that skirt."

Cindy frowned. "I don't particularly keep company with people who casually talk about someone's front or rear pelvic region."

Varsha turned to her dramatically. "Cindy, I understand not everyone is interested in beautiful bodies. Yes, the mind is most important. Yet, there are many of us who care to take a healthy gawk once in a while at a good tush."

"I'm a leg girl, myself," Annie said. "I couldn't have told you what color of eyes she had or if there were any obvious tats. I was too busy gawking at her legs. Very nice, indeed."

Cindy plugged her ears with loose papers and closed her eyes tightly with alarm. "Ohh. Sheesh, guys!"

"SOP," Varsha inserted.

Annie looked up. "What?"

"SOP. Standard Operating Procedure. A set of step-by-step instructions compiled by veteran lesbians to help newbies carry out complex routine *gawks.* SOPs aim to achieve efficiency, quality gawking, and uniformity of visual performance, thus reducing verbal miscommunication and failure to hitch up later with said visual experience. Even has a sample Velcro included, just in case you get farther up the emotional scale."

"You just made that up."

Varsha reached for a nearby book and held it up. "Three inches of *Lez Manners: The Lesbian Guide to Picking Up Women.* The proper and dependable diplomacy on how to pick up women, by women, for women."

Annie snatched it from her. "Your mother could use this book."

Varsha grabbed it back. "As a matter of fact, she's getting one for Christmas."

"Then again, some women actually like being talked rough to. Aren't you afraid it would actually make her a bit...boring?"

Varsha looked sideways at Annie.

"I mean, really. If you think about it, Varsha, your mom's whole personality is her kinda, sorta, tender gruffness. The butch mystique is written all over her. Lots of women go for that. This book doesn't speak to women like her, does it?"

"There's a whole chapter on butches and how to add a bit of classy Suave Rico to their failing ventures."

"I think you mean Rico Suave."

"I've heard his music," Cindy chimed in. "He's pretty good."

Varsha changed her voice. "Try not, says Yoda. Do, or do not."

Annie stared at her. "That was not Yoda. That was a foreign exchange student from Bolivia."

"Maybe I could use a copy of this book," Cindy said.

Annie laid a hand on Cindy's shoulder. "My dear girl. In the battlefield of life, one can apply only what one knows. To be the best, you must set yourself apart from the rank and file of the world. This—this book is a grand start to the making of any legend."

Cindy stood in awe as her eyes scanned over the book and its colored edges. "Is there a part two?"

Varsha placed another thick book atop the one in her hands while Annie printed off a receipt.

"Here. I put it on your dad's account," Annie said.

Annie and Varsha watched Cindy toddle off with the heavy books.

"Thanks, guys."

Varsha crossed her arms. "I believe we have a Supergirl in the making."

Annie balked. "Eh. More like a Teenage Mutant Ninja Turtle."

"Miss Freckle," Annie's boss announced.

Annie sucked in a frown and smiled with a turn. "Mr. Tiddle."

"It's National Heimlich Maneuver Day, and we need this sandwich board posted on the corner, ASAP."

Annie read the sign aloud. "Spit it out. Tell your friends about the latest Medical Help book from Dr. Davey Feelsupgood. At your favorite neighborhood Yodel's now." She lumbered with the board, taking a chunk of wood out of the doorway with a grunt. "Geez'o, what is this thing made of, for cripe's sake?"

"Drywall," Varsha called to her.

"What?"

"His neighbor was remodeling and was going to throw it out." She shrugged.

"Oh, my God." Annie backpedaled and flipped around into the stride of a woman in a business suit. "Oh!"

The woman yelped with a halt. It was obvious her mind was on so many other things. She had just lowered her cell phone.

"I am so sorry I startled you." She was a dream. Not a magazine knockout—more the imperfectly perfect human material of wholesomeness only a decent life of reality could bring. Her soul spoke by the way the midmorning sun glistened on her light brown hair and bronzed her cheek. She was a delight to the eye.

The woman paused with a slight smile before dismissing Annie. "You're fine."

Annie halted her with hesitation. "That is such a fine outfit, I have to say. But if you will allow me. There's just one…thing… here." She brushed off some drywall dust from the woman's sleeve.

"Really, you didn't have to worry about it. But, thank you."

Annie nodded and watched as the woman passed. "Sure."

Annie walked back inside, only to halt to Varsha's hands in the air. "Sure? That's it?"

Annie's chest tightened as she swept by her. "What?"

"You could have given her your name. What about asking for her number?"

"Don't be silly. I almost clobbered her with drywall."

"That was a true-blue, heaven-sent meeting. Your true love moment, and you blew it, Chica."

"What are you talking about?"

"You've got the goods, the singing, the hip poetry moves. You just have to deliver. Supplies are running out!"

"I'm not looking."

Varsha murmured behind Annie's every step, "Well, maybe, just maybe she is. Ever think of that?"

"It was a blink. A moment. How have I had time to think, with you blabbering to me? Besides, did I mention I'm not looking?"

"I saw that look."

Annie met Varsha's eyes. "What look?"

"That look you have when you see something that sparks your Inner Being."

"Yeah, well, maybe she's a kindred spirit from some past life or something or other. That happens, you know."

"For a reason."

Annie paused, recalling of the woman's eyes, skin, and awkwardness. "Nonsense."

"Bet you can't control your brain after this. Especially if the universe puts her back in your life, say, at your coffee shop tomorrow."

"You wouldn't dare call that in on me, Varsha."

Varsha smiled like a spoiled child in response.

"Stop it."

CHAPTER FOUR

Annie closed her car door and breathed deeply before entering her dad's house through the open garage. A gust of wind wound his American flag around the pole, which was attached to the brick wall. She carefully loosened it to fly free. She never thought about separating her father's identity with the flag. He too stood for law, freedom, and the other fundamentals that the flag protected. Now, if he could only be as unbiased.

"Okay. Snow White and the Seven Curmudgeons. Who are we going to be today? Gratifying Grouch? Malcontent Mule, Balmy Bear, Naysaying Niggler, or the ever-popular Poopy Partisan?"

She cracked open the door. "Raise your beers, happy hour is here!"

The Dobermann was on top of it with pounces and growls. She managed to open the door enough to fit a large rawhide bone through. She struggled with her half as it caught on the doorframe, before watching it jerk behind the door and out of sight. Silence. Success. She quietly entered the laundry room and closed the door with her back.

Her dad grumbled, "He'll bury that damn thing in the yard, and I'll run over it with the mower."

"He'll eat half of it before we're done with breakfast."

"Coffee?"

"Sure. Black, please."

He sat a cup of coffee down in front of her. It had cream. Annie hid her irritation by turning to the wine glass he left beside her orange juice. She poured the juice and attempted to keep the unstable pile of mail from falling into her plate.

Her dad pushed himself away from the table and stumbled into her chair, catching himself.

"Easy there, soldier. Can I do something?"

"No."

He wobbled his way over to his floor-model stereo and flipped a switch on the CD player. Annie knew she'd have to hear his praise and glory over the din of Vaughn Monroe.

"He died an alcoholic, you know," he said.

Her father had a natural predisposition to find discussions with her he found relative to her own life, or so was his perception. Most were always in bad form.

"Yeah. You've mentioned it before."

"I saw him in concert a couple of times. He was something else. Had his own orchestra and everything."

Annie mimicked along with him. She had heard the same story several times, weekly. She nudged his chair closer to him as he began to sit back down.

Her father gulped his coffee with a satisfied sound. "Good coffee. How's your breakfast?"

Annie found several raw pieces of bacon in her egg-and-potato skillet meal, and she slid them under a piece of toast. "Good."

"I drafted an inventory sheet." He shoved aside a small box of pens and tapped at a notebook stuck between a box of mini flashlights and another pile of mail. "There's about twenty thousand dollars here if you and your brother sell it all."

"I can get boxes for you if you want to start boxing up anything."

"I don't want boxes."

"Why don't you want boxes? What do you think we're going to do with it?"

"You're going to sell it." He took a bite of toast. "I won't be here to see it."

"You need to box all this stuff, Dad, if you want to carry it outside."

His voice raised. "No, you don't. You get an auctioneer. I swear, you don't know anything. You call the auctioneer and they'll handle it. All of it. They'll move it all outside and set it up the way they think it'll all sell. And then they'll sell the house."

"You can't possibly believe this house is going to sell as-is? You need to clean the house first, Dad. No one is going to buy a house that smells like tobacco from ceiling to floor. And we'll have to replace the carpet—"

"No, you don't, Annie," he said, growling her name like it was a curse word. "You don't do anything. Never put money into a house you're going to sell."

"That's absurd." Annie couldn't believe they were having this conversation. This man was not her father. He wasn't making any sense. Something was off-kilter in his head. "This house won't sell for a nickel unless it's cleaned up. And that can't happen on auction day. You have to box some of this stuff just to clean it, for God's sake."

"No, you don't." His bark began to have a bite. "Christ, you are so hard-headed."

"You're one to talk."

"That's right! I've done this before. You haven't."

Now, Annie was thrown. He knew how many places she'd lived over the years. "I've moved more times than the Reds have lost in a season, Dad. People want a clean space. Unless you want to sell to the folks who buy ugly houses."

Her dad pounded a fist on the table. "You just won't listen. Why won't you listen? Don't mess this up or I'll haunt you. You hear me? You better do right by me."

The idea dawned on Annie that, after being raised with such crotchetiness, she should be used to it by now. This episode, even though somewhat senile, was no different. Yet, as always, it was a fine razor that cut her down every time.

* * *

Annie walked into Yodel's and headed over to the desk where Varsha was tagging a box of books.

Varsha stared at her. "Hey, aren't you off today?"

Annie couldn't shake off her moodiness. "Yeah. I just didn't feel like going home right now."

Varsha's shoulders slumped. "Your dad again?"

"Yeah."

"Sorry."

Annie raised up a bag of gourmet donut holes and and waved them at her. "Energy balls? Packed with serotonin."

"Um, can I try them later? I'm working on a potato farm in Minecraft. I have to be mentally prepared for starch."

Mr. Tiddle approached her, wide-eyed and cooing. "Ooh, you have those new energy balls at your coffee shop? I must try one. I hear they are exquisite."

"All for you." She let him swipe the whole bag in his arms. She took a drink from her bottle of herbal tea before Mr. Tiddle let out a loud whine, startling her.

"Oh, my God. You don't want to drink that. It contains xanthan."

Reading the label, Annie asked, "What's that?"

"An emulsifier. Causes colitis and weight gain. You really don't want to eat that popcorn either."

Annie eyed his insistent gaze. "What?"

"Oh, geez. The higher up the phrase 'partially hydrogenated oil' is on the list of ingredients, the more trans fat it contains. Look at that. You're a heart attack awaiting its hour, sweetie."

Annie whined, "This is organic. Expensive crap. Expensive means better for you."

"You would do better with a soda and a bag of Cheetos."

"He's lying," Varsha interjected. "He doesn't really know this stuff." She shoved a brochure at Annie. "Here. Fill out this app for a credit card and you could win a round trip to Poopy Caca."

"Punta Cana. It's pronounced Punta Cana."

Cindy walked into the bookstore.

"Here's your friend," Varsha whispered to Annie.

Mr. Tiddle frowned. "Doesn't she have a job?"

"Maybe she's homeless," Varsha added.

"Nah," Annie said. "Her dad owns four pizza joints and the Quad restaurant."

Mr. Tiddle's face turned pale. "The Quad? With the four famous chefs? That Quad?"

"Yep."

Cindy held up a tray of goodies. "Nutter Butter truffles?"

Mr. Tiddle and Varsha glanced at each other, quietly delighted, before following Cindy away to another counter.

"Unbelievable," Annie muttered. "Hey, what happened to emulsifiers and starch, huh?"

* * *

Annie drove over the Ohio River on the Brent Spence Bridge and into Kentucky to visit her mother. She enjoyed watching the bridge's metal trusses lazily pass her by. Rolling down the window, she took a deep breath of the fresh air as she ascended up a great hill, far and away from Cincinnati. The drive helped ease the stress of her everyday life. Not until moments like this did she realize her world was one big whirlwind of shrapnel, all the shards of her life whizzing by her until she went numb. She loved imagining the shrapnel turning to paper and settling neatly in place when she got further away from it all. Like a pop-up book that held all the bits of her past, turning it into a beautiful tree with a few leaves being the odd childhood memories that she savored in a different light. Unfortunately, it all scattered whenever she drifted near home again. She hardly even noticed when she drove into her mom's driveway and walked in the front door.

Annie snapped back from her daze, realizing her mom was hugging her. She pulled herself from her mom's embrace and stared into the parlor mirror at herself.

"I thought you told me my boobs would shrink when I turned thirty?" Annie said.

"Mine did."

"Well, you have tadpole eggs. And I still have these obnoxious things. What the hell?"

Her mother threw a hand up. "Maybe it's a throwback from your grandparents."

Annie followed her mom into the kitchen. "Mom, everyone in your family is small. Unless you count Great-uncle Zeb—those man-boobs could have run a Playboy girl out of business. Come to think about it, Grandma Diel's boobs were pouring out of that frame on Dad's bedroom wall."

Annie's mom handed her a peppermint tea. "So, how's your father?"

Annie felt her shoulders tighten just at the thought of him. "An ogre. An absolute ogre."

"A Lord of the Rings ogre, or a Shrek ogre?"

Annie delighted in the taste of her mom's fresh-leafed tea and returned to the question. "I wouldn't mind if Dad were a Shrek ogre. I would just be the donkey to him. Alas, this ogre smells a good game of Whac-A-Mole, and comes at me with a spiked club."

"He has all sorts of physical issues going on. He's afraid, hon. If I were him, I'd be scared to death too."

"He sure has a funny way of showing it." Annie took another sip of tea and noshed on a cookie her mother offered her. "He's living in filth and clutter. Oh, my God. Such clutter."

Her mom shrugged. "You should have seen his first bachelor apartment. Cringeworthy."

"And the dog—'e's a swell dog, Mom, but geez'o Pete. He has to switch the channel whenever a commercial begins. Gunny charges at the TV."

"Every commercial?"

"Cars. Animals. People in Hawaiian shirts. Anything Fox News. At least Gunny has taste. Oh, then there's the beer commercials."

Her mother broke a cookie in half and took a bite. "How can you stand visiting him?"

"Beer commercials don't bother me. But the folks in Hawaiian shirts..." Her mom stared over her glasses as Annie reached for a plate of sliced apples. "I make sure I have a bone for Gunny, and I just pretend I don't see the condition of the house. I have to. He gets lonely. Someone's got to do it, and since the two of you divorced, he doesn't have anyone else to visit him. Scott can't stand to go over there anymore. He's disgusted by it all too."

"Have you offered to clean the place?"

"Ever hear the expression, an ounce of prevention is worth a ton of manure?"

Her mom gulped at her tea and winked. "That doesn't apply to sloppy ploppy cow manure."

"My point exactly. I couldn't keep up with the old beaver and his piles of this and that. Let alone Gunny tracking in mud on every rainy day, bringing every stick and stone and three-million-year-old fossil he'd dig up. I got to keep the fossil, by the way. So cool. Anyway, Dad scrubs the carpet with a wet sponge mop and sucks up the excess water with a shop vac. He's already ruined two vacuums because he stuck a garden hose down them. To 'flush out the clods of dog hair,' he said. I didn't have enough energy to clean my own place. I told him he had to hire someone else."

"Did he?"

"Only once and never again," Annie grumbled through a mouthful of grapes. "Claimed the maid was some crackhead who stole his bugle. I found it in the garage a week later. He forgot he left it in there after playing reveille in a mole hole. Honestly, Mom, I don't know how much more of this craziness I can take. I can tick off half a dozen symptoms between stage three and stage four dementia noticeable in Dad."

"Well, if he keeps it up, he won't even have you. He needs help."

Annie sighed. "I love him. And I want to respect him because, well, he did his best to raise me, and I'm grateful. But he's becoming such an ass. I lied last week and told him I couldn't come because I had too much work."

Her mom gave a lopsided grin. "Have you tried bribing him with a breakfast at Bob Evans for his favorite sausage and gravy plate?"

Annie bobbed her head. "At least three times a month. I've even tried getting him to meet with other veterans for a day. He'd rather mope around, isolate himself, and complain that nobody loves him anymore. Some days I just don't have the umph to put up with him."

Her mom pulled a blueberry pie out of the oven. "Annie. You and your brother are all he's got left. I wish I could say it was different between your father and I, but it is what it is. He's going to be gone, and you're going to regret the days you decided not to go. Do you really want the last image of your father to be his bacteria-infested sponge mop?"

"Actually, it's better. I'll recall the day I borrowed the neighbor's electric wheelchair to race dad down his street with his own, the one that he never rides. I told him we should blow out the exhaust and see what that puppy can do. It was a true Ben-Hur chariot race. He won by his hazard flag because I didn't see the pothole."

"How could you not see a pothole?"

"Dad acted out his Charlton Heston role like a true Oscar winner, and started slapping me with a towel. We had a blast. Then we ate popcorn and watched the movie."

Her mom's face brightened. "Is he still driving his car?"

"Of course," Annie chortled. "Drives himself to doctor's appointments, the grocery store, the bank. He is becoming more and more fearful of going out. Then throws the guilt card at Scott for not offering to do more for him. Calls Scott two days after they have dinner and wants to know why he hasn't called. What can possibly happen in two days to have a meaningful discussion about?"

Her mom turned around and leaned against the sink. "You tell him about your day. It's a fifteen-minute call about all the hours that mean absolutely nothing to you—hours you take for granted. He lives vicariously through other people's lives now. It's all he has left, love. Scott can do the same thing."

Annie placed her plate in the sink. "I've got to get back."

Her mom reached into the fridge and pulled out a take-out container. "Here. I made another blueberry pie yesterday. Take these slices home. I know they're your favorite."

"Thanks." Annie scanned the dining room table full of peach and blueberry pies. "Why all the pies?"

"Oh. My bridge club is having a bake sale, with proceeds going to an orphanage for displaced guinea pigs. One of the members, Mr. Schnitzel, is turning his garage into such a home. You know those little shits breed every three weeks? Jezzus Crimany. He's a little weird. Needless to say, I don't believe I'll ever accept a backyard barbeque invite, if you know what I mean. Still, this is for a good cause. I really love this retirement community. And you know I love baking."

"As long as you're happy here, mom. That's all that matters, right?"

"Absolutely. Here, give me a hug." Her mom embraced her. "I hope your life gets better for you, sweetie. I'm sorry you're having issues."

* * *

Annie was soaking in her bubble bath to Mary Ford's '61 cover of "Wrap Your Troubles in Dreams" as it played on her vintage suitcase record player. In Mrs. Winkle's apartment below, there was enough clatter and bedlam and barking going on for several episodes of an Animal Planet documentary. Moments later, the doorbell distracted Annie from thoughts of running away with her cats, Pork and Beans, to the Grand Canyon, where no one would hear a sound. Then again, Beans would get carsick, just as he did whenever she took him to the vet.

Donning her Star Wars Yoda-ears fleece robe, she pattered down the hall in her bare feet to answer the repeated ring. "Just a minute."

It was Mrs. Winkle. Annie's green ears startled the poor lady, who yelped at the sight of her.

"Oh." Annie pulled her hood back off her wet hair. "Sorry. The cats like to play with the ears."

"Did I come at a bad time?"

"No, you're fine. I always dress like this during Pride month." Annie brushed bubbles off her sleeve.

"I see. To keep the protesters away."

"I don't know about that, but it sure keeps the gnats and Republicans away." By the woman's slight wringing of hands, Annie could tell she was distracted. "Is everything all right, Mrs. Winkle? I heard some commotion."

"Which part? The *kapow* or the *crash*?"

"Oh, I don't know. They seemed pretty comparable."

"Let's start at the beginning."

Annie hunched over. "All right."

"Now, which did you hear first?"

Annie had a feeling this wasn't going to be a quick visit. "Well, at first I heard a clambering, then a clanging—"

"A slamming or smashing kind of clanging?"

"More like clattering and thumping."

Mrs. Winkle nodded. "Oh, that was the babies. Did you hear the crash?"

"I dunno, it was all muffled. There were a lot of noises. Like twanging and thwacking and pouncing and screaming and shattering kind of noises."

"I see. Was that before the thwacking, or after the shattering?"

"It was all before the wallop."

"Oh," swooned Mrs. Winkle. "I didn't know there was a wallop."

Annie closed her eyes and counted to three. "Um…Mrs. Winkle."

"Hmm?"

Annie took a breath. "Are you all right?"

"Yes, of course."

Annie smiled. "Good. And the babies? Are the babies all right?"

"Yes, just fine."

"Good. I'm so glad we cleared that up."

Mrs. Winkle clasped her hands and smiled. "Oh, they're so sweet, aren't they?"

"Yes, very."

"A lovely couple of companions." Mrs. Winkle glanced away. "A bit rambunctious at times. Oh, not so much with old Ms. Bones anymore. She's a dear. Has her bursts of energy. But dogs will be dogs. Won't they?"

Annie smiled again, now a bit less patiently. "Alrighty then." She started to close the door as Mrs. Winkle turned to leave. "See you in the morning."

"Oh, just a minute," Mrs. Winkle said, turning about. "I knew I was forgetting something."

"Yes, ma'am."

Mrs. Winkle lowered her voice an octave and stared at Annie with a look that would pause the Terminator. "I could use your help."

Mrs. Winkle and Annie slowly peeked around the doorway into Mrs. Winkle's kitchen. Her little Chihuahua tippy-toed between Annie's Ewok slippers and looked up at her, while Bones waited safely in the living room.

"What exactly are we looking for?" Annie asked.

"The mouse."

"Mouse?" Annie stood up and smiled to Saqi. "You hear that, Saqi? If that's all it is, then—"

A hulking, dark shadow twice the size of the dogs appeared on the far kitchen wall. A creature darted toward the women, and Annie hollered like a five-year-old. The two ran and danced with flailing hands. Annie hopped around the room with little Saqi enjoying the game.

"Mrs. Winkle." Annie was still finding her breath. "That wasn't a mouse. That was a rat!"

"And I was blaming Bones here for eating the pork roast."

Bones sat ill-humored behind the couch, reminding Annie of the one-eyed salmon at the market.

Annie cringed. "That thing could drag off the whole pig. No wonder they're afraid of him."

Mrs. Winkle handed Annie a spatula. "Go in there and kill him."

"I can't go in there. He might have a gun." Annie pulled out her cell phone and started typing.

"Can you not play a game right now, Annie?"

"I'm Googling, Mrs. Winkle."

"I don't need you to Google me. I need that rat out of my house."

"Research. I'm researching how to catch a rat."

"We're not catching anything. We're killing."

Annie held her phone up to Mrs. Winkle. "Says here that poison is never a good idea. Not every rat that eats poison dies. And the ones that do crawl back up into the attic and create a terrible stink."

Mrs. Winkle frowned. "Then, what'll we do?"

"Traps. Traps or a BB gun."

"I have traps."

Annie felt very leery about this option. "Let me change into something more appropriate."

Feeling like she was in a 1940's gangster movie, Annie returned, wearing all black and sporting a black beanie and gloves. She crawled around in various nooks and crannies with a flashlight between her teeth. She placed traps throughout the house and attic. She wiggled between studs and caught the rat staring at her with its beady eyes at the attic door. Then she saw it under the fridge, and again along the baseboards near the back door. Barricaded behind cushions in the corner of the living room, Annie, the dogs, and Mrs. Winkle waited.

Mrs. Winkle eyed Annie's Tupperware bowl. "What's that?"

"Backup. Just in case."

SNAP!

Bones barked and Saqi hid further under the table. Annie looked to Mrs. Winkle's nod before quickly crawling around the corner and feeling like an FBI agent. Annie saw the overturned trap. She took Mrs. Winkle's cane and reached out to flip it. A towel was caught in it. She looked over her shoulder in disgust, just to spy the rat sitting up and staring at her from the other end of the kitchen.

"You think you're clever, do ya?" She noticed it was waiting for the right moment to run to the hole in the wall between them. Every inch of baseboard was covered with traps. "Go ahead." She held up her Tupperware. "If I can't getcha, those will, sucker."

The rat feigned right, then left. Annie pounced. Then, Mrs. Winkle hit Annie over the head with a broom.

"Ow! Ow! Stop! It's me!" Annie hollered.

"Oh, get it! *Get it!* It's over there!"

The Tupperware barely missed the rat as he dashed around Annie's thrashing about and Mrs. Winkle's broom swats. Traps were going off everywhere in the kitchen, and before the battle was over Annie was wearing them all. No sooner had she caught her breath, she heard gunfire. She ducked, rolled, and braced herself against a wall while Mrs. Winkle followed the rat down the basement steps with continued fire.

"Come here, you little asshat!"

Annie groaned as Bones and Saqi came to her rescue with kisses. "Better than date night or a silly TV show, eh?" She painfully removed a trap from her nipple with a yelp and tossed it aside. "What I wouldn't give for that boring afternoon."

An exclamation echoed from the basement after another round of shots. Mrs. Winkle whooped and cried with a high, repeating pitch, like the Modoc warrior women celebrating their tribe's victorious battle over the US Cavalry. Annie guessed the old gal retained her sharpshooting skills from the turkey shoot of 1954, when she out-shot her challenger. The man was so impressed, he later asked her to marry him. Mr. Winkle was a smart man. Best to have a woman like that on your side.

CHAPTER FIVE

Annie walked through her dad's garage and stiffened to the sound of excited barks. After a few unsuccessful attempts of pushing and banging against the Dobermann's constant jumping, she cracked open the door. She managed to avoid the large, black schnoz and drooling mouthful of teeth enough to wedge a bone inside. She entered as soon as the coast was clear, and she checked to see that she still had all her fingers.

The house carried a familiar smell of dog breath and stale tobacco. She sat down at the table and winced at the loud holiday swing.

"Christmas in July. How savory."

"The VFW sent it to me," her dad said. "Your French toast is ready. I hope it's still warm."

"I'm sure it's fine."

Annie gazed at her dad. He looked unusually worn. "What's been going on with you?"

"I drove up to visit my old boss."

"The one you said his wife had to call 911 on?"

"Yeah. She said he threatened her. That's the first stage of Alzheimer's. Aggravation from paranoia. They fly off the handle. Argue about stupid stuff. They don't make sense. He's in a nursing home now."

Annie was going to comment on his same behavior her last visit. But she decided to keep her mouth shut. "You were okay to drive?"

"Yeah. Had one hell of a time finding the place. Took me about an hour up there. I'm bushed today. Took a lot out of me, I guess."

"Did he recognize you?" Annie poured syrup on her French toast.

"I think so. I had his attention for about five minutes. Then, he turned away and stared at the television. *Bonanza*. I lost him after that."

Annie nodded. "Hoss does that to people." She decided to distract him from the slump she sensed he was in, not believing it was all physical. In between bites, she asked, "So. How many pieces of mail did you get today?"

He perked up. "Thirty-seven. That's a record."

"I'd say it was."

He held his hands out. "The stack was this tall."

"All that fit in your mailbox?"

"Nope. The carrier had to carry it to my door all wrapped in a rubber band. I throw at least ten letters out daily. I know what they want. They want money." His phone rang.

Annie took advantage of that distraction to flip a raw piece of bacon to Gunny, who was sitting nearby in a puddle of drool. She couldn't help it. His eyes were so sweet. Moments with this dog were precious. Yet, others were mostly irritating. Annie was sure he couldn't help it. He'd never known anyone else but her father.

"What?" her father yelled into the phone. "What do you want?" her father scoffed into the phone. "Go to hell." He put the phone down. "I'm being nice today." He munched on a piece of French toast and asked, "You have anything going on after this?"

"Bird-watching."

"Bird-watching?" He snuffed harshly. "For what?"

"For the pleasure of it. For the needed break in my day so I can recover after visiting your grumpy butt."

He frowned. "Whatever. I was wondering if you'd take me to the grocery."

"Out of your coconut cookies?"

He nodded. "A few other things, too."

Walking slowly behind a motorized cart, aisle by aisle through the grocery, was always a painful process. Annie had to seal her lips to make sure she didn't drool, staring off into space. With every step, however, she tried to put herself in his place and remember what her mom had said. He was full of fear about his living condition. He was doing the best he could with what he had left. *Patience, Annie*, she reminded herself. *Allow him to be who he is, and don't let that keep you from being the person you need to be.*

"You need anything?" he asked her.

"No, I think I'm good. Thanks anyway."

"Look at that slab of meat." Her dad pointed at a hunk of beef. "Doesn't that look good? What is that, a roast?"

Annie inspected it closer. "Beef rump. Great, I'm surrounded by asses."

"That's good. Put that in here."

Annie made room in the cart that was already overflowing with food and paper products.

"Get that other one for yourself."

Annie shook her head. "Dad, really. You don't have to do that."

"I thought you liked pot roast?"

"I love pot roast."

"Then get it."

Annie knew her father well enough that when he wanted to be generous, to not argue. Just accept it. She smiled at him. He had a grin on his face she hadn't seen in a while. He was really enjoying this. How could she turn him down?

"All right. You talked me into it." She placed the other roast in the cart and kissed him on the forehead. "Thanks, Dad."

At the checkout, the bag boy grabbed another cart to put the overflow of grocery bags in.

Annie reached for it, but not before her father barked at her.

"I don't need that. Stick it in here. I can get it all in here. I always do."

Annie shrugged her slight embarrassment off and attempted to stuff his soda case under his legs. The large pack of paper towels was another issue.

"What are you doing?" he retorted. "Put 'em on the side. Right here."

She followed him out to the car, loaded up the trunk with the bags, and opened the passenger door for him, gesturing him to get out of the motorized cart.

"Don't worry about it." Her father waved her away. "I'll drive it back up there."

"Why don't you relax? I can do it for you, Dad. I'm sure you're worn out."

He looked down his nose at her. "You don't even know how to drive this thing."

"Well, it can't be any harder than a kid scooter."

She helped him into his seat, shut the trunk, and then sat on the cart. With hands on the steering bars, she studied the instructions on the cart's board.

"Okay. Looks easy enough." She moved the bar about. "Left. Right. This must be the go." She pulled on a trigger and the cart jerked forward. "Whoa! 'Kay. We've got this."

She pulled on the other trigger, and the cart leapt backward and clobbered her bumper. After a series of trial and error, jerks and jolts, Annie managed to drive through the parking lot aisle without disturbing too many pedestrians walking to and from the store entrance, not bothering to notice her beyond their own distractions of phone interactions. Annie wasn't confident the bag boy was too charmed at her ability to maneuver the thing into a spot once inside the doors. Good thing there was a brick wall to back up into. Any confidence Annie had left evaporated, considering she had parked too close to the next cart to make a liberating exit. She made an awkward leg and arm tumbling escape, slowly sliding from one seat onto another, down the line of the next seven carts before catching her breath and standing next to the bag boy. She was certain she broke a sweat.

"Have a good day, ma'am," the bag boy shouted.

* * *

Annie spent her morning at Empire Café having patrons line up to watch and videotape her barista art of rainbow-colored firebirds and celebrity 'mug shots' as she called them. Several times a week this was her second job. And she loved it.

"Pretty Muppet," she called out one coffee. "Here's your Einstein. Have a great day."

"Awesome," the happy patron remarked.

Annie was in her element. She loved the sound of steaming milk, grinding coffee, and the hubbub of the environment. Her devotion resulted in being called upon for most specialty drinks. Drops of food coloring in the frothy milk flowered into designs upon the foam like a cheap van Gogh. Her coworker Jimmie was just as talented. She watched as he created an Eiffel Tower with a silhouette of a cat on a wall, all with a toothpick. A passerby caught Annie's eye—a woman she knew from her drinking days. This poor woman had never gotten off the streets. Always, Annie's heart tugged at the sight of her. With the crowd thinned out, she felt confident she could take off her apron. Annie touched Jimmie on the sleeve.

"I'm going to take a break, okay?"

Jimmie looked in the direction of her nod and smiled at her. "Sure. Take your time."

Annie returned the smile, relieved. She dug her hand into their tip jar and pulled a short wad of bills, paying for a breakfast sandwich and black coffee. The woman outside looked surprised to see Annie squatting down beside her on the curb. The woman's hardened features were worn from a hard life. A homeless life beset with addictions. Her drab clothes clung to her body like a breath. The fingerless gloves she wore were torn away from the palms of her dingy hands as she held them like a downward prayer.

"How's it going, Rita?" Annie asked.

Rita flashed a toothless grin. "Annie. Damn. How you been, child?"

Annie rubbed Rita's back and handed her the coffee and sandwich. "Thought you'd like your favorite breakfast."

"God better take care of you. 'Cuz you always caring for people."

"I pay it forward, that's all." Annie placed a napkin in Rita's lap. "Makes me sleep better at night. Tell me, where have you been?"

Rita dismissed her with a wrinkled nose. "Marching to my own drum. Gotta do me, you know? Satan don't take no time off. Always trying to stay one step ahead of him. But he's got watchers. And the Four Horseman got cousins."

"No master plan today for building an army and conquering?"

Rita spit a guffaw. "Go on. How you doing, child?"

"Better today, just for today."

"I hear that."

Annie always felt uncomfortable describing her life to people like Rita. All her moans and groans dissipated under the light of their sun and shade, their park benches and bridges, their Vine Street and 15th Street berating. Living in muck and nooks and slum rooms no bigger than a closet just to shoot up or hit a crack pipe or meth bowl. Truth always smacked her in the face in moments like this, that her life could have ended up just like Rita's not so long ago. And that the only difference between them was that Annie discovered the spirit of hope and found a way out. She always wondered if the universe planted folks like Rita in her life when she needed to be humbled about how far she had come. People like Rita never believe in anything better than the spirit of struggle they've become. It would be so easy to be a Rita, she reflected. The same mind that finds a happy moment can discard fear and make you believe going back out one time wouldn't hurt. The insanity is you'd believe it.

"Still sober, ain't you?" Rita asked.

"Yes, ma'am."

"You better be. Damn good thing you got out when you did. Look at you. Doing so good in this place. People like you here, girl."

"Aww, now."

"No. I mean it. Sweetie, you got talent."

It was Annie's turn to laugh. "That's not talent. That's coffee."

"Honey, I can't do that. Shoot."

"Doodling froth isn't art. It's a dollar-store greeting card in a cup."

Rita leaned back like Annie had two heads. "Take some credit, woman. You got talent. It's paying, right? Girl, you better wake up. Hear me? You never know what you got 'till it's gone, gone. Then it's a bitch if you ever get it back, because you never appreciated it enough."

Annie nodded. "You used to be a blues singer, right?"

Rita murmured into her coffee, "A long time ago. I was good too." She strained the word *good* like it came from a faraway country packed with boxes of travel memories. Rita crossed her fingers. "Kay Starr and me were like this."

"Huh. She was one of my dad's favorite singers."

"Yeah, baby. She was genuine too. Chill. A real cool cat. Agents down from Chicago, club owners from Louisville, millionaires in Boston, and veterans in Vegas. They all came to Cincinnati to hear the young girl with 'the voice' sing her heart out about dusty roads, smoky caverns, jazzy whore bread-bars and two-timing rambling jacks." She cackled. "That's what I called my ex. A rambling, bramble-ass Jack."

"You should be so proud." Annie hugged Rita from the side and kissed her forehead. Then, she stood up. "I've got to get back. It's my turn to disinfect the bathrooms with a top notch, expensive-ass, lemongrass-scented cleaner, and add an Andes Mint to each stall."

"You kill me," Rita cackled.

"Only the best for our patrons, Rita. You know that. I even tape a new motivational meme on the mirrors every day."

"Your boss's idea?"

"You betcha. Creates quite the conversation."

Rita squinted. "Saying what?"

Annie pulled out the postie note from her pocket. "Well today, it's, 'Please keep your muses to the toilet and your tampons in the trash.' Also got, '#Free the Pee,' and, 'Fans of clean jazz hands.'"

* * *

Annie was rushing around the hot bar, preparing three different coffees, when a coworker slid beside her.

"I'll be right back," the woman sniveled.

"Wait. Where are you going?"

"On break."

Annie's heart skipped a beat as she stared at the half-dozen customers standing in line. "You can't. Lunch crowd. We're kind of busy here."

The woman twitched a dead response and slinked away. Exasperated, Annie finished up the drinks and hollered out the names. "Sassy Whiskers, Jaded Jewel, and Dick Without Harry." Before looking at her next customer, she slid up to the bar with pen in hand. "Thank you for waiting. What can I get…you?"

Annie stuttered as her eyes met the dream she ran into the week before.

"Oh. You. I know you," the woman replied. Her head cocked with curiosity, her eyes glazing over.

"Umm…Yodel's Bookstore," Annie coaxed. "Drywall."

A smile gleamed across the woman's thin, delicate lips. "Oh. Right! Hi."

Jimmie leaned close to Annie. "Umm. Hello. Customers."

Annie snapped out of her dream world. "Right. Um."

"Yeah," the woman laughed. "Sorry. I'll have a salted caramel frappe. Soy."

"Size?" Annie asked.

The woman had already lowered her head to text for a moment, but then she looked back up sheepishly. "I'm sorry. That was rude of me. What did you say?"

Annie realized her eyes had drifted to the woman's cleavage, just slightly visible, hinting at the tender skin under her unbuttoned collar. She cleared her throat. "Small or grande?"

"Oh. I'm a grande person. Always grande."

Annie presented a larger cup. "We have a new one. The almighty titan. Thirty-two ounces."

"Ah. No thanks."

Oh, God, her nose is so cute when she wrinkles it up, thought Annie.

"A bit much."

"Got it. Grande it is. And who is it you wish to be today?"

The woman's eyes darted to Annie's pen, poised over the cup.

Annie leaned toward her. "The fun part is that you don't have to use your real name here."

"Oh, I see." The woman's brow knitted.

"I think some people come here just to be entertained by the names."

Her smile was delightful—a smile Annie was certain she had felt the warmth of before. But not in this lifetime, this reality. Hers was a smile one could never tire of kissing, a face ever beautiful to see every season's glow upon. A subtle dash of magic sparkled in the corner of her eyes. The kind of magic that knew how to hold onto confidence and call it humility. Eyes like a jeweled glass of cognac, delightful eyes perfect for staring longingly into a campfire on a crisp autumn evening, as a poem of rippled waters and wide sunsets was read to her.

"How about Sweet and Spicy?"

Her comment snapped Annie out of her vision. "Oh. Good one."

Her coworker Jimmie ripped off the receipt and handed it to the woman. "Don't forget your receipt," he said.

Sweet and Spicy kindly acknowledged him, took the slip, and stepped aside.

He placed a hand on his hip. "When are you going to dip into that hors d'oeuvre?"

"An exotic delicacy I couldn't possibly afford."

"Mm. I'd just bet she's a rebellious, kinky, Scottish Goth behind all that demure, Lands'-End-slash-Jane-Austin image."

Annie ruffled her brow and leaned away. "Excuse me. I have a coffee to make."

CHAPTER SIX

Hyde Park Square was a bustling, posh neighborhood where shops and shoppers met with mutual approval of the best foods, businesses, and demands. Apologies never helped the individual who took to the sidewalks under an eye of disapproval to the latest fashion trends. Annie always felt a bout of constipation surge within her gut when viewing an older woman wearing yoga pants and heels with a fashionable scarf, like she was on the catwalk. She never understood the interest in yoga pants anyway. Even on those who might pass wearing them, she found them as unacceptable as wearing pajama pants in public. Yet, to paint them onto a figure that had bouffant hair, Botox cheeks and lips, plastic chin and neck surgery, it was exhausting to just watch them. Must be exhausting being them. Being told this is someone who feels good about themselves seemed to fade behind the word oxymoron. She was grateful to hide out as an ordinary, white bread, unfashionable gal without such luxuries.

But, what did she know? She hated how her body fit in clothes, and plucked at premature gray hairs on her head, while living vicariously through 1940's movies. She preferred to believe herself a more refined version of the shy teenager who liked books, doodling, and waving back at the silvery leaves of cottonwoods. The old-world romantic never left her. But the innocence certainly did. She collected vintage books, books on sober living, and cerebral biographies on dead writers, while developing an earnest attempt every day to feel that something was worthwhile in all of this chaos called Earth.

Once, she had looked into a shop window and wondered if she was just jealous at the women who wore tight pants without anyone's need of approval or interest in their criticisms. Nah. Yoga pants were simply indecent, no matter how she looked at it. She chalked it up to a grand distaste of something that would be considered a fashion faux pas by the next generation anyway, like the mullet-wearing 1980s making fun of the '70s afros. She really couldn't wait to blog, "*I told you so*," on social media. It would make her day. But, for now, she had to live with the mundanity of a world filled with gray and rain and disgust at the usual crowd of rude drivers barely allowing her to close her car door before swiping close by and pressing her into her hood.

Stepping onto the curb, an elderly woman nearly ran her through with her extra-sharp umbrella that was poised to poke anyone's eye out who stood in her way. Annie dutifully waited behind the old lady as she stepped into the boutique beside Yodel's Bookstore. Annie wasn't in a hurry to work, anyway. Besides, what good was working with one eye?

Varsha met Annie at her desk. "You're here early, aren't you?"

"Yeah. A little bit. I've got a lot of paperwork to do." Annie shook off her raincoat and hung it over her chair. "Made the mistake of parking out front."

"You're living an unusually dangerous life today. Is it real paperwork or YouTube?"

"What?" Annie wrung out her shirt sleeve.

"I saw you yesterday watching lesbian short films and TV clips."

"Oh, that. Yeah. Why is it, when you've searched for lesbian shorts, YouTube throws in a video on how to remove giant ear acne?"

"That's so gross."

Annie pulled out a mirror from her desk and began to finger through wet, brown bangs. "See, it's crap like this that starts society down the wrong freakin' path about cultures. I mean, who cares about Lady Gaga-like shoes when all you want is to watch fan videos on your favorite TV characters? That's how stereotypes happen. Just like the '70s, with buzz cuts and flannel shirts. When I came out to my mom, she waited for me to show up with a flannel shirt, just like she learned in the '70s. She got tired of waiting. Did I ever tell you? After seven years out of the closet, she finally bought me a flannel shirt. 'If you're going to get your feet wet,' she said, 'you'd better go all the way.' I had to tell her, 'Mom, flannel does not make the woman. That's a myth. It's not a gay thing. It was never a gay thing.'"

"But, you're wearing a flannel shirt now."

"Yes. Very observant of you." Annie dried her glasses off with the shirt.

"And I believe you have several flannel shirts, don't you?"

"Yes. Nowadays." Annie returned her focus on her paperwork. "Don't distract me."

"Do you feel gayer?"

Annie raised her chin. "I feel comfortable."

"Bruh, it's July."

Annie was losing the spirit of the conversation. "He has the air turned up in here. I'm freezing. I would look silly wearing a parka."

Varsha looked at her askance. "But, you don't think you look silly wearing flannel in July?"

"Do I look silly wearing flannel?"

"In July."

Annie felt the barb this time. "Well, your shoes look silly."

Varsha puffed her cheeks. "I just bought these. I got them on sale. They're puppy flats by Lady Gaga. She has her own line of shoes out now. Look at these. You push a button, and the tail wags."

"Oh, God."

Varsha demonstrated. "Look. Isn't that cute? I saw them on YouTube." She looked out the window. "Hey, did you see that little dog that lady had?"

Annie was attempting to find a distraction in the bills before her. "I was too busy trying not to get impaled."

"She obviously didn't see you."

"Obviously. Her eyebrows were too tightly sewn to her forehead, holding her skull upright so that her plastic nostrils might have been in a dangerously risky position of drowning her had the oversized golf umbrella not been extended."

Varsha leaned arms across Annie's desk. Her eyes glazed over in a blank state of daydream. "I hope by the time my day comes to look old, the science of surgeries have advanced."

"Yes, Varsha. It'll happen overnight. One day—boom—you're old."

"I've heard that. And I'll probably be just like that lady. Vain and proud of my design, wearing it like a cosplay goddess."

"Forgive me for not applauding your low standards."

"My, but we're cranky today. Cutting people down? What gives?"

Annie sighed, hoping to expel some of her unplaceable irritation through her nostrils. "Everything. And nothing."

"Now, you know when you give me those Buddhist quotes, you lose me."

"There's a big difference between a Buddhist and an alcoholic, Varsha."

"What's that?"

"The Buddhist knows his mind is full of crap."

* * *

Annie had spent the better part of the day paying the bookstore's accounts online and keeping an eye on Varsha, whom the boss insisted was fine to stand atop an eight-foot stack of books to reach places others had never bothered with.

"OSHA would have a field day with us," Annie hollered to Mr. Tiddle.

Annie neatly piled the outgoing mail on the counter. The ding of the little bell ensured her timing was perfect. The mail carrier approached her with a dimpled smile and handed her a stack of mail.

"Thanks, Flapjack," Annie said. She handed him the pile of outgoing letters. "Trade you."

He nodded and stuffed her pile in his bag before heading back out.

Varsha sprung down from the stack of books like a superhero and brushed off her hands. She approached the desk and looked down at Annie's empty lunch container. "Brussels sprouts? I like brussels sprouts."

"You enjoy watching them at various levels of decay, you mean."

"Life gets very boring after my Tuesday night show."

Annie turned to eye the clock. It was after 4:00 p.m., and her stomach growled. "Yeah, well. They don't last long in the system." She stood and stretched. "I'll be here a while longer. Guess I should go get a sandwich or something."

A delivery driver dressed in brown opened the shop door and scanned a small package as he approached the desk. "Varsha Christ?"

"Khrist. Sounds like crisp, except with a T."

"Right. I bet it was rough growing up, with people making fun and all. Christ jokes and stuff like that." He laughed.

"Yeah. I just figured anyone who did that was just an immature asshole."

He cleared his throat and handed her the package. "Have a nice day."

She winked at him. "Back atcha, cowboy. Might wanna polish them spurs. Stay on your horse, now. Hear?"

Annie walked down the main aisle toward Mr. Tiddle's office in the back of the store with a letter from the IRS and another from the Taft Theater. She rapped on the door. Sounds of clicks, latches, and chains ensued before a motorized whine made her jump.

Mr. Tiddle's nose peeked out at her as he opened the door. "Oh. Yes, yes. Come in."

Annie slid around the door and inspected his paranoid assortment of locks and gadgets.

"Just in case of a tornado," he said. "This office is perfectly safe and sound. What do you think?"

"Uh—Mr. Tiddle. Yes, your door is quite imposing and impressive. You do realize anyone can punch a hole right through your walls, though, right? They're just thin drywall. They wouldn't stand up to a six-year-old, let alone a tornado. Besides, Cincinnati is sitting in a safe well that pulls tornadoes outside the city limits to the east, over the river from Kentucky, and into Adams and Brown County."

"Tornadoes are unpredictable. Don't let yourself believe that myth."

"It's science, actually. Just look up the patterns of tornados that have ever crossed over here." Annie held up her phone with a meteorological map. "That's why people are naming Cincinnati one of the best places to live."

"We just had a terrorist march into a downtown bank and blast a half a dozen lives away. We are not safe, Miss Freckle. No safer than any other city. This city's mayoral administration is out to cause a ruckus to keep fear in our hearts and believe we need to allow homies and rednecks their firearms."

"Did you really just call black people 'homies?'" Annie knew not to encourage him any further. He'd just continue to rant and rave in his obsession the rest of the hour. "Ah, look. I'm going on break, okay?"

Mr. Tiddle was caught up reading his Taft letter, but he looked up at her. "Ah, the tickets. I was worried they messed up. The concert is Thursday. I'll be taking off early. Make sure you have your key on you. I'll need you to lock up."

"Sure thing." Annie craned her head, about to eye his wagging tickets. "Who's playing?"

"Low Blow. They're from Brazil. Tony is flying up tomorrow and wanted something new to do. I thought he'd like it."

"He likes jazz, right? Low Blow is hard rock."

"Oh, he'll love it."

What did she know? "Good. Okay. Have fun. I'm going now."

Annie walked back into the store to hear all the locks and plates buzz shut with clanks and clacks. She shivered from a passing thought. What if he couldn't get out? Oh, well. She shrugged it off. Annie spotted Varsha among a stack of fresh inventory in the Self-Help aisle.

"Hey, I'm going to Arthur's for a sandwich. Want anything?"

"No thanks. Look at this."

She held up a page from a book with a color wheel of emotions. "Have you seen this words wheel? Oh, look. Abandoned, disappointed, awful, despair, powerless. How depressing. Oh, but if I turn it, I get powerful, provocative... ooh, aggressive."

"Varsha."

"Huh?"

"Stop that."

Varsha closed the book. "'Kay."

* * *

Annie walked down the street, grateful the rain had slowed down to a misting. It was still enough to mess her glasses up with spots. She had spent a good part of the last few years appreciating everything that had life, pulse. A mentor once told her to look outside her eyes. Pay attention to everything around her. The world was here for her to be a part of, they'd said. Nature was easy to accept. She always felt closer to nature and animals than to the human race, and everything created by humans was, in her opinion, a manufactured attempt at perfection. Nothing was as imperfectly perfect as the stray blooming weed that stuck out of the crack in a sidewalk. She could stop and study it with admiration for hours and feel perfectly content. The task lay in adjusting her perception to humanity the same way. The hard part was letting herself see it created something just as beautiful. She admitted to herself that her life was still a work in progress.

She smiled at the flower photo now on her phone and walked past a shop with a poster posted in its window. *Are you ready to turn a new chapter, Annie?* it read. Annie grinned with curiosity and continued on a step before stopping with a sudden fright. She turned about and slowly gazed at the sign again.

Are you ready to turn a new chapter?

Annie caught her breath and snorted a laugh. She shook it off and headed to Arthur's for her sandwich. As she walked back, she couldn't help glancing at the sign again, just to make sure she wasn't seeing things.

We're ready when you are, Annie.

She staggered a step. Annie drew herself closer to the window and squinted. The shop looked empty except a row of chairs and a counter.

"Annie," an older gentleman's voice rang out enthusiastically. His smile was a bit unnerving, like a used car salesman, although he looked normal enough. He was holding the door open for her.

"I'm sorry. Do I know you?" Annie asked.

A grin wrapped around his long face and eyes sparkled with such a keen observance it was hard not to feel his honesty. "They've been expecting you."

With a cautious approach, she leaned past him and peeked into the shop. "I don't need a new phone. Wait. Is this a cult? Because I don't do cults. And I don't do dating services."

Annie was hesitant and felt a fresh wave of gut talk. *Oh*, she thought to herself. *I should really eat something*. She turned about. "You know, maybe next time. I really ought to—"

The man disappeared. Annie found herself alone, looking around for any sign of him, when a woman's voice alerted her to turn back to the counter.

"Welcome to Guardian Services."

Her less-than-enthusiastic announcement wasn't much of an encouragement. Annie felt like she was the only customer left at a government office, with an employee who was waiting for someone to relieve her.

A man wearing a bowler hat pedaled a unicycle around her and tipped his hat, from which spilled a fountain of stardust. His figure shrunk as he rode into the air, leaving miniature clouds all around him, and he disappeared in the blush of a tiny nebula. The store then burst alive with colors, popping lights, fantastical creatures, climbing vines with sparkling fairy wings, and other magical creations. Annie watched as an excited woman headed out the door, giggling and holding up a sparkling wind chime.

"Come on," the clerk said. "Ain't nobody here to push you out of the way, child. It's you. It's all you, Annie. Get yourself up here, now. Come on."

Annie waited for her stomach to twist and fear to overwhelm her. But, the only sensation was a childlike urge to follow her curiosity.

"Yes, ma'am?"

"Now. How can I help you?"

Annie and the clerk made a series of facial exchanges, questioning each other's expressions. A mouse on a motorcycle zipped across the counter, and Annie watched as the woman leaned against the counter's edge as if she hadn't noticed it.

"Are you ready?" she asked.

"I'm afraid you have me at a disadvantage." Annie scratched her head. "I'm not sure why I'm here. But that guy said you were expecting me."

"Oh. Right. Sorry." The clerk pulled out a form and pen. "Now, this doesn't really say. Was it the eyes, ears, limbs that you need a miracle for?"

"Oh, I don't know. I'm getting this overwhelming feeling that it's all in my head. Sort of like this place. Overwhelming. Is this what happens when you don't get enough fiber? It's like the whole of social media and all of Pinterest is right here in this shop, in a constipated way. Why am I so calm?"

"Welcome to your world."

"Wow. Dr. Seuss meets Cirque du Soleil. There's so much wackiness out there in the world that wants my sympathy, money, attention. From bald sick puppies and Trump supporters wearing wax lips buttons, to being told I've been wearing my underwear wrong, and why I shouldn't snap the ends off asparagus. I'd better go to another A.A. meeting. I'm sicker than I thought. Okay. Tell me, how does this work? Is this like having a therapist on call or something? An extra-curricular heavenly point, maybe?" Annie made a humored noise that wasn't reflected. "Just kidding."

The clerk didn't blink. "Picture a burger drive-thru owned by Annie Leibovitz. We give you the bag with better sauce and a deeper-than-imagined point of reference."

Annie watched as an elderly woman appeared behind the clerk, walking a giraffe on a leash. The elder waved, and Annie returned the woman's gesture with slightly less enthusiasm. "Maybe I need my eyes checked. I'm feeling very awkward right now and I don't know how to respond. What exactly is going on?"

The clerk smiled deeply. "Okay. Let's start at the beginning. The services contract one guardian for four months. Their visits are based solely on your personal needs. They speak your language. We have several types of guardian personas for you. Would you like animal, human, or alien?"

"Uh…I'm not really into little green people with big black eyes or stuff like that. And planetary people remind me too much of a neighbor I used to have. Guy took way too much meth."

"Animal?"

"No—I don't want Mrs. Winkle's dogs talking to me. That would be pretty frightening."

"Human it is. Male or female?"

"Doesn't matter. Female-ish, maybe."

"We'll just mark it optional. Now, would you prefer a child, old sage, fairy godmother, angel?"

Annie shook her head. "I'm not sure I'd respond well to a child after just watching *The Omen*."

"Adult then."

Annie held up a finger in question. "Are those wingy things on cherubs really real?"

"Michelangelo makes them look so good. Doesn't he? Alrighty. If you just sign here, then we'll get you started."

"What's this?"

"A release form stating you understand fully that your guardian will get all up in your business, and when you least expect it. It's part of their contract. They're all-knowing, you know."

Annie felt a twitch in her eye. "How much 'in my business' is 'all up in my business'?"

"Home, office, car, DMs, texts, highway blackboards, cable news, and all private spaces."

This started to sound a bit intrusive to Annie. "Private spaces?"

"Their favorite time of meeting up is when you're in the bathroom."

"Bathroom."

"Yeah, you know. On the pot. In the shower. Brushing your teeth. Really freaked me out at first. But, I got used to it."

Annie heard something behind her and almost tripped on a vine when she turned to see a carnival man in a red suit blowing flames from his mouth. Three crows tap-danced behind him, cawing whenever he spit fire.

"It really is the only time we're responsive and fully alone in our thoughts, if you think about it," the clerk added.

"Yes. I get distracted easily, I guess."

A woman with purple hair streaks chased a whirlwind of scattered papers in the corner of the lobby. And in the distant room, library books were talking and moving like puppets to a small child. Annie breathed deep before turning back around to the counter to sign the paper. She pulled out an insurance card and handed it to the woman.

"Oh, we don't take insurance. We're kind of a nonprofit."

"Okay. Right. How do I get in touch with these guardians?"

"Oh, we have an app."

"Really? An app."

"Uh-huh. It was already installed on your phone when you signed." The woman leaned over to Annie's phone and pointed. "There, see? OMG."

"OMG."

"Uh-huh. It's a metaphor."

"You mean an acronym."

"No. A metaphor. Like our reality that's not really our reality. Don't worry. You'll catch on later. And if you need face time—you know, a one-on-one kind of chat in the flesh—then you just ask."

Elephants danced with tambourines and woo-hooed. Annie turned back to the clerk. "I see. Out loud?"

"Yeah. Out loud."

"Any hidden fees?" Annie asked.

"The only expenses you incur is your time."

"Okay. How do I know if this is really for me? Can I just unsubscribe, like, forget I ever walked into this place? You know, *bada bing*. Gone, like an oopsey hit on a website selling crocheted huggees for rocks."

The woman leaned an elbow atop the counter and held out the receipt between two fingers. "Honey, you need this."

Annie focused in on the receipt. It was a strip of paper from a fortune cookie.

Your life. Your choice.

She frowned and glanced up. The clerk had disappeared. In fact, the store was completely empty and silent, just as it had been when she walked in. A shiver ran down her spine as she slowly turned toward the door. The doorman was there. He held the door open for her as before, with his ever-present smile.

"You're on your way," he said as she passed him.

"This has been the craziest hallucination I have ever created. Have you—" She had turned to him, but he was gone too. "Of course you're not there."

CHAPTER SEVEN

Annie pinned up her little fortune cookie message on the cork board above her kitchenette table. "*Your life. Your choice,*" stared back at her in black and white, with as little luster as if it had been cracked open over a plate of chow mein with a bad blind date.

She brushed her teeth and spit into the bathroom sink, nervously glancing past her features in the mirror. No visitor, yet. She pushed aside the shower curtain and peeked in, as if searching for some dorky figure to frighten the wits out of her. Her toes began to curl at her own jumpiness.

"Stop it," she whispered to herself.

She headed out to the kitchen to perform the usual ballet with Pork and Beans eating from separate bowls, and enjoyed the thought of sitting down to a bowl of oatmeal, toast, and orange juice while the cats looked on expectantly. At the first sip of her juice, a looming figure appeared next to her.

"Hi."

Annie choked and spewed the juice across the room. Her heart pounded and her throat tightened as she shot out of the chair to gag and cough over the sink.

The man's voice hummed with a deep base. "Startled ya, huh?"

Annie was still trying to catch her breath through a series of coughs. She glanced at him and smacked at her chest with a nod.

"Gotta work on that." He handed her a glass of water. "Here. Drink this."

Annie hadn't noticed his features before now. She gratefully took the glass and wiped the wetness from her eyes to clarify him in her sight. A hulking man stood before her wearing a V-neck white T-shirt, red plaid boxers, and a pink tutu. A pair of garters held his long, black socks up.

"Nice touch," she gasped. "Geez. You kinda look like my Uncle Tom."

"Tom. I'll go with that."

"Tom. So, you're…you're?"

He shrugged. "Got a cigarette?"

"No."

"There's no place to put a pack in this getup. So here we are."

Annie shut the drapes over her kitchen sink. "Can anyone see you?"

"Nope. Just you. I'm sorry. Does this offend you?"

"Actually…no. No. You're fine. Fine. Really. Whatever melts your butter." She pushed herself away from the sink, took another gulp of her water, and sat back down at her small table. She cleared her throat a few times, and the two exchanged a few strange looks toward each other.

"I can't stay. Just wanted to introduce myself. We've got a soccer game to go to."

"I don't understand. I thought I asked for a woman?"

"Ish."

"Right." Annie struggled to understand if this was the real reality, or if she finally snapped into mental illness. "The whole shop experience was a bit far out of my range of imaginary belief system."

"Actually, you created—"

"Created that," she chimed in with him. "I was afraid you were going to say that."

"See. You're already leaps ahead of your gut."

"You haven't seen me on the highway," she said before realizing she had absolutely no idea how to approach this guy. "Right. So. Tom. What happens now?"

"So. We're fresh out of godmothers until August." Tom gestured to the two of them. "We're in a unique situation here. I think you'll be surprised at the outcome."

"I already am."

"You're quick. I like that."

* * *

"Life happens in the most unexpected places," Varsha said.

Annie was going to add a realistic presence of thought to Varsha's comment, but decided it best not to insert anything.

"You know? Like, I was just chilling on this bench, in my own zone, right? Then, this dog's ball smacks me. Boom! Shocks me out of my quiet space. But then, this hot girl comes up to me and apologizes. I tell her it's no big deal, stuff happens, you know. She had this awesome German shephard that just bonded to me." Varsha showed Annie a photo with her and the dog. "We rolled around on the ground, played with the ball for a while, then the girl insisted on buying me lunch."

Annie glanced at her from her paperwork. "And you're dating her now?"

"No. It ended there. But I've got her number. I figured the ball thing was just her way of getting my attention."

"Ah, a ploy."

"Yeah. See, I had fun when I thought I was going to be bored. So, it worked out."

"Huh."

Varsha sat on the corner of Annie's desk. "You need to have fun more, Annie."

"I have fun."

"*When* do you have fun? When was the last time you had fun? Just impulsively doing something for no reason?"

"Well, I...take Mrs. Winkle's dogs for a walk, a swim."

"I said impulsively. Nothing to do with chores or serious suck-up time."

"I beg your pardon. That's not suck-up time. She's old. She needs help with those dogs sometimes."

"Okay. So? When have you had fun?"

Annie honestly couldn't think of a moment recently that she hadn't worked hard or made time away from expectant duties from Mrs. Winkle's dogs or random requests. "My life's pretty plain. I like watching puddles gather in the rain."

"You're quoting a song? Really?"

"I truly just did, didn't I?"

"Hasn't anything ever happened to you just out of the blue?"

"Oh." Annie scratched her head. "Yes. Actually. Quite recently. But—um...It's complicated."

"Uh, yeah. You need a great escape from your life. Such as it is. Just get out. Not with Mrs. Winkle's dogs or grocery runs. You need to explore this world, woman," Varsha stressed as a customer approached the counter. "Beyond coffee bars and bookstores."

Annie stood from her chair and walked over to greet the elderly woman. "Hi, Mrs. Proust."

The Prousts were a well-off family in Cincinnati, renowned in the past for their philanthropy and generosity, donating large amounts to the city's hospitals. Mrs. Proust was always present to make certain her late husband's name was spelled correctly when another wing was added to a building. Word on the street was that, after the market crash, Mr. Proust died of financial loss, due to his advisors putting a large sum into the wrong stocks, leaving Mrs. Proust to downsize in the poor neighborhood. Her idea of downsizing was going from a multi-million-dollar estate to a posh, fourteen-room townhouse with a library that overlooked the river.

"I need to see Mr. Piddle, please."

"It's Tiddle."

Mrs. Proust bent down to her bag, hoisted up a large, hardbound book, and slapped it on the counter. A cloud of dust swirled up and scattered, making both women fan the air and cough.

"I'll get him," Annie hacked. She walked over to her desk, pushed the intercom, and held the phone up to her mouth. "Mr. Tiddle to the front, please."

Annie dismissed herself for a restroom break. The mirror's reflection showed shadowed pieces of aged paper that had drifted on her shoulder. "Aww, man. This is a new cardigan." She brushed dust and paper off with a huff when her fairy godmother appeared in the corner, shaking her from her senses.

"Ho!"

Annie twirled around and grasped onto the sink basin, then bent over with hands on her knees, her heart pounding. "Okay. I really have to pee, now. Can you—um." She crossed her legs and waved him out.

Tom's face turned from a smile to a look of surprise. "Oh, yeah. Sorry."

Annie soon walked out of the restroom and leaned on the closed door behind her. She attempted to rub the tension from her forehead, but it didn't seem to be working. She walked along the aisles in search of him. Instead, she found a book lying on the floor in a book nook. She bent over to pick it up when a large hand met hers.

Annie wasn't used to jumping out of her skin, let alone so many times. She stopped herself from flailing about after a series of unsettled jeebies and heart poundings. "Jesus—Tom. We've gotta work on this. Okay?" She wiped the newly acquired sweat from her brow. "Got any Valium dust in that tutu?"

"Oh, you don't want that. It'll cause muscle spasms and irritability."

"I already have that, thank you. I'm sure diarrhea will follow soon. Look, I know I've just got to get used to this. Right?"

"We've only got a month." Tom adjusted his tutu.

"Wait. A month?"

"Yeah. It's a monthly club. When you signed the paper—"

Annie winced. "A lot of stuff was happening, okay. There were giraffes and fairies, and circus crap dropping everywhere around me like bad magnets on a refrigerator. My discussion with the clerk ended up being a bit of a blur. A month? That's a bit rushed for a relationship. Don't you think?"

"We found it works best this way. Different entities offering different perspectives of your desires."

"Aren't you all the same entity?"

"Yeah. But, humans don't see us like that most of the time. You all tend focus on what your Now Reality shows you."

"Now Reality?"

Tom held the book up to her and pointed to the title, *Self-Care Empowerment*. "Do you practice this kind of stuff?"

Annie shook her head. "I always envisioned self-care teachings like two doves trying to mate. One hopping around after the other. Just bopping along, never really understanding the process, and hoping the process just kind of gives in and allows him to catch up. Seems like a lot of work. Besides, I follow a 12-Step program. That's a game-changer right there."

"One can never have too many spiritual tools." Tom refiled the book. "Sometimes, words, affirmations get stale. You get bored. Why not tell me about yourself."

Annie tucked in a stray flap of shirttail. "Aren't you supposed to be all-knowing, or something?"

"I want to hear what you believe about yourself." He sat down on a stool and rested willowy arms over rangy legs.

Annie was still getting used to Tom's appearance. He didn't even try to look natural in it, and when he daintily crossed his legs, she struggled to stifle a laugh. "Honestly, I don't know about me. I can't tell you everything about me, because I haven't met all of me just yet. I know Past Me, which is yucky and stupid and full of bad choices. I know Now Me, which is full of okay thoughts and less-than-stupid life decisions, most of the time. Still, I feel like I'm pushing against something. And I know What-I-Want-To-Be Me, which is filled with hopes and dreams and success. I don't know Thirty-Five Me, Forty Me. Midlife Me. And if she's anything like Last Week Me, with the stiff back after two days of lifting seventy-pound boxes of books and eating pear and goat cheese tarts, farting over the pothole bumps on Vine Street, I kind of get the idea how Old Lady Me will turn out to be."

Annie was so intent on describing herself to Tom, the voice of Mr. Tiddle behind her took her completely by surprise. She let out a little shriek as she spun around to face him.

"If you're finished reciting this chapter of your memoirs, I would like you to assist me in removing a very inconvenient situation that has developed in the front of the store," Mr. Tiddle said.

Annie turned back around and scanned the nook for any sign of her fairy godmother before following Mr. Tiddle. She was grateful for the disappearance, at least for the moment. She still couldn't wrap her head around the fact that no one else could see Tom.

Mrs. Proust was still standing at the counter. But now, volumes had amassed in piles at her feet and stacks upon the counter, with such a weight that Annie could hardly believe the desk hadn't already crumbled to splinters. Mrs. Proust's chauffeur shot a surly lip at Mr. Tiddle before wheeling his dolly out the door and slapping the dust off his pressed suit.

Mr. Tiddle whispered to Annie, "Signed first editions of Charles Darwin's journals."

Annie wheezed. "Holy crap, Batman."

Mr. Tiddle tapped his fingers together. "Aren't they glorious?"

Mr. Tiddle was a sucker for first editions, knowing the resale value would catapult his store into the limelight of online shoppers. The inconvenience of this situation, though, was quite traumatic for the poor store's finances.

"We can't afford to buy these from her, Mr. Tiddle."

Mr. Tiddle moved a hand over his thin beard. He always toyed with his beard when he was thinking, and Annie knew she was about to launch into a series of Q&As with him.

"Can we negotiate payments on our other debts?"

Annie shook her head. "We've reached our maximum allowance after that signed first edition of the *Book of Mormon* was purchased last month."

"401k funds?"

"Penalized already from early withdrawal."

"How about the IRA account?"

"The tax you're paying on that withdrawal already put you in a higher tax bracket in April."

Mr. Tiddle stomped a foot and handed her a card.

"Why are you giving me an ATM card?"

"It's a high-yield savings account gifted to me from my grandpa's estate. He died last year," he said.

"Aw. Are you sure you want to do this with it? I mean, he had to have worked hard, long years to save this up. I'm sure he had higher expectations for it besides bail money."

Mr. Tiddle rolled his eyes. "Haven't we sold those papers yet?"

"Nobody wants to buy the grumblings of a circus ringmaster."

"Miss Freckle. The creative jaunts and travels of one man's genius marketing skills are hardly grumblings."

Annie faced him. "P.T. Barnum was a liar, a thief, an extreme racist, and he single-handedly dealt a cruel blow to humanity in exploiting other people's handicaps for entertainment. Not to mention the animal abuse. He was a horrible man. A Nero of his era."

"Drama is money, Miss Freckle. I want you to sell those papers."

"Rome burned, and Nero died. Just remember that." Nero turned to leave, but Annie held a hand out and stopped him. "Mr. Tiddle. I have a fiscal responsibility to keep this ship above water. Do you understand that, if you do this, you are risking an IRS audit, and might face the eventual possibility of being shut down completely?"

Mr. Tiddle gave her a snide look. "Mentioning the fact that I have a college degree in Accounting and Business, and you have nothing, I'd say only one of us is capable of knowing the true statistical risk and answer to that question. I know what I'm doing. Keep your eyes on what I pay you to do, and leave the rest to me. 'Kay?"

His remarkably cocksure attitude was enough to hide from anyone else the fact that his confidence was as flimsy as his countertop, which suddenly cracked and lurched before her. Annie simply sighed to the heavens.

"I'm going to have to find another job."

Tom appeared next to her, leaning against a bookshelf. "I thought you loved this job."

Annie dipped her head in his direction and stared at him. "There won't be anything left to pay me with if Mr. Tiddle goes through with this deal. Besides, he's forgotten that he hired me because my mother taught me accounting and gave me my first job."

"Never justify yourself to someone who doesn't value your opinion. How do you know this deal isn't something that will launch your future into something you've always wanted?"

"I don't recall asking for something that resembled homelessness. I'll have to get back with you on that."

Tom stood and focused on unwrapping a piece of taffy. "Your choice is either going to drain you or provide pleasure. It's that simple. If you want a better life, better your choices."

Annie watched him pop the taffy in his mouth.

"The power of choice," he mumbled.

"I love what I do. I'm damn good at it. I love this bookstore. I can see so much value in it, if he would just turn it around. That's what I want."

Tom laid a heavy hand on her shoulder. "That's the spirit, Annie. We love it when you are defining yourself. Do more of that."

Varsha approached Annie in a panic. "Mr. Tiddle is having an asthma attack after an argument with Mrs. Proust over the first editions."

Annie snuck up beside Mr. Tiddle. She pulled him aside and handed him his inhaler. "That sucking sound you're making is your esophagus telling you to retreat. Retreat! Retreat! Remember, professionals are predictable. It's the amateurs that are dangerous. If your attack is going well, you've walked into an ambush."

Varsha interjected, "She was about to give you the dead husband story. Look at her! It's the sad widow face."

"I've already fallen for the sad widow face," Mr. Tiddle uttered. "It won't happen again."

Annie observed the woman coughing into a handkerchief. "Oh, she's about to pull out the old Polish grandmother story."

"What Polish grandmother story?"

Varsha smirked. "She'll wave a hankie, her Polish grandmother's hankie. Stitched it herself during the old war. She'll tell you she's dying and doesn't want to visit her grandmother's grave without explaining she can never see her again because of her failed attempt to sell her husband's treasured collection to afford the bus to Jersey."

"Oh, for Christ's sake," Mr. Tiddle countered.

The women watched as Mr. Tiddle approached the woman with stiff, professional poise. Then watched as his shoulders fell.

Annie cringed. "Oh, no."

"He's not going for it," Varsha reassured.

Tiddle leaned against his counter with his hands set far apart.

"Stay strong," Annie whispered. "Soldier up."

Tiddle slouched. Annie cringed. Tiddle raised up and threw his shoulders back. Annie exhaled. Tiddle tapped his pen on the counter.

Annie sucked in a breath. "No…he's calculating. Stop that."

"Maybe he's winning," Varsha said. "Maybe she'll agree."

Mr. Tiddle's head dipped to one side.

"Oh, the tippy head," Varsha cried.

Annie turned away with anguish and dread. "Damn, not the tippy head. He caved. He caved!"

Varsha rubbed her back. "There, there. Maybe we can sell it to a newbie collector someday at a ridiculous price."

Annie heard the tingling bell at the door and turned around. Mrs. Proust was leaving the store, and Mr. Tiddle had stepped away from the pile of books with the woman's Polish grandmother's handkerchief, crying and wiping his tears.

"What was it this time?" Annie asked.

Mr. Tiddle whimpered through tears. "Her derby horse lost. Her daughter refused to send a car, so she spent her last dollars hitching a ride with an eighteen-wheeler, listening to the driver's bad karaoke country music, while being forced to eat stale Twinkies. Do you know the shelf life of a Twinkie? It must have been there since 1969!"

Varsha pouted. "That's so sad."

"Very sad," Annie agreed.

* * *

Annie decided to take Mrs. Winkle's two dogs on a river cruise. When on the Ohio River for lunch, it was best to indulge oneself and ride upon one of the old paddle boats. The big, red paddles would pick up the heavy, dark waters and churn them back out with a delightful *shwamp, shwamp, shwamp*. Little Saqi and Bones seemed entranced by it all. Annie enjoyed the ragtime band on the balcony above them; the music drifted her to a far away, long ago time when such travels weren't a luxury as much as a necessity for the people of nearby towns headed for work across the water.

After the tasty meal, Annie was grateful to use the convertible option on her little car so Bones could sit up and get the full-face wind experience she deserved. It was a quirky, one-foot-wide convertible slice, but Annie had fallen in love with her yellow car. Saqi sat safely between Annie's arm and the door. The sun was high above them, and the winding drive through the large park was peppered with children kicking balls and getting tied up in kite strings, and parents wishing they'd invested in contraception. It was a great day to be a dog. Annie made sure they played ball, ate ice cream cones, danced to songs, and clowned around her as she rolled down the hill. The kisses and pounces were enough to help her forget all about her sore ankle.

Leading them back to her car with a hobble, a familiar and beautiful smile met her.

"Hi."

Annie's voice cracked. "Well, hi there. Sweet and Spicy, right?"

The woman dropped her head with slight acknowledgement. The sun gleamed upon her auburn hair gently, reminding Annie of her favorite orange marmalade. She was holding onto a small gym bag, which she adjusted to reach her hand out to Annie. "Catrin."

Annie had juggled the dogs, leashes, and door before accepting Catrin's hand. "Oh, that's such a nice name. Fits you, I think."

"Does it?"

"It's in the eyes." Annie adjusted her glasses. "You know only two percent of the population have green eyes?"

"I did not know that." That comment seemed to enliven Catrin's cheeks to a near-blush. She shifted her stance and changed the subject. "Are you injured? You were limping."

"Oh, it's nothing a little icing won't cure. You know. The extra whipped and creamy vanilla kind."

That got a laugh out of Catrin, and Annie's grip on the door eased.

Catrin dug in her bag. "I have a wrap."

"No, no. You're fine. Thank you, but—"

"Here. I insist. Trust me, I'm klutzy too. I can never look as graceful with most yoga positions as other people do. I have this grand illusion that it's still helpful, somehow. So, I carry on and keep all the necessary accoutrements on hand, just in case I fail to look good yet again."

It was Annie's turn to grin. "I don't think you need any help looking good. Any time you want to break out of that dulled illusion, just let me know. I'll be glad to remind you."

"Thank you."

The reply was so soft, Annie could have sworn a feather had landed by her heart.

Annie's ears warmed up. She pointed to the dogs and cleared her throat. "I'd better get them back."

"Oh, they're so cute together." Catrin reached out and petted them both, muttering unintelligible baby talk.

"This is Saqi."

"Saqi?"

"Yeah. Short for Sasquatch. For a bitty fella, trust me, he has huge paws that you can hear all over the house. Don'tcha?" Annie rubbed his little head. "And this big baby is Bones. She's patient with me."

Bones held her paw out and Catrin shook it. "Well, nice to meet you, Miss Bones."

"It's Ms. We have a few days a week together. They belong to my landlord. She's elderly, so they don't get out much."

"How sweet of you."

Annie shrugged the comment off. "I do it because it's the right thing. And the only time her son comes over is once a year for her to sign tax papers."

"Wow."

"Yeah."

Catrin paused with a thought, then shoved the wrap in Annie's hand. "Well, here. I've got to run. But, take this and be safe."

Annie shook her head. "Really. It's okay."

"I insist."

Annie met her eyes. "I've a feeling you insist often."

Catrin laughed and looked away. "Sorry. Guess I'm used to giving people what they don't want." She twisted about and presented her bag. It had a large, silk-screened symbol of the Postal Service on it.

"Ah." Annie knew she was defeated and happily shoved the wrap in her jeans pocket. "An important job, nevertheless."

"Not everyone would agree. Especially if you're any part of the tech world."

"Tradition dies hard. I appreciate having a mailbox. Where else can we Americans abuse our individual freedoms and create tacky art to describe our personalities?"

Catrin met Annie's smile and walked on. "Enjoy your day," she called over her shoulder.

"You, too!" It then dawned on her that she'd never introduced herself to Catrin. "Hey, um—sorry. I'm Annie."

Catrin backpedaled a couple steps and smiled. "Enjoy your day, Annie."

As Annie turned back to the car, both dogs were staring at her.

"What?"

They turned their heads toward Catrin's departing figure.

"Don't even go there."

* * *

Annie was sitting on her comfy chair with legs slung over the arm, playing a ukulele to the rapt attention of Pork and Beans while she sang an old 1920's tune, "Louise," with a few personal changes.

"Every little breeze seems to whisper Pork and Beans
Birds in the trees seem to twitter Pork and Beans
Each little rose tells me it knows I love you, love you
Every little beat that I feel in my heart
Seems to repeat what I felt at the start
Each little sigh tells me that I adore you, Pork and Beans"

A loud thud and scrambling from the ceiling broke her concentration. Pork and Beans turned their ears about to varying degrees, and Annie watched as their irises swelled with curiosity.

"Oh, great. Tom? Is that you? No, that's silly, Annie," she answered herself. "What would a fairy godmother be doing in an attic? Oh, geez. I hope it's not another rat."

Annie set the rickety ladder up in the hallway and clutched a small flashlight. She carefully climbed up to the attic hatch, then looked back down to her assistants, attentive with their happy tails.

"If I don't make it back, you two can have my tuna salad and Yoda ears. Beanie, you take care of your brother."

Beans responded with a drifting pout and a stare down the hall. A quirky flip of the tail added to his rebellion.

CHAPTER EIGHT

Annie clicked the flashlight on and lifted the panel to the attic. Slowly, she scanned the perimeter and drifted naturally into her imagination. Maybe it was a squirrel. *No*, she thought. *That thump was too heavy to be a squirrel.* Maybe some part of the old roof had started to deteriorate. The pink insulation had discolored after enough years up here. She might have to discuss that later with Mrs. Winkle. As soon as she had summed up the noise as nothing to concern herself with, she twisted around to slip the panel back in place and came face-to-face with a flash of bright, pointed teeth and a hissing that scared a series of cursing exclamations from Annie. The ladder creaked wildly and collapsed, scattering Pork and Beans, leaving Annie to hang and drop herself clumsily to the floor. She decided it was best to weigh her options while lying on the floor. She exhaled a hard breath and opened her eyes. Her fairy godmother leaned over her with a dippy grin.

"Oh. Hey, Tom."

"I see you have a friend."

She pulled herself up off the floor, feeling her back ache, and shook off the feeling of her skin crawling. "There's something up there in the middle of a metamorphosis. A creature with huge fangs, with fat, pink claws, and an unbelievably horny tail. *Eeeeaaaaah*—not to mention the horribly malodorous breath. It must have eaten every rodent in a twelve-block radius." Annie squirmed and twitched at the thought.

Tom crossed his arms and listened with a blank face. "You mean that baby possum?"

"Possum? That's not a possum, that's a monster."

"It's a baby possum, and it needs your help."

Annie threw her shoulders back in defense. "My help? Oh, no, no, no."

"I thought you loved animals."

"Cute, fuzzy, *loveable* animals. Animals like baby lambs, goats, puppies, kittens, bunnies. I'd even settle for a llama. Okay, maybe even salamanders and turtles. But not something that looks like it survived a roadkill incident and government radiation experimentations from 2006."

Tom replaced the ladder. "All creatures, no matter their appearance, are sacred and have meaning on Earth."

"What meaning does this thing have?"

"That's for you to find out."

Annie looked down to find some semblance of support from Pork and Beans, who sat in the doorway of the living room. Simultaneously, they turned and left her.

"Thanks for your help, guys. I'll remember that."

Tom was on the ladder ahead of her and motioned her on. "Come on. We'll do this together. I'll show you how easy it is to earn the trust of someone who isn't used to humans."

Annie began to wonder if everything she had conceptualized about this entity in human form was influenced by watching way too many *Seinfeld* episodes, drunk on mimosas and bourbon, smoking cheap cigars.

She turned away with a cringe. The pink tutu did nothing to hide his plaid boxers from the angle of her position. "Can't you just beam yourself up there or something?"

"Nah. I wanted to have some fun."

"Yeah. Loads."

"Hey, you know what? I think I'm—I'm stuck."

"Oh, hell no."

"Can you just give me a shove?"

Annie scratched her head with both hands. "No, thanks."

"No, really. I think I need some assistance here."

Annie watched as his enormous frame barely moved inside the opening. She had to admit, he was tucked in there pretty well. An arduous sigh escaped her lips.

She scaled the rungs and tried to discover as many options of not touching him as she could possibly imagine. Nothing came to her.

"I don't think I'm qualified to make this magical transition," Annie exclaimed, wrapping an arm around his legs.

"Lift me. I'm not as heavy as I look."

Annie couldn't budge him. "That's what they all say."

"Push."

"I am not touching your butt."

"Then use your shoulder."

She feigned nausea after swatting down his tutu. "There's a multitude of other things I could be amused by right now."

She braced her shoulder under his butt and lifted. In a shot of sparks, she easily launched him into the attic. A big grin soon popped into view.

"See. What I tell ya?"

"Amazing." Annie couldn't help but wipe her hand incessantly on her jeans.

A soft rap at the door shook Annie's senses. She jerked her head around and stared at the familiar silhouette.

"Crap. It's Mrs. Winkle." She breathed deeply before her toes curled in panic mode. "She owns a gun, and she knows how to use it."

Annie cracked open the door and met Mrs. Winkle's smile. "Oh, hi, Mrs. Winkle. Did I disturb you? I'm so sorry."

"I heard this large bang. Thought I would investigate."

"Oh, it's fine. I just—fell."

"Fell? Oh, my."

"It was nothing."

"Are you sure?"

Annie rubbed her back and blew out a guffaw. "Yeah. Fine. Just a little sore, that's all."

A loud scratching noise resounded from the ceiling above them. Mrs. Winkle squinted her face up and pushed the door open. "Is that noise coming from the attic?"

"What noise?"

"It sounded like a scurry."

"Scurry, or scuttle?"

"I don't know. I'd have to—" Mrs. Winkle whooped. "There it goes again."

"What?"

"Don't you hear that?"

"Umm."

Mrs. Winkle pointed at the ladder. "Have you been up in the attic?"

"Attempted, actually. That's where I fell."

"Oh, you poor thing."

Annie patted the tiny hand that reached out to her, and smiled. "I'll be all right."

"Is one of the cats up there?"

"They could be. Possibly. Yeah." Annie realized she was caressing the edge of the door in her nervousness. "I was just checking the insulation. You know, winter's coming soon. It's the best time."

"It's nearly August, dear. It's stifling up there right now. Terrible time to think of such a thing."

Little sounds hastened overhead.

Annie dashed past Mrs. Winkle. "You know, I'll just go have a look. Pork, Beans, that you?"

No sooner Annie repositioned the ladder and placed a foot atop a rung, Mrs. Winkle replied, "They're right here."

Annie gazed over her shoulder. Mrs. Winkle was petting the both of them.

"Here you are, pretty babies. Yes you are. Handsome little boys, aren't you?" She stood with hands on her hips and pressed her lips together with a determination Annie witnessed not long ago, with the rat incident. "Now, move aside. I'm going up."

"Oh, geez, Mrs. Winkle. That's probably not such a good idea. Why, with your balance issues…"

"Balance? My balance is just fine."

"Legs, then. Hips? Have you renewed your AARP membership? Watch that last rung. Hold on."

"Annie, for heaven's sakes. Stop that. I'm perfectly fine. Now, hand me that flashlight."

Annie surrendered with a gulp and handed Mrs. Winkle the flashlight. Her heart shuttered inside her like a Catalan rumba. "Please don't see it," Annie whispered to herself. "Please don't see it. Please don't see it."

"What is this?" Mrs. Winkle asked with a wheeze. She pulled a multicolored article of clothing that was wedged between the attic panel and ceiling and held it over Annie's head.

"My sock?" Annie quickly looked down. She was wearing only one sock. "How'd my sock get up—" She caught herself, realizing it had to be Tom's doing. She took it and slipped it back on her foot.

Mrs. Winkle lifted the small panel and scanned the beam of light around the dark hull of space and stared into shafts with an eagle eye. "Well, I don't know what that sound was. But, I can't find anything moving now."

Annie felt instant relief. A second later, chaos reigned. The baby possum had been standing atop the panel and dipped his head down to greet Mrs. Winkle, upside down. Her holler joined his hiss, and she dropped the panel.

Mrs. Winkle climbed down the ladder with the agility of a determined killer. "Oh, doesn't that give you the heebie jeebies?"

"Mrs. Winkle, I'm sure we can handle it."

"You bet your sweet bippy we can."

"Bippy? My bippy?"

Mrs. Winkle turned back to Annie at the door and shook the flashlight at her. "I'll be back. You keep that thing right there."

"No, no, no, you—Mrs. Winkle, you don't really want to do that."

Mrs. Winkle slammed the door behind her.

Annie panicked. "Crap. Flashlight. She took my flashlight." Annie opened the closet and dove into the dark, tossing about every cluttered piece she had on the floor, finally coming up with an incandescent lantern. She flipped the switch, smiling as it lit up. Then, she dashed up the ladder and lifted the panel carefully.

"Tom? Tom."

Tom sat in the corner of the attic with the baby possum. "We're right here. She's a little shaken up, but she'll be all right."

"She? How do you know it's a she?" His cocked head was convincing enough. "Right. Never mind." Annie hoisted herself up and into the attic. "Okay. Come on, missy. We've got to get you out of here. I really don't want you looking like Swiss cheese after Mrs. Winkle is done with you."

"Better move fast," Tom said. "She's a good shot."

"Can't you just poof this little thing out of here?"

"Poof?"

"You know, make her disappear."

Tom looked amused. "That's your job."

"What the hell are you here for?" Annie caught herself yelling. "Sorry."

"You said you were bored."

"You were listening?"

He shrugged. "Comes with the job."

Annie started to crawl between the insulation with hands and knees on the rafters. It was a precarious situation and very straining to the muscles. She raised up to look at the possum and bonked her head on the roof above.

"Oww!"

A riveting jolt seized Annie's back. She lurched on her back and burst into a whimpering ball of tension. "Ho, back spasm. Back spasm." She was so intensely involved with the moment, the scant feeling of something tickling her stomach passed without much notice. "What is that?"

Tom expressed soft glee. "Aww, she likes you."

"What?" Annie managed to roll over more on her back to spot movement inside the pocket of her T-shirt hoodie. Her voice cracked with alarm. "What…what is she doing? Tom? Oh, my God—oh, my God—oh, my God."

Tom moved closer. "Just breathe a minute and listen."

She felt the possum curl up in a ball and put its head down.

"Oh, my God. Shoo. Oh, geez'o. What the hell?" Her back started to loosen up, and she relaxed into several harder breaths. "Okay. Okay. Ohh…kay. That's good." She glanced down to the little bulge on her belly. "Huh. Well, would you look at that. I guess it just wanted a mom. Right?"

Tom grinned and nodded.

"Really? Baby kangaroos, right? I'm a mom. Who'da thought?"

Annie's laughter and relief halted as she heard the front door slam.

"Ah! She's back."

Tom pressed her. "Move. You have to move now."

Annie began to sweat with profuse vowels escaping her, spitting and gasping as she agonized over each rafter, sliding on her back toward the open panel. A sudden meeting with Mrs. Winkle's gun barrel scared the both of them. They yelled in sync.

Mrs. Winkle caught her breath, then frowned. "Where is it?"

"Just let me come down and you can have your fun, okay?"

"Well, get out of the way."

"Mrs. Winkle."

"What's the matter with you? You look ill."

Annie was sweating and she knew she must have looked flushed. "You know, I think I'm overheated. Yeah. And…uh…" She grasped onto the ball of movement in her pocket. "My, my stomach isn't feeling too awful well right now."

Mrs. Winkle looked agog. "Oh. Right. Well."

She headed back down the rungs of the ladder to allow Annie space to flail herself out the hole and onto the ladder. Desperate not to startle the little creature out of her pocket, Annie slid down each step, holding onto her shirt. She felt the possum twitch and tried not to show her repulsion.

"You look awful," said Mrs. Winkle.

Sweat ran from every pore and crevice. She had never sweated from her crotch before. And now that she had, she decided she'd prefer if it never happened again.

"I'll be all right. Say, I'll just disappear in the bathroom for a while, okay?"

A line appeared between Mrs. Winkle's brows. "You go on. I'll take care of this."

"Yes, ma'am. Thank you."

Annie stepped away and headed to the bathroom door as Mrs. Winkle shot up the rungs of the ladder, refocused on her mission. Annie looked down at her shirt. The possum's tail was exposed. Horrified, she twisted about, feeling like a pregnant woman about to burst, and slipped inside the bathroom before closing the door. She expelled a few more whispered vowels in an attempt to poke and insert the tail back into hiding. Once the tail was tucked in, she peeked out into the hall and up the ladder.

"Mrs. Winkle, you okay?"

"Yes, yes. It's hiding. You take care of your business. I've got this."

"Okay, good."

Annie stepped out and closed the bathroom door behind her. She tiptoed to the front door. The latch clicked, and the door creaked with slight resistance. With one more look back, Annie slithered out the door and down the steps.

"Tom," she said, hushed. "*Tom.* Where are you?"

Tom scared the wits out of her as he appeared around the corner of the house.

"You did it!" he said. "Isn't that great?"

"Yeah. Great. Now what? What the hell am I supposed to do with it?"

Tom followed Annie as she walked with much haste up the winding street. He directed them into the nearby wooded tree line. They sat on a small fallen tree trunk.

"Well, I guess this is as good a place as any. Right?" Annie peeked into her pocket. Little beady eyes stared back. "Ahh! Cripes almighty." She settled her senses then took a fresh breath.

She opened her pocket and waited. "Come on. Come on. You're safe now." She pointed her sweaty pocket over the trunk. "Why isn't she coming out?"

"Perhaps, you can pick her up and pull her out."

"Pick her up? Are you crazy?"

"Go on. Give it a shot. What have you got to lose, except a couple of fingers?"

Annie gritted her teeth.

"Kidding. Trust me, she likes you."

"I am definitely giving you only three stars on my review, Buster, even if I make it out of this with all my flesh intact."

Annie's hands shook the closer her hand got. She slid a hand in before jerking it out, not having even touched the little animal. Then, she held her breath and slid a hand in again. "Where are you? Eww. Okay. Here you go. There you are. Oh, boy. Oh, boy. Okay, here we go." Annie wrapped her fingers around the little bundle of belly and began to pull the possum out of her pocket. "Holy cow."

The possum clung onto her forearm.

Tom handed Annie a banana. "Here. She's hungry."

"A banana?"

"Young possums need calcium."

"Really? Huh." Annie noticed she wasn't as scared as she thought she'd be. "Well. This…this isn't so bad, is it?" She drew the tip of the fruit closer to the possum's mouth and watched as it sniffed then eagerly began to bite a piece off and chew it with vigor. "Oh, my. Look at you go. You like that, huh?" Annie mimicked her little head held high with big chews and laughed at her little pink paws. "You are kind of cute, aren't you? Look at your ears. You have Yoda ears. And soft. Ish." Annie snapped her hand away. "We have to work on your buzz cut though, girlie. Maybe a pink or green swatch of color. Just like Varsha. Give you a butch tat on the tail or something."

"You should give her a name," Tom said.

"Name? I can't keep her. Mrs. Winkle would find her in a hot minute and turn her into a potato skillet."

"She's an orphan. She hasn't got a mother anymore."

"Why? What happened to her?" Annie felt the message in Tom's eyes. "Oh." She held the possum up to her face and met her dark eyes. "Hey, chickie. How about Chinese? Want to split a chow mein?"

* * *

After a couple weeks of hiding the little possum, Annie had found a Wildlife Rescue Center on the west side of the city that accepted possums. She rubbed the little head as the tech checked her little toes.

"What's her name?" the tech asked.

"Wonton." Annie watched as the tech inspected Wonton's ears and played with her belly gently. "She loves wontons. And Gatorade. Grapes, carrots. She's a true food disposal. It's fun to watch her spit out cooked celery and grape skins."

The tech grinned. "They can certainly put it away, that's for sure. Did you search the Internet to find information on her?"

"Inside help. At first. Then, yeah, lots of research hours and videos. And hiding from the landlady. After two weeks, it's been quite an adventure."

"Well, you took very good care of her, I'd say. You were a great mom."

"I'm going to miss her, really. A lot. She became part of my two-cat family."

The tech looked surprised. "Really? They got along?"

"Well, I didn't find any murdered bodies or missing fur."

"That's awesome."

"The cats just thought she was a strange-looking cousin at first, then let her in on the food and games. She likes balls with bells in them." Annie then remembered the tiny, baby-blue blanket in her backpack. "Oh. Here. She loves to snuggle into this. Can she have it?"

"Of course."

Annie felt a sob forming within her. "Okay. I'd better go."

The tech winced at Annie's attempt to hide her sadness. "We'll send you updates on her, if you'd like. Video clips and such."

Annie turned, excited. "Oh, that would be wonderful!"

"This must be your first foster child."

Annie felt another pang of sadness. "It is."

"It gets easier."

Annie smiled, a little soothed. "Will she be released back out in the wild?"

"We'll see. Most are. A few never acquire the necessary survival skills, and become permanent residents here."

"Oh. I see. How long do they live?"

The tech smiled as Wonton sniffed the blanket and curled up into it. "Normally, possums have a lifespan of about two years."

"Only two years?"

"If they're happy and are physically well-off, possibly three."

Annie's heart ached. "Dang. Guess I'd eat as many bananas and ice creams as I could get my hands on if I was told I only had two years to live."

The tech met her eyes and nodded with a small smile. "Right. Kind of puts our lives in perspective, doesn't it?"

Annie reached out and pet Wonton between the ears. "Thanks for putting up with my failed humanness. Just because you're different doesn't mean you're not loveable, right?" Just as she turned to leave, she reached out to shake the tech's hand. "Thank you."

"Thank you. For saving her. She wouldn't have survived without your help."

Annie left feeling good about herself. Saving animals was something she'd done several times in her life. Whether it was a bird who had run into a window and needed a few minutes of cuddling time to get their senses back, or a stray dog who needed to find their worried owner, or a turtle who needed to cross a busy road, she didn't discriminate. Wonton would surely become one of her more cherished memories. She walked out to her car when a text appeared on her phone.

Ready when you are.

She halted. It was from OMG. "Ready for what?"

"Well, come on. Let's ride."

The voice spooked her. It belonged to a short, elderly woman with wrinkles like stickers from around the world on a worn piece of luggage; full of life's color and design from an exotic life. Her fashion of dress could only be described as stylish disorder, with thick, bottled, round glasses that cut quite a fitting figure with the cigar in her mouth and her shocking pink hair.

"You don't really light that thing, do you?" Annie asked.

The godmother frowned. "Heavens no. Why light a perfectly good Churchill?"

"I guess you're Pinky?"

The woman shrugged.

"Well, the hair actually works with that outfit."

"Of course it does. Can't say the same for you."

"What do you mean? This is my favorite shirt."

Pinky groaned. "Oh, not with those shoes."

Annie watched as Pinky walked around the car and made her way to the passenger side. Her sneakers lit up with every step.

"Helps me down dark alleys," Pinky said, as if knowing Annie was staring.

Annie slipped behind the wheel and closed the door. She paused before turning to Pinky. The woman's outfit had changed to a pink skirt over tights, and a tank top with the word, *Sharpie* crushed around sagging breasts that looked like they'd been placed on a mammogram tray way too many times.

"Do you do this often?"

"What?"

Annie hid a comment under puffed cheeks, met Pinky's eyes, then shook her head. "Nothing."

"Let's go to one of your favorite parts of town. You know, the one with the irritating drivers and shoppers looking for the next miracle facial scrub."

"You mean the Commons? Got it."

"It amazes me how much people have to pay for jars of sugar and kitty litter," Pinky cackled with a slap to Annie's arm.

* * *

Annie drove through the neighborhood of shops and stores of the outdoor mall as Pinky expounded on the clusters of ambitions humans acquired without even a hint of belief in them coming to life.

"You gotta make your own miracles, Sally."

"It's Annie."

"Make your own gold. Let the world be what it wants in all its shit. You gotta make your own way. Don't worry about the bunk everybody else is living in. That's theirs to own."

"But, if I can offer some advice, you know, share my experience…"

"Most folks that ask never really want an answer, Amie."

"Annie."

"They just want to tell you their sad victim stories and want everyone's pity. Attention. They want attention. They don't want happiness. They certainly don't want your happiness. Your happiness irritates the crap outta people like that. They'll never get it that way. They have to be willing to live it, too." She slapped Annie on the knee and inhaled with a wide grin. "Come one. Let's go find an ice cream shop and a beautiful, baby-blue convertible."

Annie stepped out of the car and followed Pinky to the sidewalk. Pinky was now dressed in large beads, bangles, chunky bracelets, and cowboy boots. A baby-blue, modified motorcycle with a 1950 Bel Air rear pulled in front of them.

"Eh, close enough," she said.

"How cool is that?" Annie said, swooning over the machine.

"Hecate!" the man on the seat shouted.

Pinky winked to Annie. "He always calls me Hecate to seduce me."

Annie cringed at the thought. "And what's his name? Hermes?"

"No. Harold, of course."

"Oh, of course. Wait. He's a godmother, father, something? Someone else's?" Pinky shrugged. "And I can see him?"

"Stay present-minded and you'll see a lot of stuff you've never noticed before in your life. Busy now." Pinky waved him off. "We'll chat later. Now, I think we ought to talk about your sex life, darling."

"Sex?" Annie felt a flush rise up within her. "Do we have to talk about sex?"

"Oh, I know. I have very little to say about sex, myself."

"Well, I should think."

"Your place or mine?" Pinky laughed.

"Really? Godmothers don't—"

"Don't have sex? And you believed we didn't eat. Remember that later, honey. Everything you are, we are, because we are all one and the same. I know, I know. You won't get that right now. But you will." Pinky ogled a young blond woman as she walked by. "I think twenty-three is about right, don't you?"

"Uh-uh. I don't do younger."

"Younger? I was talking about her IQ. Haven't seen so many in a generation in all my life. Hell, there's droves of 'em." Pinky laughed. "Oh, I'd have a ball. Male, female, ishes and wishes. Doesn't matter. Whoever they want to be, we'd hang with them. We love a good story with hidden gem adventures. Just be, Agnes. Live!"

"You're really grooming that mood, aren't you?"

"Why not? Life is meant to be fun. Diversity in one's life is imperative. You gotta allow life to mix you up a little. How you supposed know what you want otherwise?"

Pinky's accent reminded Annie of her great aunts from Chicago. She loved sitting with them around a big table, telling their stories, sharing their lives and laughter. Annie tucked the car keys in her pocket. "Are we still talking about sex? Look, I'm happy for you. But, I'm enjoying my solitary time, thank you very much."

Pinky halted Annie with a hand and turned to her. "Very honorable, indeed. But, without the rut."

"What rut?"

"Honey, you've got to expand a little. Get out of your head once in a while and out into the world where there's color.

Beautiful flushes and blushes. All there for the taking. Love for the fun of it. Kiss for the fun of it. Bask in life, for the fun of it. You people are way too serious."

"Wait a minute. Aren't you folks supposed to love me just as I am?"

"We do. We love you very much. We are here to help you see all that you are and all that you have stored in your hopes and dreams. Yet, here you are, pushing them aside as unimportant check marks on a page in a journal. Dreams are meant to come true. The stars are out there for you to count. Check off all you want, and have all you want. And the more you want, the more are born. You are a part of a great expansion. You're just not keeping up with it. So, we're here to give you a little push. Now, come on. Let's have some fun."

Annie sighed and took a step, noticing her shoes had changed. "Whoa. Hey!" She was wearing a pair of yellow Converse shoes. "Oh, look at that. And in my favorite color."

Pinky smiled. "Oh, this'll be good."

They passed a shop window that displayed several outfits on mannequins.

"What are we looking for?" Annie asked.

"Not we, you."

"I...I don't need anything."

Pinky rested her fists on her hips. "Now, for this to work, you have to be in a receptive mode."

"Receptive."

"A really remarkable translation here is *wanting it*. You have to *want* something for this to work. Focusing on what it is you really want is absolute. Otherwise, you're just living by default, honey. Don't be like politicians."

"But I—"

"Ah, ah, ah. Just go with the flow here. And imagine being able to have whatever you wish."

Annie shifted her weight with ambivalence.

"Go on. Give it a shot. What have you got to lose?"

"Last time you folks asked me that, I encountered possum teeth."

"Not every situation in life will feel like an encounter with possum teeth. Go on. Flatter yourself with a more liberal hand. Color outside the lines once in a while. Hell's bells, woman, use the whole box."

"Okay. Okay." Annie sucked in a fresh breath, dropped her shoulders, and nodded. "You're right."

"Of course, I'm right."

"What the heck. Let's do this."

Pinky lurched close to Annie's face with a huge grin and lightly punched her arm. "That's the spirit."

Annie scanned the sidewalk and parking lot for women and their attire. "I really don't ever think of stuff in windows as something I'd wear. I'm more of a 'gosh, that's a nice jacket' kind of person." She pointed to a woman with an outfit that Annie was clothed in before she finished her sentence. "Whoa, this is freaky wild."

The outfit switched to a dark pinstripe suit and bright white blouse as Annie and Pinky began to walk. They passed a woman with torn jeans, white ripped T-shirt and a short-brimmed felt fedora, which Annie spun about in excitement to be sporting. One after the other, shirts changed, as did hairstyles, shoes, sweaters, jackets, and pants, with or without suspenders. Annie lost all sense of anxiety and engaged in the moment with complete entertainment, as if it all was a grand feast.

Later, the two enjoyed an iced coffee float and a ride on the baby-blue, modified motorcycle, with Pinky driving and Annie hanging onto her in joyous fear.

CHAPTER NINE

By the time the sun had kissed the Ohio River with its cantaloupe gaze, Annie had settled into her night shirt and pajama pants and found a comfortable position on the couch between the pillows. With her slippered feet up on a footrest and a popcorn bowl in her lap, she was ready for her evening of documentaries. Pork and Beans loved the popcorn game. She enjoyed tossing pieces in the air for them to bat around the room. She had just started flipping through program selections when her phone rang. She mumbled her displeasure between chews. It was Mrs. Winkle. She put the phone back down and tried to ignore it. After the third old-fashioned phone ringtone sounded, she succumbed.

"Hi, Mrs. Winkle."

"Hi, dear."

"Is everything all right with you and your babies?"

"Oh, we're fine. Just fine." There was a pause to Mrs. Winkle. "I just thought I'd call you while I had a moment. I'm not disturbing you, am I?"

Annie focused on reading a description of the disturbing consequences of too much social media and its effects on the individual. "No. Not at all. I'm just streaming a few Netflix episodes."

"Oh, I used to fish in a stream a long time ago. Was it fun? You didn't fall in, did you?"

"Flix. Netflix. Streaming. Watching multiple episodes of a TV show in succession. I'm sort of an addict. Well, not sort of. I am. An addict. Recovering from a few issues nowadays. Sugar abuse. Isolated thinking. Attracted to distractions. Is everything all right?"

"Oh. Well, I was just thinking. If anything should happen to me…"

"Uh-huh." Annie knew someday this subject would surface.

"God forbid. But, if anything should happen to me, I've been thinking about what to do with the dogs."

"Oh. Right."

A heavy breath hissed through the phone. "I know this is a bit weird to talk about right now. But. Well, that's what one does, I suppose."

"That's perfectly fine, Mrs. Winkle. Nothing has to happen this red-hot minute. We're just talking about it. It's okay. You love your dogs. And you want good care for them."

"Yes. You're right. Well, Saqi's issue is easy enough. My sister in Phoenix will come for him. But, you'll need to put Bones down."

"Excuse me?"

"She's old," Mrs. Winkle continued. "On her last breath here, so to speak. Just if anything should go awry."

"Oh. Well. Of course." Annie's body tightened.

"I'd want you there with her. You've been such a dear."

"Oh. Gosh." Annie's brain attempted to visualize the moment of watching a beloved animal's last breath. She felt honored, yet grappled with the emptiness of not seeing the entire universe in those eyes any longer. "Sure, Mrs. Winkle. I wouldn't want any less for her. I mean, she's been my pal for so long. It's only right that I should be there for her. Of course. I would be happy to be with her, if that's what you'd need."

"Well. That's all I wanted to say, then. I'll not keep you."

"Thank you, Mrs. Winkle. For thinking about that. Because…I…I haven't."

"All right, dear. Enjoy the rest of your night."

Annie tossed out a piece of popcorn for her cats to clobber in the air before scattering themselves about like contentious hockey players. The conversation left her a little mopey. She didn't feel very zealous for her evening of television anymore. When the boys came back for their second round, she decided it was better to put herself in a better mood. She clicked on her music channel, grabbed their feather toys and plopped down on the floor. It was an intense moment of catch it, missed it. They knew how to get her to feel better.

* * *

In the ensuing weeks, Pinky took Annie and Mrs. Winkle's dogs on wonderful adventures around the city. Everyone was dressed to the nines, with Pinky dressed in the nineteens. Bones liked her sunglasses and scarf. Saqi enjoyed prancing in his Hawaiian shirt and goggles. First along the Ohio River, in the misty morning, where they and Annie were the colors of the day and brought smiles to the passersby. Then, Annie and Pinky rode Segways across bridges and around the streets. Bones rode in a basket on wheels behind Annie, who kept Saqi in a daypack slung across her chest so he could take in the sights and bark at the street trolleys. The hot air balloon ride wasn't Annie's favorite, as she and Saqi clung to each other in the middle of the basket with one eye opened. Pinky and Bones, however, were leaning over the edge and enjoying every hill and dale the city and countryside offered. At least, Annie could chalk it up as something she'd always wanted to do, despite her fear of heights. She looked up to the white, poofy clouds and tried to relax her racing heart and swallow down her mind's attempt to start a vertigo spin.

All the roads were beautiful from up there, away from the hustle and bustle of her life. Annie eventually looked down and gained a new appreciation from a safe sitting position.

"Look, Saqi," she said, peeking through the basket weaves. "Farmland and fields and lots of woods past all those white ribbons of highways. I bet there's a nice, shallow creek down there you could catch minnows in."

She looked up and realized how perfectly content the sky was, in all its cloud formations and change.

Pinky sat next to her and looked up with a smile.

"You know," Annie mused. "It's a whole other game up here, isn't it?"

"Yep. That's the idea. Things do often flow in a free and easy way when you aren't forcing to make something happen."

"I feel better looking up." Annie couldn't help herself. She had to break out and started murmuring the lyrics to "99 Luftballons."

"I really do like watching clouds. Ever since I was a kid. Laying in the grass. Watching bunnies and dragons float by. I really can't believe how awesome it is up here." Annie let a few more minutes pass of relaxing under the gentle movement of clouds. "There's nothing up here. And yet, there's everything. Up here, I really feel it. I feel it all. Or maybe I just have to pee. Yeah. Can we go down, now?"

* * *

At Yodel's Bookstore, Varsha plopped down an armful of books on the bookstore counter with a heaving grunt.

Annie looked up from her calculations and adjusted her glasses. "What are those?"

Varsha caught her breath. "These are all mislabeled. Religion. They were in the Occult."

"It's all about perspective, isn't it?" Annie sat the label gun on the edge of her desk. "Freshly loaded with new tags. Just for you."

"You'd think we all should walk around with our own label guns these days. Everybody's got so many titles and labels nowadays. I don't think I want to look like some businessman's stickered passport. Do you? What do you call yourself, anyway? Lesbian? Dyke? Queer?"

Annie professed, "I prefer Annie. I don't believe in labels. I'd rather not be an abbreviated version of myself when there's so much more to me to share with the human race than that. Although, I get it that our government needs boxes checked off for census reports. I truly respect folks who love labels, and feel defined by them. Like tattoos. I have my firebird. Just in case my body in death is unrecognizable. At least, they'll have that to go by."

"I've always been worried about drowning. I wouldn't look like myself. I try to imagine the toe tag. What would they call me then?"

"Bloated. I could never drown. I've got too much muffin top. My belly button would be searching for air faster than a porpoise in heat."

Annie raised her eyes from her computer. Varsha stood paled, her hands balled up into fists and her face scrunched up like she was in extreme pain.

"Are you holding in a fart?" Annie asked.

"No, I'm suppressing an impulse to scream," Varsha whined.

"About what?"

Varsha launched an impressive gesturing finger toward the floor to a tiny spider near Annie's desk.

"Really? It's a harmless spider."

"You know I can't stand spiders, Annie. Please…"

"Oh, for Pete's sake." Annie pulled a small plastic container out from a desk drawer, scooped up the little creature, and capped the container. She stood up and eyed it near Varsha's cringing figure. "You're safe now. Relax." Annie took the container outside and released the spider upon the windowsill. "There you go, little one. Try to stay out of trouble."

Varsha met her inside the door. "See? Easy peasy, butternut squeezy. Thanks, Annie."

"Lemon."

"What?"

"Lemon squeezy. The phrase is, 'easy peasy, lemon squeezy.' Butternut is a squash."

"Hey, see? It's squeezed and squashed. Even better."

"I didn't squash the spider. I released her into the wild of brick and mortar where she could build her webs in more successful nooks and crannies that have more drafts than what your hysterical limbs are flailing about. I have to admit. I don't mess with the really weird jumpers. Those babies are pulverized into the next dimension."

Annie returned to the front counter where Mr. Tiddle was waiting.

"Hey, Mr. Tiddle. What's up?"

"Is that woman drunk?" he said, sneering and gesturing toward a woman on the other side of the store.

Annie watched as she sat on the floor cross-legged, rifling through a small pile of vinyl records.

Varsha turned her head in her direction. "I didn't smell anything on her. Then again, I didn't talk to her."

"That's her own business if she is," Annie grumbled, stepping past him to her desk. She hadn't yet obtained a tolerance for people who judged an alcoholic lifestyle with disdain, as if theirs was anything to brag about.

"She is drunk," he stated. "Look at her."

Varsha shrugged. "Hmm."

"You think she's in a blackout?" he whispered to Annie.

"What is she doing?" Annie asked.

"Singing."

"You believe she's in a blackout because she's singing."

"Look at her."

Annie leaned over his shoulder. The woman was holding a broken, unlit cigarette between her lips and murmuring a Beatles tune.

"That's Marti Douglas. She loves to sit and scan through our albums. She's a big collector of sixties music. She's probably been here some time." Annie glanced at her watch. "I'm sure she'll catch the same 2:20 bus she did last week."

The woman moaned in recognition of another album title, before starting to reminisce about another song out loud to herself. "God. This is so freakin' awesome. I was here, man. I saw him in concert. He was so good."

"Is she always drunk?" Mr. Tiddle asked.

"Why don't you ask her?"

"Miss Freckle. I need you to go smell her."

"Excuse me?"

"I thought you might have a better nose than the rest of us, since you used to be a drunk yourself."

"I beg your pardon?"

"Oh, don't get all touchy-uppity with me. You people have this reputed ability to recognize your own, don't you? Just like a gaydar, you have a drunkdar. Am I right?"

"You must have mistaken my eye twitch to you as a sudden spasm of sympathy for her."

"If she smells like the Rhinegeist brewery, I need you to get her out. We can't have her running our legitimate customers away with her stench."

Annie mumbled a disagreeing curse before making her way to the woman. "Hi, Marti."

"Huh? Hi. Oh, hey. How you doing? Look. Look at these. Aren't they fabulous?"

Annie crouched down to her and whispered, "The bus will be here in five minutes. You still ride it, don't you?"

"Oh. Right. Right. Gotcha. Thank you. Mustn't miss my Zumba yoga class."

Annie helped her to stand and gather her fringe purse, long scarf, and half the items that fell from the purse, scattering around them.

Marti stumbled and squat. "Oh, damn. Sheesh. Hey, fifty-two pick-up." She cackled. "Flashlight, keys. Hey, there's my travel lighter and hair spray. Never use them together. Oopsy-daisy, and tampons. Golly, you know, I've had these things for years. Never use them anymore. Menopause, right? I just carry them around in case another chick needs them. Would you like them?"

"Mm, no thanks. Not my week. Come on. Gotta go."

"Maybe your little helper would like them."

"I'll ask her later. Here." Annie put the tampons back in Marti's purse. "You hold onto them for us, okay?"

"Say, say. Can you hold these albums for me?"

"Sure, I'll put them aside for you." Annie took the albums from her and slipped them under the table.

"You sure it's okay?"

"Absolutely."

"I've always wanted to travel to Liverpool." Marti beamed. "I've heard so much about it. I love that you have the old baroque music too. You're always so nice, you know that?"

"Comforting, isn't it? Just like Beatles and baroque. Peanut butter and pickle sandwiches."

"Oh, my grandma loved those," Marti laughed. "Oh, you're something else, Annie."

Annie smiled at her. "You're welcome to come back when you have more time."

"Well, thank you. I'll…I'll come back. When I have more time. Next week."

"That'll be just fine. I'll be here."

Marti reached back to her. "Don't lose my albums, honey."

"I'll keep them for you. I promise." Annie walked her out to the sidewalk just as the bus arrived. She assisted Marti up the first step and gave the driver a couple dollars. He nodded with a kind grin and wave, holding his hand out to assist Marti's uneven pace.

"Thank you."

Annie backed up and watched as the bus traveled on its way. Crossing the street was a pleasant figure to help Annie restore her mood. Maybe it was the layers of cinnamon hair that caught her attention. No. Catrin was a woman whose inner being spoke volumes more than features could ever attempt to. She was the delicate kind. The kind who could hide among the masses. Undeservedly neglected. She could easily be overlooked, until she smiled. Then, she was the prettiest flower in full bloom.

"Seems I'm always catching you in kind gestures," Catrin reflected.

"Hmm? Oh, that."

"Yes, that. Wasn't that Marti Douglas?"

Annie cocked her head. "Oh, you, you know Marti?"

"Yeah. She was my philosophy professor at UC. Until she got ill. The department threw her a massive retirement party at the local ice cream shop. She had so much fun with us."

"How wonderful for her. You know, it pains me that most people see her as a troublesome alcoholic. She hasn't had a drop in years. Marti is simply experiencing cognitive difficulties in her disease."

Catrin adjusted her stance. "I guess it's easier to judge than care that she has Multiple Sclerosis."

"Hmm."

"It's nice to see you were willing to help her."

Annie let out a self-deprecating sigh. "I have my moments. They feel good. I should probably do more of those. Say, what brings you to this neighborhood?" Annie noticed Catrin was wearing her post office shirt and shorts.

"Flapjack is on vacation this week. Looks like you have to tolerate my visits."

"Oh, I think I can endure them with much less agony than you'd believe. I have to say, you look so much cuter in that postal uniform than he does."

Catrin smiled back at Annie, then dug into her bag. "I'm a little early on my route."

"The mark of an incurable type A."

"There's a means to my madness." Catrin handed Annie a few pieces of mail. "I haven't had my lunch break yet and was hoping to grab something around here. Any ideas?"

Annie nodded across the street. "There's a great sandwich shop owned by a hearty little fella who claims to be of Tuscan descent. Makes his own pecorino and sausage, if that's your flair."

"Oh, I love sheep cheese."

"Then you'll love his wife's pickles. Wait. That didn't come out right."

"Care to join me?"

"I'd love to, but—umm..." Annie's gut clenched. Her eyes darted away, hoping the unease didn't give her away. She spotted Varsha's figure in the shop window. She had a wide, over-expressive smile and was holding up both thumbs. "Well... you know what, I...I should."

"No. I understand if you can't."

"Really. Yes." Annie faced Catrin's lovely grin. "Yes. I think we should do that. I think I can do that. I can do that. Well. Yes, I can do that. Certainly. No. No problem. We can do this. Together. Yes. Good. Good idea."

"Good."

"Good."

Catrin smiled.

"Let me just take this mail into the shop and let Mr. Tickle... uh, Tiddle know I'm going on break."

"Good. I'll run this package over next door, then meet you back here in five minutes."

Annie hardly entered through the shop door before Varsha attacked her with squeals, wiggles, butt dances, and strange gyrations; each one Annie avoided and sidestepped like it was the next slimy offering of octopus rituals.

"You two look so cute together. Oh, I can't believe my Annie is actually checking out with the green goddess. Crime is going down tonight. Woot, *woot!*"

Annie passed her by. "What in the world are you blabbering about?"

"Can't wait to read your front pages in the morning."

"Varsha."

"Hmm?"

"Stop that. It's a lunch." Annie picked up the phone and dialed Mr. Tiddle's extension.

"She's grabbin' a lunchena." Varsha wiggled. "A lunchena for a Willa."

"Speak." Mr. Tiddle's voice drew out the word with his usual deadpan.

Annie squinted and held out a hand to block the sight of Varsha's obscene gestures. "Mr. Tiddle, if there's nothing immediate, I'm going to take my lunch now."

Annie ignored Varsha's silent, expressive dance and excited facial expressions inches from her face.

"Any mail yet, Miss Freckle?"

"Actually, you received a letter from the IRS."

Silence. "And?"

"And a brochure from Secret Senior Tours, highlighting an article on the mysterious writings of cave crickets in the Sicilian underground hideout of Mussolini's bodyguards. Scientists have translated the writings as predicting an extremely high rise of US funds in early 2023."

A gasp arose from the phone. "I'm on my way."

Annie put the phone down and slapped Varsha with a folder. "Get a hold of yourself, woman. Hand me that grenade over there."

Varsha looked to the desk, then spotted a live grenade sitting in the open, casually, as if it wasn't a high explosive. She jumped back and repressed a yell.

"It's a lighter, fuzzball. It was a Christmas gift from my dad. He always finds this crap on the Internet no one needs."

Varsha rested it carefully into Annie's hand. "Looks like you need it now."

Annie lit a candle. "Don't distract me."

"Isn't that dangerous?"

Annie showed her the candle's ceramic lid. "It's only a tea candle, and it's perfectly safe."

"Oh, look. It's a little owl. With holes."

"So his belly glows. Yes. I just need to smell something good when I get back."

Varsha nodded slowly. "You mean unlike Mr. Tiddle's cologne, which smells like burnt bark and pond water?"

"Exactly."

* * *

Annie and Catrin enjoyed their matching deli lunch sandwiches of Parma prosciutto, truffled pecorino, marinated eggplant, tomato, arugula, and balsamic glaze.

Annie fell in love with her drink. "These lemonade slushies are really, really good. Never thought something could replace the lemonade at the Philly cheesesteak place."

"I know. That's so good too," replied Catrin. "You must love lemon."

Annie's muscles began to fidget. "Yes. Lemon anything. Lemon bars, lemon piccata, lemon curd. All things lemon. Yellow. Yellow is my color. Sunflowers, cheese, baby chicks, dandelions, rubber duckies, bumblebees."

"Huh. Okay."

"Yours?"

Catrin drew her eyes to a vague spot across the room. "I guess it would be green."

"You're a limey kind of gal?"

"Yeah. I suppose."

"Citrus is in. Citrus people get ahead in life. Just look at me." Annie's head was about to explode. Her hand clutched onto her phone just as the screen lit up. It was a message from OMG—her fairy godmother, telling her to relax.

"How about a little *sorbetto di limone*, gals? Huh?"

It was Pinky, her fairy godmother, serving them. Annie's face fell into her hand with a mixture of shock and relief.

"How did you know?" asked Catrin.

"It's on the house. Enjoy."

Annie watched as Pinky turned away and glanced back to her with a wink.

Annie and Catrin took turns laughing at each other's comments and covered everything from urban dictionaries to work, nature to fainting goats, bad ideas to pot holes.

After their meal, Annie discovered she was quite at ease sharing her recent accomplishments with Catrin, even though she was hiding behind her glass of ice and sucking on an empty straw.

"I've been getting out more," Annie admitted. "A couple of friends pointed out that I was living in a kind of rut, and they helped me get out of my comfort zone. In my head too much."

"It's easy to stay in a rut when you're living by yourself. I had to push myself to get involved with a group."

"I like listening to the grass grow. That's my group. Truth. Grass. Roots. Trees. Birds. Rocks. They're my people. And books! Books are my tribe. I have another group that helps breathe common sense into me sometimes. People group. Well. Often. Like frequently. A lot of the time. For years, now. Sort of a lifeline, if you know what I mean."

Catrin nodded and returned to her drink. "I have that trust in a group too. Sort of a spiritual necessity to keep my motivations in check. Her posture stiffened. "Ever take a yoga class?"

Annie snorted. "Me? No."

Catrin glanced at her watch and slipped out of her side of the booth. "You should check it out sometime."

"You teach it?"

"No. I joined last March to stretch out my cold, aching muscles from the days out in that wonderful snowy, slushy southern Ohio muck, and I ended up staying on. It's relaxing, really. I think you'd enjoy it. Something different in your repertoire. Here, let me see your phone."

Annie stood and handed over her phone. Catrin typed in the location and handed the phone back.

"We meet on Thursdays at seven. Your first visit is free. There's nothing to lose, except your time."

Annie recalled that same phrase on time being something she had heard before, and she felt goose bumps rise on her arms. "Oh. Thursday. Like tonight, Thursday."

"Yeah. Oh, but you don't have to go tonight. I get that it's a last-minute deal for you."

"Yes. But, that's okay."

"No. No. Don't worry about it. Try it next week, when you've given it some thought."

Annie's phone bleeped a notification. *You're ready for this*, texted OMG.

Annie twisted her mouth in response. "I'm free, actually. Tonight. It's perfectly fine. I didn't have much planned anyway, except another round of ukulele songs with Pork and Beans." She watched question marks arise everywhere around Catrin's head. "They're my cats."

Catrin smiled and exclaimed a sighing, "Ahh. Are you sure tonight's going to work for you?"

"Let me see. Feed the cats, shower, read. Or back-to-back episodes of an ad nauseum cut-and-paste crime drama fave. Yeah, I'm sure."

Catrin touched Annie's arm. "Gotta go. But it was nice having lunch with you."

"Oh, absolutely. Thanks for asking." Annie glanced at her phone. "Yoga Pug?"

Catrin smiled. "The owner's dog and assistant trainer. You have to go, if just to see the pug. He's so cute. I'll see you there."

* * *

Annie wore a light pair of gray sweat shorts and a vintage Yes band T-shirt, feeling awkward on her yoga pad in her attempt to stretch with the others. That is, until a little blond pug marched around to her side.

"His name is Potato," whispered Catrin.

Potato stretched out his back legs and lifted his head. Annie hesitantly followed in like. Her legs and back strained to the position.

"Okay. If a potato can do this, so can I. Right? Oh. Oh…I feel that. Yep," she gasped. "That's very good." She whispered a thank-you to her little helper.

If for no other reason, the yoga session was a great escape from her usual evenings. The various positions were nothing but set after set of flips and flops and unbalanced waggles, wobbles and the occasional teeter-totters, which she managed pretty well, considering it was her first struggle at such a frenzied experiment. She heard Catrin's laugh when she teetered on a more complicated one-foot position, falling into a cluster of fake houseplants. At least she was grateful and not too embarrassed with Catrin's rescue.

The next morning's alarm disturbed her from a dream of a cuddly pet fox that turned into her dad's Dobermann and began attacking her leg. Pork and Beans both meowed at her wrestled endeavor to reach for the clock, exciting them that she even stirred. Her calf then delivered a severe charley horse and tossed her out of the bed with a whack upon the hardwood floor.

Annie's morning routine was filled with moans and grunts as she dressed, lifting arms and legs with painful undertaking. Even her teeth hurt.

Annie knew her bedroom noise would alert Mrs. Winkle. Soon, she was making her way down the hall toward the ringing of the doorbell, with much effort to appear normal. She quickly withdrew her unpleasant expression, which reflected in the mirror to a more tactful mug.

She opened the door with a forced smile. "Morning, Mrs. Winkle."

"I heard a loud thump. Is everything all right?"

"Yes, Mrs. Winkle."

"Are you certain?"

"Yes. Fine, thank you. I'm just a little stiff today."

"Well, what on earth was that?"

"I fell out of bed."

Mrs. Winkle drew back, aghast. "Why did you do that?"

"Well, I haven't done it in a while. Thought it sounded fun."

Mrs. Winkle folded hands before her.

"I had a bad leg cramp. Yoga."

"Oh. He was such a cute bear. I didn't know you still had him."

Annie pulled her aching shoulders back. "Not, not Yogi. Yoga. It's a series of Hindu bodily postures widely popular with people, unlike myself, who can easily adapt at untying themselves from booby traps, pickles, and precarious tippies."

Mrs. Winkle swooned and winked an eye. "Oh, we were doing that sort of thing back in the sixties. How many partners did you have?"

"What? No. No, no, no." Annie pressed her palms up to her ears. "La, la, la, la! Never mind."

"Well, I'm sure you gave it your level best, at any rate. Why, I remember many evenings of bongos, beads, buns, and loads of mushrooms tucked up in Tommy and Jillian's psychedelic extremities."

"Mrs. Winkle!"

She laughed. "We were cool cats back then. Anything went in those days."

"Yes. Well. Thank you for checking in." Annie began to close the door, but halted to Mrs. Winkle's puzzled sidelong stare. "I'm sorry. Was there something else?"

"Well, I thought so."

"Uh-huh. Well, if you happen to think of it before I leave within the next half-hour, just call me."

Mrs. Winkle searched the ground for an idea.

"Have a good day." No sooner she closed the door and turned around, Mrs. Winkle knocked again. Annie cracked her neck before opening the door. "Yes, ma'am."

"Could I borrow your screwdriver? I seem to have misplaced mine."

"Sure." Annie walked over to the closet, opened the door, and looked down despairingly at the toolbox on the floor. "Oh, that's such a long way from here." Her muscles twinged in sad anticipation to her next move.

Her legs were so stiff, Annie had trouble manufacturing a position to bend down and get the screwdriver. The slant and side bend didn't get her close enough, and the dipping at the knees with arm in front of her crotch only got her a few inches nearer. She decided the stepladder would be an option.

"Did you find it?" Mrs. Winkle asked.

"Just a minute, Mrs. Winkle. I'll be right with you."

Annie opened up the stepladder and dropped herself upon it with legs dangling. After catching her breath, she grabbed the screwdriver and shot up off the ladder just as she heard footsteps, dancing with tiptoes to a stop out into the hall.

"Shoo. There you go," Annie said, handing Mrs. Winkle the tool. "I really should organize that closet sometime soon, huh?"

Mrs. Winkle joined in with Annie's distressed laugh, not as humored.

"Is there something I could help you with?"

Mrs. Winkle frowned. "No, dear. It's just my TV antenna. Needs adjusting."

"Alrighty, then." She showed Mrs. Winkle to the door. "Well, holler if you need anything."

"I'll be fine."

* * *

Annie kissed her two cats on their little heads before leaving the house. They sat dutifully together and watched her leave.

"I'll be back later. I promise. You know I'd rather be here with you, right? You boys hold the fort down. I love you."

She was confident they enjoyed the same routine every day as much as she did, knowing the time of her leave and her return. If nothing else went well for her this day, she knew there would be love waiting for her to come home to. She breathed a little easier as a July breeze curled around the tops of the street trees, and the blue skies began to deepen in hue. Her weather app showed it was going to be a day of heat and humidity. It was also a day she struggled to stay positive in anything. Her head was in a spin, wrought with office duties. Her shoes were already hurting her feet. The Lidocaine patch on her back felt like a rumpled, cold mess. She pulled it out from under her shirt only to have it stick to her fingers until she shook it off with great insistence. She watched as it flew, attaching itself to the passenger window. Annie pulled out of the driveway and wasn't even bothered by Cindy's presence across the street. She rolled down her car window and waved as she passed by.

"Morning, Cindy." It was as sincere a greeting as she could muster.

Annie wasn't halfway down the circuitous street when her brother texted her.

Just got a message that Dad's in the hospital. Been there since yesterday noon. WTF!

Annie let out an aggravated growl that built up in an aggressive choke hold on the phone. "Oh, for fluff sakes! Why can't he call somebody?"

Annie swallowed her vexation before driving to the hospital and rushing through the lobby. She concocted a friendly smile for the information attendant, who barely even glanced at her before turning away. Annie wasn't in the mood to entertain someone else's disinterest in their work, so she reached in her daypack. Pulling out the grenade lighter, she slipped it down on the desk.

"Excuse me," she blurted in an authoritative voice. She held up her wallet and flashed her Empire Café ID like an FBI agent. "Hospital Secret Security. Can you hand me that grenade over there, beside your cell phone?"

The young man's priggish demeanor melted away as the color drained from his face. He leapt against the far side of the desk, pressing himself against the monitor.

"Thank you for your prompt attention," she added, pointing to the grenade. "Maybe I'll just take that for you." She carefully lifted it before bobbling it from hand to hand. The man screeched like a little girl and wrapped his head in his arms. Annie resisted playing with him more. "It's all right. You're safe. Everyone's safe now. Quickly. I need you to look up the room number to Colonel Demetrius Freckle. We need to question him about this." She scrutinized his shaking limbs. "Well, come on, come on."

He fidgeted before hopping into the chair, typing wildly on the keyboard, and then exhaling. "Room 214."

Annie zipped up her daypack and paced past him, patting his shoulder. "Thank you for your service. Stay alert."

"Yes, ma'am."

Hospital corridors are always drafty, and full of an emptiness Annie could never quite describe. She took her time through the identical, barren halls, alone aside from the occasional passing nurse or dispirited couple. That didn't help her focus on anything but dread. Every step toward her father's room was another reminder of all of the moments she had tried to bring something positive to the table with him. Much of the time, of course, he'd responded to her gestures with his usual churlishness. Stopping before the door, she snatched up a sheet from a rolling table against the wall and draped it across her arm. A tech approached her from his room.

"Can I help you?" the tech asked.

"I'm here for Colonel Freckle." Annie watched the woman's eyes gesture to the sheet on her arm. "Oh. One should always be prepared for a bullfight."

The woman smiled and lowered her voice. "He hasn't been that bad this time. Not yet."

Annie gave the tech her sheet and stepped toward her father's bedside. "I guess you decided you needed a change in scenery?"

Her father's frown turned upside down. "What's happening?"

"Why don't you tell me?"

He shrugged. He seemed more melancholy than usual. "They can't tell me anything."

Annie sat beside him, pulled out the grenade lighter, and burnt off a long thread from his hospital gown. "How did you get here?"

"What do you mean how did I get here? I called 911."

Annie knew this was going to take some time. "And what was happening to you?"

"I couldn't breathe."

"Why haven't you called me or Scott?"

Again, a shrug. "They haven't done anything."

"Have you let them?"

His tone, predictably, became more nettled. "Annie, they want to test me for this, they want to run a test on that, they want me to stay and take this such and such liquid. It's bullshit."

Annie flared her nostrils and raised her voice. "Right. So, tell me what you expect them to do. Huh? How, in God's name, do you expect anyone to help you when you won't let them?"

"Oh, shut up."

"No! I'm getting tired of your shit."

"Watch your mouth!" he interrupted.

"What the hell's going on with you? Attention? You want attention, like a little kid. Because you feel lonely. Is that what this is about?"

Her father looked away. "You don't know anything."

"I know you yell at people on the phone. I know you argue with the home nurse your doctor is sending out now because of hospital visits like this one. I know you forget to eat. I know you haven't been in the shower for months. I know, unless I do your laundry, you forget about it. I know you're scared to answer your door, from the rifle cocked against the doorknob. You have a .45 hidden in a tissue box under your pillow. I know you call

Scotty in the middle of the night because, for the fiftieth time this month, your porn sites lock up your computer with more titties than Trump has tweets." Annie took a breath and ran a hand over her hair. Her limbs were shaking. She couldn't believe she was yelling at her dad. "Do you remember you called me by your sister's name the other day?"

Her father searched the floor and met her eyes. "No."

"Do you remember what you just told me about these tests?"

"You just got here!"

"I've been here for fifteen minutes."

"You're lying. You're lying! Bullshit!"

"You're losing it, Dad," Annie fumed, her finger tapping her temple. "You're losing it. I can't do this anymore because you're too damn stubborn to accept help from anyone. I'm done. All right? I'm done. You hear me? I'm done!"

Her father sat with hands clasped between his thighs. With a sullen nod and blank stare, he replied, "Thank you. Thank you for being honest."

His comment drew Annie to step back and lean against the wall. "Do you even know why you're here? Time, after time, after time? What is it you're looking for? What do you want from these people?"

His eyebrows drew together. "I want them to fix me."

She couldn't help noticing his eyes dim a little as his demeanor slipped into that of a little boy. It was enough to make her heart sob. She walked over to the bed and sat beside him. The idea dawned on her that his cognitive abilities may not be as up to par as they once were. She had seen him lose himself before, but only for a fleeting moment. This was different. It was in this moment she felt an odd weight in her stomach.

Annie rubbed his back and leaned over to kiss his forehead. He pulled away.

"Get me outta here," he spat.

The revolving doors began to move, and Annie could see her father being pushed in a wheelchair. She had been waiting at the lobby entrance long enough to dwell on her behavior, and beat up on herself for allowing the situation to disembowel her every fiber of serenity.

The aide assisted him into the car and closed the door.

He leaned over to her and hugged her arm in tears, pleading, "Please don't be mean. Please don't be mean. I'm sorry. I don't know why I do what I do."

Annie pulled his head to touch hers. Kissing him, she stressed, "We'll get through this. I'm sorry I yelled at you. It wasn't fair. I'm sorry. Okay? Dammit. We'll get through this, Okay?"

* * *

A couple hours later, Annie drove her father home. He sat, exasperated, in his armchair. It was the best she could offer, along with a glass of Diet Mountain Dew and a bowl of black licorice at his tableside.

"Scott came over to let Gunny out earlier," Annie said. "He was fine."

"Good."

This time he allowed her to kiss his head. "I've got to go, Dad."

"Thanks for your help."

His gratitude came out more like a sign of defeat than like the withering crackles of a bonfire in its last embers. He was clearly exhausted by whatever fiasco he'd stirred up for himself. Annie was certain this would not be the last of it.

Annie slouched against the doorknob and faced him. "You stuck it out and hung onto every prayer when I was at my very worst. Some days I didn't even know where I was and I still can't tell you how that chipmunk got in my shirt pocket at the liquor store. But you didn't give up on me. You enabled me. My greatest enabler. But God knows why you never gave up on me. I'm not giving up on you, Dad. I promise."

She closed the door behind her and stepped off the porch, walking side by side with her fairy godmother Pinky.

"You did very well, Annie."

Annie halted in step and looked at her. "You said my name."

Pinky's lips slowly turned up, and her eyes twinkled.

"And I didn't do well at all. I sucked. I failed. I let him get to me."

"Ever wonder why it is that you have days where your head just feels like it's under water? Things just blah? Don't want to go to work. Don't want to help your dad. Don't want to give your attention to anything because nothing seems fun? You're all caught up in doing things out of obligation rather than asking yourself if that's what you really want to do. So, you become resentful. You bury it well. But you're rebelling. Can't you feel that? You're teaching people they can have their way with you. And you're teaching yourself there's no other way to be there for them."

"It's called being of service."

Pinky opened the car door for her. "It's not serving either one of you if you're not enjoying what you're doing."

Annie slid behind the wheel and closed the door. Pinky was already sitting beside her. "You need to understand that life is not happening to you, it is happening through you. You will notice the world will begin to change around you when you start to honor who you are and who you are becoming. You've got to find some boundaries, Anita. For your emotional health. It's that simple. You're not meant to be all things to all people. And stop beating yourself up for blowing up at your father. Seeing someone you love change before your eyes is tough. Not everyone will accept that with grace and a smile on their face. Those that do, have no love for that person. Honor the fact that you do have love for him."

CHAPTER TEN

Annie was finishing up coffees at the Empire Café, topping them with chocolate shavings and whipped cream. After she set them out, she called out the names. "Peter, Peter, Pumpkin Eater; Baby Squirrel Earl; and Lickin' Dickens."

Her coworker Jimmie nudged her. "What happened to your baby bumblebee?"

"I'm sorry. My what?"

"Your car?" He raised his chin toward the window. "I see you're driving a freaking Mustang. Coffee and books can't be paying you that well."

Annie returned to the coffee machines with a huff. "My *bumblebee* found a pothole the size of Detroit. Heard its demise all the way to the next stoplight." Annie put much resentful play into the hissing sound that extracted from her lips. "It's getting a new tire. In the meantime, I'm driving the owner's Mustang. He lives in my mother's neighborhood. Has a crush on her. I was grateful for the gesture, at any rate."

"Brownie points."

"Yeah," she sighed.

She had been in her own little world, not paying much attention to anything or anyone around her all morning. Climbing out of an emotional tailspin was hard work. Allowing herself to be focused on the job and not the tire, or the fact her alarm didn't go off, was a little relieving. She had begun the practice of meditation in the mornings. It was easy for her to find mindlessness because her brain wasn't turned on first thing in the morning, anyway. But, running late like she was, she made the poor decision to play the meditation CD in her car. She'd never admit to another human being that she found herself on the wrong side of the street, breathing one, two, three, and detouring across the Purple People Bridge, a pedestrian-only bridge. Swift instincts and a rude awakening were her only saving grace. Her Fortwo clipped the cable-car rail just right to send it on two wheels, missing the few pedestrians and rolling through the cement posts at the exit in perfect alignment, like a daredevil. She landed on the levee and in a pothole with all four wheels down just before a mother was crossing with three children and a baby. If it wasn't for the applause, she would have felt worse about the start of her morning.

A sink of dirty containers awaited her and she sunk herself into the good, jazzy music playing over the speakers, when a large shadow appeared. An armload of pitchers and cups fell into the sink, dropped from the arms of a hulking figure who made her jump aside with a yelp.

The man's stoic face barely acknowledged her before he turned back to his chores.

"Who is that?" Annie asked her coworker Jimmie.

Jimmie turned from his steamed milk and nodded toward the man. "That's Harry Leto. A new hire."

Harry was a big, lumbering middle-aged gentleman with a thick neck and tiny ears. His appearance reminded Annie of a cartoon character she recalled who used to beat up an Ichabod Crane figure in one of many television shows from her childhood. Far from attacking, Harry leaned over the hot bar, attempting to make teeny, tiny coffees with his large, pawed hands.

Annie slid up next to him. "Hi. I'm Annie."

"Shhh," he responded.

"If you need any help, I'm—"

"Shhh."

Annie wasn't sure how to respond to a shush. "Okay."

Jimmie turned up the music and approached Annie as she backed away from Harry. She sucked in her lips and looked at him, wide-eyed.

"Music tends to distance murderers and victims with its ability to untangle any afflictions in the mind of the murderer."

Annie turned to a coffee with a slouch. "He's not a murderer, Jimmie. Else he wouldn't be working here."

"You don't know that."

"He's a new hire, right? Maybe he just needs time to concentrate."

Harry was singing and murmuring into the little cups as he topped each with a frothy spoonful of milk. His accent sounded Italian to Annie. "Does he speak English?"

"Oh, yeah," Jimmie said. "Broken. It's better than some folks around here, though. Get this, he used to be a gondolier in Venice, Italy. But he weighed the boat down so much he was rowing wheelies around the canals. Apparently, tourists lined up for him like a Disney ride. I guess the mayor wasn't too humored, and he was asked to retire the business to his son."

"How did he get from Venice to Cincinnati?"

"He fell in love with the Rubber Ducky Regatta, apparently. He volunteers to pick the little ducks out of the Ohio River every year."

"How cool is that?"

Harry grunted and leapt toward Annie. She shrieked and clung onto Jimmie. Harry was headed for the radio behind Annie and turned the volume up.

"'Going Up the Country.' Canned Heat," Jimmie whispered. "It's like his favorite. Anyone can mumble to it efficiently enough. Makes him feel good."

"Absolutely. We want him to feel good. Right?"

"Mm-hmm."

Jimmie showed her his phone. "I looked up his last name. Can you believe it means cheerful?"

Annie shrugged. "Maybe I should be hanging with him."

* * *

Thankfully behind the wheel of her own car, Annie was sitting at a stoplight, texting in reply to Mr. Tiddle's question about the P.T. Barnum papers. *I was researching last night*, she typed. *I wrote down a few leads. Left them at home. Let me stop by the apartment, and I'll be in shortly.*

She pressed on the gas pedal when the light turned green, and immediately stomped on the brake again as a figure appeared before her. It was her fairy godmother. Annie was still catching her breath when Pinky climbed in the car.

"You know," Pinky said, "you make it quite difficult to get your attention when you're texting and driving."

Annie started driving. "I was sitting at a light."

"Miles away in something you hate thinking about. Instead of discovering the subtle hints the universe gives out to redirect your passions in a direction that will make you feel better where you are."

"Let's not talk about the meditation CD, all right?"

"We didn't do that. You did that. Own it."

"Okay. Okay. Out of curiosity, what subtle hints were you throwing at me?"

"Like the smiling cloud you missed. The dragonfly that buzzed past your windshield. The excitement in your boss's text with the anticipation of a great sale."

"What? Wait. Wait. How's that supposed to make me feel better?"

"Humans get so busy fretting about how their own desires and wishes aren't coming into their reality, they miss how important their lives are to someone else's dreams. You're all working together in this global community, Amber."

Annie felt a familiar ache in her forehead.

"You get what you want when you help others get what they want. It's all a part of the big picture."

"Yeah, but he seems to think his whole career in this bookstore is balanced on this one set of papers selling. That it could make him or break him. And I just don't know that it's true."

"It's true for him. It doesn't have to be your dream. But, doesn't it feel good to be a part of someone else's ambitions? Just imagine getting all your desires accomplished without the help of other people. You won't get far. The universe will put people and situations in place to help you in the most wonderful ways. Your job is to simply believe in your desires and trust that we'll manage the rest. He irritates you, because you can't believe in your own ambitions the way he believes in his. Think about it."

Annie gritted her teeth. "So, I'm jealous?"

Once she turned the corner onto her street, Annie groaned. There was Cindy, her faithful stalker, leaning against her baby-blue Jeep, across from Annie's apartment. She was holding her phone up above her head and staring at something across the street. Annie pulled in the driveway and climbed out of her car. She glanced up to her building's roof, following Cindy's angle. Mrs. Winkle was on the roof, tottering around a giant antenna. Annie fell back against her car and felt her feet give out from under her as her heart leapt from her throat. She must have yelped in terror, because Cindy jumped and covered an ear.

"Keep it down, Annie. I'm trying to videotape this."

"Jesus, Cindy. Are you kidding me? How long has she been up there?"

Cindy shrugged. "A while now, I suppose."

Annie's skin broke out in a sweat. She dashed across the street and called out to Mrs. Winkle. The old lady's frail body wheeled about and tripped. She caught hold of the long bar and began swinging about.

"Aaahhhh!" Annie held out her hands, as if that would help. "Hold on, Mrs. Winkle," she screamed. She ran over to Cindy and yelled again. "For Chrissake, Cindy. Where the hell is your brain? Stop that goddamn video, you dumbass, and call 911!"

Cindy's nose wrinkled. "Golly, do you have to talk to me like that? I vowed I would never expose myself to such offensive verbiage."

Annie raised her eyebrows and exploded. "Well, for shit's sake, woman. If that's all it takes, listen, and listen well, Petunia Pants. I'm upping the ante, hear me? Social media can wait. Call the fuckin' fire department, bitch! Find a real job, and be of real help to somebody, you lazy ass. You're about as useful to humanity as belly button lint. Just go find a hole and stay there. Jezzus."

Annie ran around the side of the house and danced around the yard in distress, attempting not to burst from the emotions that flowed like pieces from a busted kaleidoscope.

"Oh, my God—oh, my God, oh, my God." Her hands shook uncontrollably, and she spun in circles. "What the hell do I do?" She slapped herself. "Ow! That was not it. Get a hold of yourself, dammit. She needs you. Get your ass up there, soldier." She closed her eyes, then took a breath. The antenna ladder was simple enough to climb, even with trembling limbs.

"Hang on, Mrs. Winkle. I got this. I'm coming. I'm coming."

The leg swing to the edge of the roof was awkward trick, as Mrs. Winkle shuffled to guide Annie up.

"The roof is weak there," Mrs. Winkle said. "Plant your foot just to the right."

"Got it." Annie's leg began to cramp again, just as she tried to shove herself off the ladder. A series of bleats erupted from her lips as she grabbed her leg. "Crap. I'm stuck. I'm stuck. Um…I'll be right there."

Pinky appeared on the ladder just below her, scaring her, then shoving her in the butt. Annie took a screaming fly roll upon the roof, and she landed on her back safely.

"Oh. That was helpful, actually. I'm good." Annie wheezed and clung onto the gritty shingles. She turned over and crawled closer to the antenna. "What the hell are you doing up here, Dottie?"

"I told you, it needed adjusting."

"But you didn't tell me it was this one."

"I'd prefer it if we discuss this at a later date, don't you agree?"

Annie realized she was raising her voice. "Yes," she said, a bit softer. "You're absolutely right." She grabbed onto the rod and held a hand out to her. "Give me your hand."

"I don't think that's wise, do you?"

"No, Mrs. Winkle. Your other hand." Mrs. Winkle grabbed onto Annie's hand, shaking slightly.

Annie overheard Mrs. Winkle's release of stomach gas on several occasions.

"I'm sorry this is stressing you out. We'll get you down safely. I promise."

Mrs. Winkle nodded. "Do you know how old this antenna is?"

"Honestly—"

"I bought it in 1968. The Reds had just finished their season fourth in the National League, with a record of eighty-three wins to seventy-nine losses."

"Gee, that's swell. I hate to bother you, but can we tidy this up a bit faster here?"

"Oh. Well, you'll have to come closer, dear. Watch that gutter. Don't slip. Careful now. Don't look down. There's a cable there."

"You know, Mrs. Winkle, none of that is of any help right now."

Annie reached further out than she was comfortable doing. With one hand on the chimney and the other just inches away from a bar on the antenna, she heard the old aluminum start to creak. The antenna was bending away, with Mrs. Winkle on the other end. Annie's foot slipped. She leapt from the chimney and grabbed onto the bar. She heard Mrs. Winkle scream, and Annie tried to keep them steady, but it was too late. The two looked like wet linens spinning around on a whirligig clothesline, hollering in unison. The antenna slowed to a jerking halt, the bar bending them to hang over the roof and against the face of the building.

A fire truck had arrived at some point, and a fireman leaned out of Annie's living room window, coaxing Mrs. Winkle to step onto the ledge. "I gotcha," he said. "Come over here and give me your hand."

"Oh. Have you got an antacid? I have the most horrible heartburn."

"Yes, ma'am. Let's get you to safety first, okay?"

"Well, I'm all right. Just get Annie."

Annie was busy attempting to lift her foot up around the antenna's rods. "It's all right, Mrs. Winkle. It's all good. Oh, look. See? There's a nice fluffy bush to catch me if those other firefighters are late with their—"

The antenna's bar snapped, and Annie fell into the bush with a series of winded curses.

* * *

The Life Squad truck had a nice, wide step for Annie to sit on while a paramedic placed a bandage in the middle of her forehead. She smiled at the generous cup of coffee handed to her from a firefighter's thermos and snuggled under the rescue blanket. The paramedic walked away to reveal Pinky's figure standing before her.

"Well, that went well," Pinky said.

Annie touched the bandage on her forehead lightly. "Injured my third eye. I think it was out of focus anyway." Annie whimpered in pain and wriggled away from the doorway. "A few bruises and scrapes. I think I'll have to replace the bush, though." She looked around. Vanessa Young, the blond newscaster from Channel 5 was standing before the house, pointing to the crooked and broken antenna. Cindy was standing beside her, being interviewed. "Great. Where did everybody else go?"

Pinky sat down solemnly.

"Is Mrs. Winkle safe? Did she make it inside safely?"

"She made it in safely, yes. You helped her a great deal."

Annie felt a tug in her gut. "Then, what's the matter?" She looked toward the house, where a couple firefighters exited in conversation. "What is it?"

Annie tore off the blanket and rushed over to the steps that led to her apartment.

An EMT stopped her. "You can't go in there just yet."

"Why?"

An older firefighter stepped out of the door with a face that could sink a ship. "I'm sorry. We tried to revive her."

"Revive her?"

"Once I got her inside, she collapsed. We tried to bring her back." He gently rubbed Annie's arm. "I'm sorry."

His solemn voice forced tears to streak down Annie's cheeks.

"I'm really sorry," he added.

Annie turned away and sat on the step. "Oh, God. It was too much. I knew it was too much."

He sat beside her. "Too much what?"

"Excitement. Gives her gas." She choked on the words and accepted a tissue. "She always said it would get her in the end." Annie blubbered fitfully into the tissue. "I gotta pee."

CHAPTER ELEVEN

Hours ran together and the days numbed by Mrs. Winkle's passing. This day felt especially hard to cope with. It seemed the worse she felt, the worse Annie's day became. She dumped a large box of Q-tips in the linen closet and conked her head on the protruding wire basket on the door. She tripped over a rug at the front door, missed the bottom step of her landing, dropped her keys at Mrs. Winkle's door, and clonked her head on the cowbell on the rise back up. She fed Mrs. Winkle's two babies in an attempt to feel their unconditional love and live in the moment, only to watch Saqi puke on the rug by the back door as Bones pooped on Mrs. Winkle's slippers.

Tossing Mrs. Winkle's moldy leftovers in the trash, Annie lifted her head up and found herself staring at a half bottle of Maker's Mark bourbon on the counter. She realized she hadn't thought of drinking for a very long time. The pause of thought was probably longer than was healthy. It seemed like an eternal moment. She balked at the dust on the shoulders of the bottle and wiped it off gently. "Well, that never happened to any of my bottles." The events of the day flashed before her eyes in bits that seemed to suck more life out of her. Until Pinky's words about subtle hints from the universe rang in her ears.

Annie took her eyes off the bottle and looked out the window. A robin was sitting on the shepherd's hook close by. A strange feeling of relief settled in her chest and melted her to tears.

"Robin. New life. New beginnings. Not so subtle a hint." Annie nodded. "I'm sure that's a brick. I needed that." The robin turned to her and began to preen itself. She unscrewed the cap and poured the liquid down the sink. She didn't even feel remorse. She felt nothing and that made her feel good. She dropped the bottle in the trash and looked out the window again. The robin was gone. She glanced up to nothingness. "Thank you."

Annie followed up her afternoon by mowing the lawn and tripping over a hole. A rosebush grabbed her every motion, catching on her shirt, her pants, pricking her wrist, and pulling her hair. Once she'd freed herself, Annie was certain she looked like she'd just gotten mugged. She took a bag of trash out to the street corner. It burst on her halfway down the driveway.

Later, she sat before a hedgerow and started to trim it, when she noticed a pale set of legs through the bushes. A deep sigh escaped her as she recognized the red Converse shoes.

"Are you kidding me?"

Annie looked up to meet Cindy's shy smile.

"Hi, Annie."

"Hi, Cindy. What's up?"

"I just thought you'd want to know that I'm going to stop coming around."

"Oh?"

"Yeah. I found someone who likes me. Kinda. I guess. We'll see."

"Oh." Annie never imagined having this conversation with Cindy. Her brain tingled with something she wasn't used to feeling. "Well, um. That's...great. That's wonderful, Cindy. I hope it works out."

Cindy smiled and walked away, leaving Annie's stomach in a knot.

Annie felt like an ass for behaving badly that awful day. Cindy was just being Cindy. She knew that was no excuse to launch an attack at her. Cindy was not a violent person. Just a human who was socially inept. Annie didn't see herself as anyone better. She knew she was no better behaved than Cindy in that moment, and it cracked her.

"Cindy," she called out. Cindy turned around. Annie stood up and took a step toward the bush. She drew a blank. She froze. She couldn't do it. Should she do it? Should she apologize? What if she did, and Cindy took that as a come-on. An approval of mutual interest? Too much effort. She pressed her mouth in a hard line. "Good luck."

She watched as Cindy drove away. She huffed at herself in frustration. Annie turned around and stepped on a rake. The handle swung up and smacked her across the nose, flipping her off her feet and onto the hard ground with a painful grunt.

* * *

Annie listlessly fumbled about her apartment, tending to her attentive cats. They acted like they knew she was sad. They watched her every move. Pork rubbed her arm to distract her from staring out the window too long at the backyard, empty of the playful romping of Saqi around Mrs. Winkle's feet, empty of the happy ease of Bones helping Mrs. Winkle weed around her favorite rosebush. Beans knocked over a pen on the desk, along with a notebook and a stack of papers. Annie finally agreed to pay attention when she heard her phone hit the floor.

"Stop it. That's enough."

Pulling herself back upright, she spotted a car in the driveway. She readjusted her glasses and caught movement from the corner of her eye. Looking again, she saw that Saqi and Bones were being pulled harshly through the yard to a county dog pound truck.

Annie ran out through the yard, hailing the dog warden. "No, no, no. Wait. Wait. What the hell are you doing?"

The pale fellow barely acknowledged her presence. "My job, lady." He held his nose before letting out a series of sneezes and curses. "Bless it, these allergies."

"Allergic to dogs, huh?"

"Yeah."

"Why do you even have this job? Didn't get the modeling gig at Macy's? Look, you can't take these dogs. They live here. I just fed them. They just settled down for a nap."

"Pat yourself on the back."

She pointed at Bones. "This one needs her medication."

The man cast a smug squint toward her with a disgusting coughing flinch that only a forty-year smoker with greasy hair could accomplish with such acoustic echo off grimy rusting metal doors. "Look. I was called and told the owner is deceased. This is what we do. Now, if you don't mind, I've got a job to do. Excuse me."

Annie stepped back and watched with helpless abandon as her beloved friends were shoved into the oversized kennel. Yellowed nail nubs of tobacco-stained fingers clenched around the door and slammed it shut.

"How the hell did you get in? Who do I call to make a complaint?"

The dog warden threw a thumb over his shoulder. "I'd start with that guy. He's the one who called it in."

Annie turned back to the house. Mrs. Winkle's son, Keith, was struggling to lock the front door and pull his stuck key out.

She approached him and bellowed, "Keith!"

"Oh, good. Here. Get this key out of this door for me."

"Why should I help you when you're sending two beautiful souls to their deaths? It's a kill shelter. Do you realize that?"

"Not my problem." He stomped in a snit and resumed his struggle with the key.

"Fine. Hate them. But, it's not their fault that you're not an animal lover."

"Allergies. Not that it's any of your business."

"You should go have a drink with that guy," she said. "Have you tried lizards?"

His eyes drew to her with a ferocious twitch. "I'm not here to carry on a conversation."

"Besides, aren't you being disrespectful of your mother's wishes?"

"What wishes?"

"That Saqi be sent to her sister in Phoenix."

Keith turned around to her. "She's in a nursing home. No pets allowed." After ceaseless attempts at the door again, he threw his hands up and stepped back with a growl. "Remind me to change these locks to push-button."

Annie searched deeply for a shred of sympathy, understanding that even though he had the personality of a mop, she wouldn't wish to be in his place. "Oh, for cripe's sake. Here, let me." With some effort, she knew it was stuck. "You have to jiggle it." She started to break a sweat before she invoked the only help she knew could assist. "Pinky. Tom. Somebody. Look, I'm still under contract, right? Can you just give me a moment of your time, here?"

"You'd better not be having other people staying in this house rent-free," Keith announced with a finger in her face.

"Honestly, Keith. Do I look like I'm interested in entertaining anybody right now? I loved your mom. She was a good friend. I've taken quite a hit, here."

The key released, and Annie fell back off the step and onto the yard. Keith's hand reached down and plucked the key from her still-grasping fingers. Her breath was knocked out. A piece of paper floated down over her face. Thankfully, she felt her lungs fill with air again, and she coughed, peeling the paper off her face.

"What's this?" she asked.

"Your eviction notice. I'm selling the house. Thirty days, and you're out. Better start looking."

Annie watched his shadow disappear. For the moment, she really didn't care about that as much as she did reclaiming her breath. A loud syncopated vibration of a motorcycle's muffler resounded up the street and into the driveway after Keith left.

The presence of a face shadowed hers. A woman with a tangle of short, black hair hovered over her. Annie was distracted by the shock of electric pink and green that burst from her temple, beside an ear full of piercings. It all went well and was quite impressive against the string of stars tattooed on the side of her neck.

"How's it going?" the biker asked.

Annie saw the word "Oz" tattooed on her wrist. "Oh, you know. Trying to embrace my inner shit day."

She helped Annie sit up. "How's that working for you?"

"About as well as eating a salad from a mason jar."

"Did anyone ever really like mason jar salads?"

"I don't think so."

Annie wiped the tears from her face and held her nose that started aching. The stinging simply added to how she felt on the inside. "I bopped myself in the nose when the key came out. I think it's broke. I already injured it with the rake."

The woman sat next to her and stared closely. "Naw. It's not broke. You know, you can redirect this negativity any time you want."

Annie turned to her. She wasn't some Good Samaritan off the neighborhood street. That kind of talk could only come from one source. She eyed the woman's features and her "Oz" tattoo again. She pulled herself on her feet.

"Oz, is it? Listen. There's a lot more stuff going on here. I'm trying to deal with it, but it's not easy being human. You people don't seem to get that."

"We're more of a collective consciousness, really."

"You're all happy and crap, or just plain weirdly detached and expecting us to be okay with this awkward nonsense. 'Don't worry, be happy. Be happy and happy things will come to you.' Well, it's not working out, dammit!"

"Has it never worked out?"

"Don't distract me. I'm trying to prove a point here."

"Just as a side note, you allow yourself to be distracted by things that don't serve you well. Have you ever noticed that? If you ever want help focusing on your value just let us know. By the way, when has it never worked out? When have we never had your back?"

"Stop turning this around on me."

"Fine. I get it. You want to sit in your hole. That's all right with us. Remember that pothole? The mom with kids? Who do you think stopped your car in that pothole? You did some awesome driving there, by the way. That was all you, Annie. Be proud. You were really focused then. Awesome stuff happens when you focus on the life you really want. Do more of that."

"Don't you get it?" Annie jumped herself to her feet. "I'm talking outta my ass to someone nobody else sees. I don't think I've been in the real world. This. Here. This." Annie flagged the sky, trees, and grass. "This is the real world. I get this. All my senses see this, feel this, smell this, taste this. I can't get around it. It sucks. It really sucks! You, I can't even talk about you without getting sent to the loony bin. I couldn't even sell you and your beliefs on the street corner. No one is buying this shit." Annie stomped on the grass. "This is real." She swiped up a fistful of clipped shrub. "This is real." She reached for her clippers and batted them against a tree trunk, screaming, "This is real! This! Is! Real! It's real! It's all real!"

She turned to Oz, shaking. She hated herself for being this upset. But her heart was full of it. She felt the warm tears stream down her cheeks and her bottom lip quiver. "What are you people doing to me?" she hollered. "I don't understand you."

Oz stood next to her. "Actually, you understand more than you give yourself credit for."

"Stop that," Annie growled at her.

"Look at yourself. You're all riled up because you're grieving. You're in a tailspin. So. Fall. Just fall. There's nothing you can do about it. Stop fighting it. Just make peace with it."

Annie peeled off her glasses and wiped her eyes with a sleeve. "I can't do this. I really can't do this anymore."

"Choices. Your life is a series of choices. Choices that you've made. And now you want us to just fix it for you so that you can feel better." Oz tilted her head to Annie's frown. "Sound like someone you know?"

Annie growled to the heavens. “I don’t believe this is happening to me. Don’t you want me to believe in you? I thought you knew me. If you knew me, you would know I can’t do this anymore. I can’t do this. I can’t. I can’t handle this.” Annie collapsed onto the ground and covered her face in her arms. “I thought you loved me, dammit.”

She felt arms pull her near in an embrace. “It’s going to be okay.” Oz’s voice was calm and reassuring. “You are so loved. We’ll get through this. Okay? You’re going to be okay. We’re right here. Promise. You’re going to be okay.”

It was a strange and beautiful experience to be held by that which cannot be described. Through tears and sniffles, Annie added, “Okay. I don’t know why, but I believe you.” Annie pulled away and sat up, accepting a tissue. “By the way. I really like your ride. That 1953 black Indian Chief, it suits you.”

* * *

Annie later sat with Oz on her balcony step and sipped on a hot tea.

Oz held out a small box. “Tic Tac?”

Annie barely acknowledged the box before holding her hand out.

“Past will creep up on you every once in a while,” Oz said. “You can’t help that. It’s a human condition. We know it sucks. It does suck.”

Annie rolled a couple of Tic Tacs over her tongue. “I guess I just let everything get me sideways. There has been lot to sort out. I feel so lost. I just can’t wrap my head around it all. I’m overwhelmed. Why has everything been snowballing on me lately?”

“Because you’ve made an art form of believing you are undeserving of anything good happening to you. Don’t beat yourself up for feeling angry. For being enraged. For feeling grief. For missing someone. But, don’t allow yourself to sit in it. You have to care how you feel. You have to be selfish enough to care how you feel, or you have—”

“Nothing to give anyone. Yeah, I remember.”

"Just chill a while," Oz continued. "Stop trying to change everything. News flash, people are not in your life to make you happy. 'If this changes, I'll be happy. If he stops doing that, I'll be happy.' Stop giving up your power to excuses. I think you can relate to this; invest in your choices. Would you invest in something rocky, or something you know will become more valuable? You get to decide if you want to be frivolous or not. You're smart. Is your choice draining your account or adding to it? Be happy, for no reason. Just for the hell of it. Find a little appreciation with where everyone and everything is. Let the rest go. Just for now. Work on you. Can you do that?"

"Oh, the irony. This, coming from Roadkill Rita meets Hardly Hardware Hannah."

Oz glanced down to her outfit. "What? Is it the chain?"

"It's a bungee cord, Oz. I can't take you seriously with a bungee cord."

* * *

For over six years, the symbol for Annie's relief had become the Alcoholics Anonymous sign at the door of churches and obscure businesses. She always felt strengthened while sitting amongst others who shared stories of struggle in their lives, yet no longer found drinking or drugs a solution to issues.

"Hi," Annie breathed. "I'm Annie, and I'm an alcoholic."

"Hi, Annie," the group responded in unison.

"I almost killed myself today. On a bike. It was a very steep street in Mt. Lookout. The chain fell off when I tried to brake for a crossing salamander." Her heart sank. "Thank God he was fast. And when this man pulled me out of his flower bed, he found a lost set of keys the ex-wife tossed years ago when she declared she was divorcing him. So, I guess it wasn't a total loss. Things are looking up. I am feeling better, most days lately. But then, little things. Little things try to crack my spiritual groundedness, you know. Little things are happening all over. I come here to realize that they're not little things. I choose to shine a light on only a portion of them. They're big things, really. Big, ugly messes sometimes. Big blessings others. Crackling all above my head like fizzing Fourth of July sparklers at various stages of existence.

"I recognize that the monster under the bed and behind me, down the dark hall, is still under the bed and down the hall. Sometimes, I used to feel it was wearing a pink tutu to humor me. It was just playing with the boxes I shoved under the bed in an attempt to cover up its existence. I've discovered it's not to be feared. It wants to help. It has a beautiful soul. I need it in my life. It's not a monster at all. It embraces me with the best-ever hug and unconditional love I never knew I wanted." Annie teared up as her heart swelled with love. "I've learned that the real monsters I believed that are outside are just reflecting my angst about me, about how well I'm not taking care of myself. Orange barrels. Broken nails. People. Flat tires. Rain. Grumpy people. More rain, sometimes pounding thunderstorms. But, it's summer. So, they go away quickly. The people, not so much. My haircutting salon decided to have a sale the day after I got my hair cut. The supermarket stopped carrying my favorite root beer. I got mad at my attempt at making naan bread the other day and threw the sticky pieces around my kitchen. I've painted them now as abstract pieces of art. I've learned there are some words I can never take back, and there are some things I have no control over. My dad's a real jerk sometimes. But he's ill, I still love him. My dear old landlady died. I miss her so much." Annie started feeling saddened again and began to sob. "And now my stalker is leaving me for somebody else," she squeaked. Someone handed her a tissue. "Thank you." She blew her nose.

The sleepy man beside her leaned over and whispered, "I could use a haircut."

* * *

After working her morning job at the Empire Café, Annie was headed for her car, when her mother called.

She answered, "Hi, Mom."

"Hi, honey. I'm so sorry to hear about Mrs. Winkle."

"How did you know about Mrs. Winkle?"

"It was all over Channel 5 news, with that blond anchor your brother likes."

"Oh. He told you that?"

"I'm your mother. I know my children."

Annie recoiled, and for a second, she thought she knew what having Tourette's might feel like.

"How are you doing, dear? Must have been horrible."

"It sucks. But I'm dealing with it. Speaking of which." Annie halted herself from asking her mother for a room.

"What was that, dear?"

"Ah, nothing. I—um—I'm having to look for another place to live. Mrs. Winkle's son wants to sell the old house."

"Oh, yes. I read that on your Instalips."

"Since when did you get on Instalips?"

"Scott set me up on it so I could keep tabs on the two of you."

"Huh." Annie unlocked her car and slid into the seat. "Guess I'll have to start saying nice things about you now."

"Oh, ha, ha. Yes, you'd better, young lady. Your brother tells me you're out of a place to stay."

"No. I still have a roof over my head for the next thirty days, Mom. I'm not worried. I'll find something. Mrs. Winkle's son lives in another state. Probably wouldn't be too great a landlord, anyway."

"But you love that house."

"Well, I don't have a choice. And I don't have the money to buy it. Don't worry. I'll find something."

"Just remember, Annie. You could always stay with me."

Annie allowed the visions of having to live under her mother's roof to flash before her. Painfully meeting all her mother's dates from Catch.com. Or the pressure to answer grueling questions about her workday over leathery, dry-roasted chicken or burnt pot roast while disengaging the smoke detectors. Even the thought of dwelling within a house full of smoke from her mom's daily spiritual rituals felt off the mark from pleasant, quality time.

"I already have a few prospects, Mom. But thank you."

"Okay. Well, I have to get going."

"Where?"

"I signed up for Mrs. Puddle's Shake, Rattle, and Roll classes. 'Cause we're all over fifty, and that's all we can really do. The last ten minutes of cooldown is really us trying to stand back up."

Annie snorted a laugh. "Mrs. Puddle, the neighbor you hate, with the Pepto Bismol-pink shutters and barking dogs at two in the morning?"

"Oh, it's all right now. After being fined for the fourth time in two months, she decided to put up the white flag and hosted a neighborhood barbecue, where everyone could get to know her dogs. They haven't barked since."

Annie was impressed. "The dogs or the neighbors?"

"Options, darling. We all have options for solutions. I don't know about you, but I can't be in the problem and be looking for the solution at the same time. Two totally different vibes."

Massive, green highway signs provided Annie with choices for on-ramps. "You know, I'm beginning to understand that."

"She's really an interesting person, Mrs. Puddle. One of those goody-goody neighbors who makes you wonder if they're a spy in disguise. Guess I watch too much drama on television. Okay. Gotta go. Love you."

"Love you too. Oh. Mom?"

"Yes."

"Thanks for checking up on me."

When her mother replied, she could tell in her voice it was a whole-hearted, "You're my heart."

Annie felt a sob of appreciation ball up within her, and she inhaled deeply with joy.

CHAPTER TWELVE

Boxes surrounded Annie while she sat and ate a bowl of Asian chicken noodle soup at her kitchen dinette. Sucking a mouthful, a noodle wiggled and thwapped a wet streak on her glasses. She made a sour face and cleaned the lens with her T-shirt. That evening had provided little interest. Even strumming on her ukulele couldn't keep her entertained. Her apartment searches only added more reluctance to continue.

It was time to change her mood. The yoga stretches she had been practicing were becoming easier. But she still couldn't manage the giant rubber band without slapping herself into the next room. A new discovery of Qigong motivated her into a pleasing atmosphere of ease. *This was the ticket*, Annie thought. She looked at Catrin's number on her phone. Thought about calling. Texting. Nope. She laid it back down on the table. The decision to work on more Qigong set her mind and spirit into a groundedness she had never experienced.

Pork and Beans were playing amongst themselves, hopping in and out of the empty boxes laying about. She sat on the floor to pet them and held up a framed photo of Saqi and Bones posing with her. She almost allowed herself to fall in a funk about it until Pork nosed her photo and rubbed her leg. She placed the photo in a box and smiled at Pork, rubbing his little face.

"You're right, Purr Purr. I can't dwell on missing Mrs. Winkle's two babies. I'll find us another place, and it'll be just as sunny as this one. I promise. We've still got some time." Something tweaked her gut. "But maybe I could just call and see if they're still there." She picked up her phone and called the pound. Before the call could be picked up, her heart leapt, and she hung up. She couldn't go through with it. She really didn't want to know. She rubbed her face. "This feels detached. I'm doing it again, aren't I? We should think better thoughts, huh, boys? Maybe somebody out there loves old dogs and adopted her. Took Bonsey in. Why don't we hope in that instead, right?"

Pork and Beans both nudged her from their separate boxes. Annie played the game of Catch The Paw and Find The Scratching Noise On The Box. An idea then came to her.

"Hey, come on. Why don't we bake some bread? A special bread for Mrs. Winkle's birdies?"

The boys assisted as best they could, sniffing out drawers and pantry shelves while Annie cleaned up the kitchen. It wasn't long into the mixing process that Annie's doorbell rang.

She dusted her hands off with a towel and opened the door to find a dark, hooded figure standing before her. Annie pulled the tip of the hoodie up and stared at Varsha's peaky demeanor. "Oh, boy. Tomorrow's going to hurt."

Varsha swept past her. "You think this is a phase?"

"Yes, I do. It's called delusional." Annie closed the door and followed her to the kitchen.

"I think I've turned a new chapter in my life here. I've been thinking some really deep stuff here lately."

"Like reusing snack bags, and turning off the water when you brush your teeth?"

Varsha waved a limp hand at her. "No, silly. I didn't even brush my teeth today, come to think of it."

"Oh, good."

"A shirt sleeve comes in handy in brain fart moments like that." Varsha shimmied over to the counter and glared at the lineup of ingredients for the bread. She grabbed a brown bottle and sniffed it. "Hey, what kind of liquor is this? I thought you quit?"

Annie watched as Varsha gulped the liquid from a measuring cup and gagged with a wiggle.

"Wow, this is strong crap."

"That's because it's vanilla extract, turtle head." Annie snatched the cup from Varsha's hand. "I'm baking something."

Varsha crooned, "Cookies?"

"No. It's a Dutch apple quick bread with dried cherries, peanut butter, and sunflower seeds for Mrs. Winkle."

"But. Uh…Annie. Mrs. Winkle is dead."

"I know that, Varsha. And you don't have to whisper. Mrs. Winkle wanted me to make her a loaf of bread when she… croaked. To feed it to her backyard birds as a sort of, 'Sorry I'm gone. But, here's something to remember me by' bread offering. I thought it was a very wonderful thing to do. I'm honored she asked me. Means a lot."

"Yeah. Wow. That's pretty deep. I'm really feeling that, dude."

"No. You're feeling your hand in my egg bowl."

"Eww."

Annie led her over to the sink and rinsed off her hand. Handing Varsha a towel, she stood back and felt herself begin to absorb Varsha's features and sensed she was reading her friend's thoughts through varied expressions. The overwhelming struggle to think, to not think.

"Here," Annie offered. She placed a food processor in front of her. "Help chop these dried cherries for me."

"Yeah. No problem." Varsha curiously eyed the contents and pressed the button on the lid over and over again. She stood back, then attacked it with a pounce. "Man, what gives? I think it's on the blitz."

"Fritz. It's on the fritz," Annie corrected her. "It's not plugged in yet."

"Ohh."

"You know what? That probably wasn't such a bright idea. Go sit down." Annie pulled up a chair at the bar. "Go on. Have a seat. You can watch me."

"Cool."

Watching Varsha raise her butt to the bar stool and slide on was like watching someone in slow motion fall up. Her hands and arms caressed the bar as if searching for a missing puzzle piece, and her legs had their own life, not knowing if they wanted to cross or not.

"What's going on with you? No wait. Let me guess. The habanero chick from Fired up Pizza with the misspelled tat that read, 'No Regerts?'"

"No, dude. That was last week. This is the bartender from Below the Belt bar."

"I can't keep up."

"Not that anything's wrong." Varsha grinned as if enjoying a vivid vision and scratched her lime and blue streak of stiffly spiked hair. "It's great, dude. It's, um…*pow-wowza* great. She's fire, spark, wild." She made a sizzling *kapow* sound with her lips and wiggled her fingers. "The sex is crazy wild, fun, kinky marshmallowy weird."

"Wow. Okay."

Varsha laughed and rubbed her neck. "Yeah. She's—damn. Good. Really, really good. Shoo. But."

"But?"

"I don't know. She's really not that"—Varsha's eyes drew a blank—"romantic, you know?"

"Romantic?"

"I mean, yeah. She rushes me straight to her bed when I come over. And sometimes, right there inside the door, man. On the floor. Like she can't get enough of me." Varsha eyed the coffee cup Annie slid to her and scooped it up in her hands. "Don't get me wrong. You know I love a good quicky as much as the next chickie. I know I'm good. I know I'm irresistible. I've had a lot of practice." Varsha crossed her fingers. "See this? Huh? That's me and my Libi. We're tight. We talk. And when she needs some attention…"

"Varsha."

"Yeah."

"What's your point, hon?"

"You got a cookie?" Varsha pointed at her coffee. "I need to dip."

Annie smooshed the corner of her lips and dug into her cookie jar.

Varsha swooned at the offering. "Ooh, oatmeal. My favorite." After a dip into her coffee and a bite, she continued, "Dude. I need someone to have deep, intellectual, philosophical conversations with my lovers. Like you and I do."

"You mean the kind where I correct your English."

"Exactly." Varsha rubbed noses and butted heads with Beans, who was pacing before them on the bar. "I thought she was really into me. Then, tonight, she started flirting with this guy at the bar. Sunk ole Libi into the depths of despair."

With her bread dough mixed, Annie plopped it into a loaf pan. "It doesn't need to rise. I'll just stick it in the oven." Annie slid her bread into the oven and closed the door.

"Damn! Is that what you did with your Libi?"

"What? No. I'm talking about the bread. My libido is perfectly fine. In the corner reading a book somewhere."

Varsha gasped. "You two aren't talking?"

Annie frowned. "We have an understanding. It's a solid relationship." Annie started washing up the dishes. "Varsha, there's nothing wrong with you and your Libi. She'll get over it. And she knows you'll move onto someone else." She checked her watch. "I'll give it forty-five minutes."

"Don't get me wrong—I like casual sex. Hell, I have to make up for the two of us, Annie. You're not doing anything."

Annie glared at her from around an open cupboard door. "I beg your pardon. Just because I've decided to stay single and celibate doesn't mean I'm not doing something. I happen to be enjoying my solo escapades, thank you very much. Unlike you, who is a magnate for marshmallowy and polyamorous partners."

"See, that's just it. She couldn't just keep that aspect to herself. She tried pressuring me into having a threesome."

"What?"

"Yeah."

"Zinkers, Batman. What did you say?" Annie poured her another cup of coffee and slid it to her.

"No. No, no, no, no. Definitely not. We already had that talk when we met. I don't do Twinkies. But she got all puppy-dog eyes on me and walked out. With the guy. And now she's not responding to my texts." Varsha cradled the cup in her hands and drooped close to the steam. "Sex was the only thing we had in common. And now it just seems…" Varsha bounced her head and waggled and made all sorts of ugly faces.

Annie sipped on her own cup of coffee. "Don't worry, Tiger. You'll find plenty of turkey legs to nibble on. You just have to learn to be more selective, now that you've turned the page on a new chapter. There are just as many women with healthy Libis as there are men with…their…whatever's in this world." Annie hated speaking about the male anatomy. "Anyway. Tell me, what does this new chapter in your life read like?"

"One without the drug scene."

"What?"

"Yeah, Bruh." Varsha gestured for another cookie. "Poison in your cup. Didn't I tell you?" Varsha nodded deeply. "This one was definitely Rocky Road suicide dipped in salted caramel asphalt. Besides her insistence in the bar scene, she was a pill popping cokehead."

"It's not like you to date addicts, Varsha."

"I know. I guess I'm getting sloppy."

"Woman, you are so much better than that. You are worth so much more in your life than roadkill. Second-hand candy and hand-me-down clothes are one thing. But you deserve only the best women."

"Quality, not quantity, huh?"

"Yes. Exactly. I know what it is. Your Libi is telling you that you could be a high-stepping, Tristate titty-topper, kitty-stopper."

Varsha crooned close to Annie's face. "No."

Annie waved the liquor vapors aside. "It's ready to move onto the big catches. It's all about where you're looking. Get back on your bike and hit the trails again. You used to love that rush. I understand there's all kinds of gals hiking, biking, and taking in that good, clean air. Healthy women, with healthy issues. Issues, none the less. But healthier than any barfly. Get my drift?"

Varsha nodded with a grin. "On the rapids, baby. Oh, I'm starting to get a vision."

"Come on," she coaxed. "Last call." Annie walked around the bar and pulled up Varsha's hood up over her head. She threw an arm over her friend's shoulders and led her to the door. "You've got clout, girlie. There's plenty of women out there. Don't worry about a sexy stray demon misleading you. There are tons of batshit crazy women right here in the Tristate for your viewing pleasure. Just keep them at arm's length until you can gauge if they're romantic material." She opened the door and watched Varsha toddle to the doorway. "By the way, how did you get here? You weren't crazy enough to drive, I hope?"

Varsha's face withdrew into something of a puffed frown, and she flicked out a bus card from her pocket. "I've always been prepared, Annie. You know that. I don't drink often. But when I do, at least I'm smart enough to allow the graces of our fair city's metro to drive me."

Annie sat back on her heels. "Wish I had been that smart when I was drinking."

Varsha waved her off. "It's easy. I can teach you."

Annie leaned against the doorway and crossed her arms. "Remember that story you told me of how Miss Bartender tried to get you to be someone you weren't?"

"Yeah."

Annie shrugged. "This story has the same ending. I can't do what you do. It's not in my DNA."

Varsha leaned back and exhaled a soft, "Oh. Wow. I get that."

"I thought maybe you would."

Varsha then fell into Annie with a sloppy hug. "Thank you for being my friend, Annie."

Annie couldn't help it. Her stiff resistance melted into an accepting slump of nurturing joy. Her heart swelled, and she held her friend tight.

"Guess it was just a false alarm," Varsha said.

"It's okay," Annie replied. "It's going to be okay." Annie couldn't help recalling when someone said those same words to her. Empowering words they were. Worth sharing.

Varsha pulled away and took to the steps. "It's still early. Think I'll get a tattoo."

* * *

Gunny, her dad's Dobermann, wasn't jumping at the garage door. In fact, he wasn't anywhere near the door. Annie's entry into her dad's house was uneventful, which made the blood rush to the back of her skull.

"Dad?"

No response.

Scott followed in behind her. "He didn't answer the phone. And I've called four times in twenty minutes."

Her mouth went dry. She stepped into the kitchen area and spied Gunny standing stiff in the living room, staring her down. He whined and urged her with a pounce of his front feet. Annie recognized his animated behavior as an attempt to translate an urgent message. Visions swarmed in her head, and none of them predicted a good outcome.

"Dad?" Annie called out.

She and Scott dashed down the hall, stopping at the bedroom door. She patted Gunny's side and pushed him back before entering the room.

"Good boy. Good boy. Stay here."

"Something smells really bad in there," Scott groaned.

Annie's hands began to shake. "I can't open it. You do it."

A heavy malodorous stench filled the room. "Whoa, oh… my God."

"Annie, is that you?" her father said.

"Are you okay?" Scott hollered.

"Scott? Is that you?" their father's voice echoed.

Annie could hardly speak when she opened the door. The image of her father lying facedown, naked on the bathroom floor, surrounded by a pile of his own excrement, was too much for her. She gasped and held her breath, inching her way over to the bathroom door. She grabbed for a sock atop a stack of clean clothes and covered her face. At least, she hoped they were clean.

"What...what happened to you?" Annie asked. "Are you all right?"

"I pooped!"

"No kidding."

"No. I mean I really pooped. Quite an explosion. Must have been those new fish oil supplements. The neighbor lady thought they would help."

"Help with what?" Scott asked.

"My constipation."

Annie moaned. "Wow."

"Successful as a Sherman tank, Dad," Scott added. "You had Gunny worried to death about you. He had us thinking you were...um..."

"Dead?"

Annie nodded. "Smells like it."

Later, when Annie and her brother had finished cleaning up her father and his bathroom, they sat down together at the kitchen table over a glass of lemonade.

"I'm sorry you had to see that," her father mumbled.

Scott looked like he was about to burst out laughing. "The murder scene poop splatter or your butt?"

"Both."

Annie watched her dad recoil as if he was embarrassed. Then, he started to laugh.

"Dad, it happens," she professed. "Poop happens. And it just so happens that the occasional live bit of flesh can't help but get involved. You forget I used to work at a nursing home. A butt like yours ain't nothin' special."

"I'm sure you've had moments in your life you wanted to moon someone," Scott quipped. "Ta-da. There you go. Scratched off the bucket list. I have to say, though, seeing your hiney was not at all on my bucket list."

"It reminded me of seeing your little baby butt, Scott, when mom taught me how to change your diaper." Annie threw a thumb at him. "Your butt stunk too."

Gunny handed her his bone. His tender eyes and steady gaze reflected something she had seen in Mrs. Winkle's sweetie, Bones. The tug in her gut returned. Already, she missed Bones. She rubbed Gunny's head with a calm acknowledgement. "You're a good boy." Gunny pawed at her leg for more attention.

"This is new," Scott said.

"He's been very calm lately," their dad admitted. "I let him curl up in that old, red recliner. He watches TV with me. Hates commercials. I have to flip the channel every time one comes on. He'll lay at my feet. Put his head in my lap several times a day now, just to get a big rub."

Annie half-listened to her dad. It was a familiar story, which he repeated often. She still smelled poop. She was afraid that smell would stick in her sinuses for the next ten years. Thankfully, she'd had the foresight to wear old clothes, as she always did when visiting her father's house. She eagerly anticipated the day when she no longer had to dress according to King Lear's biohazard contentious HAZMAT regulations. She raised her glass of lemonade and smelled the odor of dog breath in it.

"Dad, did you by chance let Gunny lick this glass?"

Her father paused, then shrugged.

She gagged.

CHAPTER THIRTEEN

Annie was in her car at a stoplight, when she glanced over to a ridge of lawn. A man and woman with two toddlers were feeding of a small gaggle of geese. The parents had actually let the kids stand close by the birds. As she continued to watch, she noticed not one of them was frightened. The geese were, in fact, very gentle and friendly. The family then dawdled away and back onto the sidewalk as if they had just visited their buddies. Annie was startled from the moment when the SUV behind her honked at her. The light had turned green. She drove on with a polite wave of apology.

"That was cool. That was very cool to see. Subtle messages of happiness. I get it. See, I saw that one! I want to create more of that."

* * *

A potential buyer for Mr. Tiddle's P.T. Barnum papers held Annie's attention on the phone until Yodel's doorbell tingled.

Varsha walked into the store with a tall blonde, whom she quietly redirected toward the restrooms. She then wiggled and danced her way to Annie and leaned against the desk with wide-eyed excitement. "Guess what?"

Annie held her finger up to Varsha's animations and grin. "Yes, sir. That's a set price."

Agitated mumblings expelled through the phone. "I'll email my offer to Mr. Tiddle," said the buyer. "That's all I can promise."

"That's fine. When should he expect your answer?"

"In a day or two. Anything else?"

"No, sir. Thank you for your interest."

The gentleman's voice cackled with quivering disregard. "We'll see."

Annie hung up the phone and eyed Varsha's waggling fingers in her face.

"What, Varsha?"

"Guess what? Guess what?"

"Sorry, I haven't the gift of divination today. I'm only psychic on my days off."

"Did you see that little hottie?" Varsha was pointing in the direction of the restrooms with an elaborate pattern of waves akin to flaggers at an airport tarmac gate. "I'm taking her to a concert at Bogart's tonight. Her name is Tanzy Liprecorn. She's visiting from Vegas. Gets paid big bucks just to wear feathers on her head and show off her legs."

"Make sure you check her basting times. What happened to getting on the bike trail for a real gal?"

"I had just pedaled fourteen miles and put my bike on the back of my car when I spotted her walking into the Trail Café."

"You have an amazing radar for certain women."

"Thank you," Varsha beamed. "Whatcha reading?"

She closed the P.T. Barnum folder as Mr. Tiddle's line buzzed. "*The Steiner-Rand Scale of Acceptance*." Annie picked up the buzzing phone line. "Yes, Mr. Tiddle?"

"Miss Freckle. I need you."

"On my way."

Varsha winked at Annie as her date emerged from the restroom. "Wish me luck."

"I would rather wish you God's speed with your little red Corvette." Annie actually felt a twinge of envy as she watched them cuddle lovingly while heading out the door. Her eyebrows begged to be unknotted. "I need a break. Or laid. Or a bowl of mango gelato in Florence, Italy." Annie stopped to stare at Oz's questioning glance as she slouched against a bookshelf. She was beginning to get used to her fairy godmothers' pop-up appearances, like annoying reminders on her phone. Annie held her hand up to Oz. "Okay, okay. I know. I need to be happy for her. I'll work on it. I'll just allay myself with the distraction of sucking peanut butter off a spoon while cozying up to a nice old Cary Grant film."

"You realize what you just did there, right?" Oz asked.

Annie surveyed her surroundings, as if hoping the answer would pop out to greet her. "What?"

"You have a wonderful way of not allowing distractions when you're focused on something you like. But, this is the perfect example of wanting to find a distraction when you feel uncomfortable, inadequate."

"No."

Oz raised her brow and folded her arms. "Mm."

"I could call somebody."

"Somebody being…Catrin?"

Annie stuck her bottom lip out and looked askance in thought. "Yeah," she breathed slowly. "Yes."

"Then why haven't you?"

"Why haven't I what?"

"Called her."

Annie blew a sound from her lips. "I'm sure she's busy. I'm busy."

Oz grinned. "You don't really believe that."

"I don't?"

"Stop believing you're unqualified for happiness. You are a talented, beautiful, energetic, compassionate being. What makes you think someone wouldn't like that in a person?"

Annie stared at her before shuffling away, now and again looking over her shoulder to Oz as she approached Mr. Tiddle's office door. She hadn't really thought about her behavior in that nature before.

She waited for Mr. Tiddle to unlatch the four bolts, two electronic locks, and a hidden mechanism that sounded like the suction release from a piece of Tupperware. The drooling agony was not unlike waiting on a hospital elevator climbing its way toward the sixth floor before returning to the lobby and believing the season had changed. The large, metal door creaked open, and a finely combed eyebrow raised from around the edge.

"Is the drawbridge down now?" Annie asked.

Mr. Tiddle's voice had an anxious tilt. "Yes. Come, come. Quickly."

Annie slinked inside as he lurched against the door, heaving it with a shuffle of his hands, his knees, his back, and his butt to close it. She then followed Mr. Tiddle to his desk as he wiped the sweat from his newly spray-tanned face. Always an indication that he was planning a date night.

"Hitting the town tonight, are we?"

Mr. Tiddle shot a wild glance at her. "How do you know? Who told you?"

Annie tilted back on her heels and puffed her cheeks. "Oh, just the familiar particulars. You're wearing your Boy George cologne, for one."

"Oh." He beamed and combed back a floppy bang off his forehead with his hand. "I have," he continued, "another pair of tickets to entertain my gentleman."

"The same guy up from Mexico City?"

"If you must know, yes. His name is Tony."

"Last time, the concert was a hard-rock band from Brazil, right? Did he enjoy that?"

Mr. Tiddle pursed his hairy lip. "No."

"Hmm. Isn't he more of a jazzy kind of guy?"

"Yes. Back-to-back jazz concerts. So, this means I'll be leaving the shop early tonight, and I need you to close up for me, since Varsha has the night off."

"Sure. I'm free."

"Of course you are."

His dry response prompted a twitch in her eye.

He looked up from his papers and waved her off. "That'll be all. Leave."

He sashayed around the desk and helped her open the door. The two had to tug it open with a two-inch-thick rope slung over their shoulders.

"Remind me to choose you for our next tug of war against the Northside Queens," he grunted.

Annie released the rope and bumped her way out the door, hearing a weird electrical hum. She looked back in a start.

He again waved her on. "It's fine. Move on through. This is timed, you know, so."

She stood there as the gears rotated and clunked and chunked and wheezed the door shut. She shrugged and returned to the front desk.

As 6:00 p.m. approached, the lights in the shop flickered. Her computer slowly came back after she mouthed a few curses.

"No, no, no. Oh, I hope this piece of crap autosaved." She sighed with relief as her P.T. Barnum documents returned. "Phew." She drew her eyes to the phone. No indication of life. She picked up the receiver. *Dead. Huh. Oh, well. At least it'll be quiet as I finish this pain-in-the-ass assignment, once and for all.* Mr. Tiddle had accepted a client's offer, and the client would pick them up the following day. All Annie had to do was complete an email to the client and send a copy of the payment information to Mr. Tiddle's email. After a final press of a key, it was finished. "Thank God," she said.

At 9:00 p.m., Annie turned the open sign over on the door. A figure knocked at the door as she was about to lock it. Opening the door, she said, "I'm sorry. We're closed."

"Annie. Hi," the customer said.

Annie recognized the voice and opened the door, meeting Catrin's smile. "Catrin."

They exchanged stares and smiles.

"Hi," Annie breathed. "What—um. What are you doing over here? Sorry. You…want to come in?" She presented her the time from her classic Micky Mouse watch. "I'm, uh…"

"Really late, I know. Just finishing up, myself," Catrin said. "Oh, nice tweed and tie. You sport it well, if I must say."

"Thanks. Trying a new style. I think it's me."

"So do I."

Annie felt her cheeks warm. "I'm rushing to catch a new episode of *Salmon Spawn*. For my boys, Pork and Beans. It's their favorite, next to *Frisky Ferals of Rome*."

Catrin nodded, bright-eyed. "Oh. Well, then. I won't keep you."

"Yes, you will." Catrin returned Annie's smile. "I'd prefer it," Annie added.

"Look, I'm having a few friends over tomorrow night and was wondering if you'd like to join us for eats? I assure you, we're all foodies, so there will be plenty to choose from."

"Wow." Annie restrained the impulse to fling herself against a wall in shock. Her head swarmed with cartoon visions of dancing babies, cats, and a drooling Bugs Bunny who panted and whistled with a wild heart thumping out of his chest. "Yes. Well."

"Oh, please," Catrin insisted. "Don't feel you have to cancel something else just for me."

"Trust me. I don't believe Saturday night with Lauren Bacall and Humphrey Bogart marathons can hold an oil lamp to you."

Catrin leaned against the doorway with a swoon. "Are you kidding? *Key Largo* was my favorite Bogie and Bacall movie."

Annie felt her hands sweat. "Really? Mine too. Well, almost a tie with *To Have and Have Not*."

"Just put your lips together and blow."

Annie's legs became water with Catrin's sexy exhale. If she hadn't been clutching onto the doorknob, she would have fallen, surely. Catrin's eyes sparkled from the nearby lamps, and her lips curled to a grin, coaxing Annie's blood to rush in a southerly direction she wasn't used to experiencing. She climbed her way back up the door and stood to full height. When she spoke again, it was a peep. "Ah." She cleared her throat. "Yes. One, one of the more prominent quotes."

"I'm sorry. You're tired."

"No, no."

"I'll let you go." Catrin turned to leave.

"It's refreshing to know someone else is as interested in the Golden Years of Hollywood as I am. I'd love to continue this conversation tomorrow night."

Catrin twisted around. "Really?"

"Absolutely."

Catrin's smile never really left her soft face. "Good. I'll text you my address and time, then."

"Great. Wonderful. I assure you; I will be much more mentally and emotionally stable tomorrow after hours of psychological preparation—and chai tea lattes. Should I bring anything?"

"No. Just yourself. Do you eat pork?"

"Bacon and I are close friends. Pork loins and I greet each other as if long-lost cousins."

"Good. I make a devilish barbecue pulled pork that would make Bobby Flay jealous. Have a great evening."

Annie slowly closed the door, hoping to catch a scent of Catrin's mystique drifting back to her. "Night."

Annie's flesh warmed with excitement over the prospect of being around Catrin again soon. Her head filled with unflinching questions. Of course, she'd go to her grave without ever allowing them to escape her lips. It was heaven's dance in all its majestic, nebulous colors to float on the breath, words, and figure of Catrin. Annie shut off sections of lights as she walked back through the shop, stopping at the back door to take a final glance around the place. A vague noise echoed from somewhere above her. Or maybe it was down another aisle. The sound was indescribable. She shrugged it off as an air duct noise, paying it no more attention, and she locked the door behind her. Mr. Tiddle's car was still parked in the back lot, beside hers.

She hesitated only briefly. "Huh. Guess his date picked him up."

A text from her brother, Scott, cut Annie's drive home short.

Dad is in the hospital again. Since yesterday noon. Can you go? I'm tied up.

"Well, boys. I guess your fishy show will have to wait."

* * *

Annie found it interesting that hospitals tended to keep loved ones like her father at the far end of a very long hall. Perhaps, to keep them at a distance from the well-behaved ones in their contentment and quietude. She didn't have to read the numbers. She could follow his barbed pelting. He was arguing with the nurse and tech.

"Halloo," Annie called out.

"That's my daughter," he spewed. "She'll tell you."

"Tell them what?" she asked.

The nurse turned to Annie. "We're trying to help him stay for a scheduled test tomorrow."

"I don't need a test," he growled. "That's bull. They're full of crap. I've been here all this time, and no one has done anything."

"How did you get here?"

"Whatdaya mean how did I get here? I called 911."

Annie closed her eyes and took a deep breath. "Why?"

"I couldn't breathe."

"Well, miracle of miracles, you're taking in all kinds of breath now and spewing it all over the place. I'd say they fixed you."

Her father's brows knit together. "Shut up and get me outta here. And what the hell is that get-up you're wearing?"

"Clothes. It's called clothes."

Her father's reply was a degrading balk with a shake of his head. "Well, at least you don't dress like a whore."

"I'm saving that for next week."

The glare from her father was priceless.

Once in the car, Annie asked her dad, "Why didn't you call Scott or me and tell us where you were?"

Her father answered as he stared out the passenger window. "I didn't remember your number."

"That doesn't make sense. The hospital has us on file. Unless you told them not to call."

"I don't know. Drop it. Just get me home."

Annie decided it best not to speak. She might say something she'd regret. After a few minutes into the drive, her father's countenance melted into the seat. He sunk down with a hefty sigh, closed his eyes and dropped his head. *Pouting*, she thought. *My God, my father's pouting.* Never did she believe she'd catch a glimpse of how he must have looked like when a child. Yet, the resemblance of behavior was mystifying.

"Did they give you oxygen? An IV of anything to help?"

The bottom lip perched out further with a shrug and shaking of the head. "They can't do anything for me. I'm too frail, they said, for heart surgery. My legs are giving out for some other reason. My kidney count is raised. I'm a mess. But they don't want to help me."

"They wanted to run tests, and you didn't want to stay."

"Bullshit. Bullshit!"

Annie started chewing on a hangnail. "You're swearing now."

"Shit is not a swear word, it's a vocal sigh."

She glanced at him from the corner of her eye. "That was one hell of a sigh."

He laughed after a moment.

She joined in. "You know, Dad, I just have to tell you that there have been so many things lately to be resentful toward you about—but I've had to give some of them up."

He slowly scanned an eye toward her. "Am I supposed to congratulate you?"

"No. I'm just sharing the fact it feels better to feel better. Not long ago, you told me that you wanted the medical community to fix you. You just want them to fix you."

"Yes."

"Do you think it'll make you happy, if they fix you?"

"That's a stupid question, Annie."

"Haven't you ever asked yourself why you can't seem to be happy and stay happy for long? You haven't truly been happy since mom divorced you and you sold the farm, do you know that?"

He turned away from her.

"You're looking for once upon a time, Dad. Once upon a time you and I were like this." Annie crossed her fingers. "That's my memory of us. But I was five. Things changed after Scott was born. Look. I know you've struggled with depression for years, and nothing seems to be working. At all. Have you ever considered the idea that medication can't do all the work? I truly believe, through personal experience, that I have bettered myself by not taking life so freaking seriously. I have these... mentors. They tell me that I'm looking for love in all the wrong places. I have to begin loving myself, giving myself a break. Not being so hard to please. I'm tough on me. Because you've been tough on me. And I think that's because you've been tough on yourself. My biggest lesson is that I've had to make peace with where I am, who I am."

Her dad turned a skeptical eye to her.

"The world isn't going to give us what we're looking for," she continued. "It can't. It hasn't lived our lives and felt everything we've felt. And it doesn't care if we're scared shitless. But I care. I care that you're scared shitless. Because I've been there. I wanted to die. You know that?" Annie held up a pinched hand and felt her eyes swell with tears. "I was this close to committing suicide. I thought I had screwed up so badly that you'd never want me. I thought that you would disown me."

Tears flowed from the corners of her dad's eyes. His sigh was deep. "Annie. I would call your brother. In the middle of the night. Crying. Telling him I didn't want to bury my daughter. I didn't know what to do. I felt helpless."

Annie reached for her father's hand and held it tight. She met his eyes and breathed, "We don't have to be scared anymore, Dad. We have each other. I love you so much. You don't have to do this alone, okay?" She released her grip and wiped her eyes. "If you can just muster a really great memory that makes you feel good, okay? Let's talk about that. Anything recent? Anything that just tickled your toes?"

"You mean like when Regan was in office?"

Annie nodded her head, stunned. "Regan. Ronald Regan."

"Yeah. Russian accents were a novelty in the '80s, and high-profile espionage arrests were as popular as Frank Sinatra concerts. God, he was good."

"Sinatra."

"Yes. Really knew how to put on a show. Especially when he brought on stage his Rat Pack. You know Dean Martin was an alcoholic?"

Annie had a feeling this was the beginning of her father's rudimentary disinterest in the last thirty years of his life, and the beginning of a dandy memory loop. She decided to detour the subject. "But he sang well."

"He did. Great years, the '80s."

"If that's when you were your happiest, Dad."

"Yeah. Those were some exciting times in our nation."

"Wow. Good. You hold onto that."

Annie turned on her father's favorite oldies radio station. The Boswell Sisters were singing "Heebie Jeebies," and Annie bobbed in her seat, which made her father smirk. It was the closest thing to a smile she had seen from him for a while. In a very weird way, this was a really good visit.

* * *

It wasn't often that Annie could meet up with her brother for lunch without either of them escaping to their jobs. The following day brought a sunny day to Eden Park, and it flushed with dripping tree limbs, babbling water, and green grass. Folks had come out for dawdles, speed walks, and puttering about. Annie sat on the short wall and looked over the vast expanse of the Ohio River. She had shared the story of her drive home from the hospital with their dad.

"Did he really link his joy to Reagan?" Scott asked.

"And Sinatra."

"Not our holidays together? Not our vacations? Not pulling us around on the antique tractor through the snowy fields, while we were clinging our half-frozen hands and butts to a piece of cattle fence tied to a rickety drawbar?"

"Those are your joys, Scott."

The overlook was always a favorite spot for wedding photographers and the like. Scott drifted back to the wall from looming near a flower bed bursting with honeybees who loved the summer-orange butterfly weed and blue asters.

Scott's reply was a somewhat distant admission. "I suppose so."

Annie handed him a pastrami and smoked gouda sandwich from the picnic she made. He took a bite, then directed her attention to the pond behind them, where a child pushed a little boat along the water's edge. "Remember the little canoe our cousin made from birch?"

"Vaguely."

"Gosh, I had fun with that," he said. "It floated pretty well on that ole pond. Until a snapping turtle raised out of the water like a leviathan and took a bite out of it. It took on water after that. The entire crew of little green army men were lost at sea. Couldn't get there fast enough to save them. War is gruesome. Bound to lose a few."

"Conquests are risky." Annie enjoyed her peanut butter and pickle sandwich and looked over the valley.

Scott sat down on the wall. She proffered a bag of grapes.

"Do you miss the farm?" he asked.

Annie's mind eagerly drew images of large fields with drifting wildflowers, tadpoles around the pond, and the old cherry tree they used to climb. "A lot of good memories there."

"All Dad does anymore is lament over moving from the farm or losing Mom, or his failing health. Constant complaining. But he doesn't want to get help. I think all he wants is attention."

Annie hid her disgust behind a drink of lemonade. "He's a manic-depressive. And has dementia."

"I tell him to get out. Just take a walk down the street. Drive to a home improvement place, get on a cart and drive it around the store for an hour. Excuses. He'd rather spew out excuses and become bitter that life sucks. It's dangerous to be in your head all the time."

"You're preaching to the choir, brother."

Scott swallowed hard on his sip of water. "Sorry."

Annie winked at him. "I say, for his birthday, we should get him castrated and throw a get-well birthday party with strippers, change his name to Lee Majors, a.k.a. the Six Million Dollar Man, and watch the city dedicate an alley in his name. Maybe even get someone with a Sherman tank from the VFW to ride him up and down his street. That should fire him up a bit."

"For about a week. Better add a few women flashing their breasts."

"Give him something else to reflect on for a while besides Fox News and conspiracy theories." Annie tired of railing against their father's behaviors. Reminded her of her own shortcomings; this being one of them. She changed the subject. "Speaking of news, have you asked that blond news anchor on Channel 5 out yet?"

Scott nodded. "Actually, Vanessa and I are going out next week."

Annie slapped his arm. "Get out. Seriously? Damn, Sam. Are you lying to me? You're lying."

Scott laughed and shook his head. "I ran into her at the piano lounge. She approached me after I played a rendition of Billy Joel's 'Just The Way You Are.' She said it was one of her favorite songs."

"And what did you say?"

His cheeks flushed. "I said I thought Billy wrote it just for her."

"Nice line."

"It wasn't a line."

"It was a line."

Scott's cheeks flushed. "Maybe just a little." He glanced at his phone after a search and added dryly, "Christ, Dad does look like Lee Majors."

* * *

A particular excitement buzzed around Yodel's Bookstore when Annie drove down the street. Two fire engines and a squad had parked before the shop with flashing lights, and a hoard of gawkers each vied for a spot before the windows.

"Oh, great pumpkin, Charlie Brown. What a cluster cluck," Annie grumbled. "What the hell did he do now?"

A Life Squad vehicle was blocking the back entrance, forcing Annie to shimmy through and into the store. She almost got run over by the rescue team as they assisted Mr. Tiddle out. He whimpered incoherently, looked quite shoddy in the same clothing he wore the day before.

"Whoa. Someone had a rough night," Annie blurted. She walked up to Varsha, who was in conversation with a police officer and the fire captain. "What's going on?"

"Annie," Varsha exclaimed. "Mr. Tiddle was locked up in his office all night."

"Are you Annie Freckle?" the police officer asked.

Before Annie could reply, Varsha leaned into her. "Sealed like a mummy in a tomb."

Annie gasped. "Oh, no."

"Damndest security system I've ever seen," the fire chief ranted. "Had so much wiring up in the ceiling panels, steel rods along the walls, not to mention one helluva door that would put a bank vault to shame. If it wasn't so effed-up a bundle, I'd almost believe he did this himself."

Annie craned her head around the corner. The wall appeared to have been clobbered by a catastrophic storm. "It was actually a relative who needed a few extra bucks. His cousin, I believe."

"Knew enough to be dangerous," the chief said. "We had no choice but to get him out with the jaws of life, and a pool noodle. Those things are an amazing invention."

Annie's head swelled with a melting feeling, and her heartburn flared. She meekly allowed an exasperated vowel to escape her lips.

The police officer stood within her peripheral vision. "You locked up last night. Is that correct?"

She turned to him. "Yes. Had I known…"

"We're not blaming you, miss. It's sealed pretty tight in there. No possible way anyone would have been able to hear even a peep from him. If he even attempted."

She rubbed her hands over her cheeks. "God, I feel awful. I knew I heard something. I don't know."

"Did you hear him call to you at all?"

"No. It was more like…"

"Like a tapping, or knocking?"

Annie nodded. "Maybe a clunking. More like a clinking."

The officer frowned close to his tiny notepad. "Clinking. Are you sure it wasn't like a pinging?"

"Pinging's good. But as I think about it, it was more like a doinking. Along with a gurgling something."

The officer pushed his pen onto the notepad and pronounced the word as he wrote it. "Doinking."

"Doinking. With an I. And gurgling."

"Gurgling. And when was this?"

"I was closing up. About nine." Annie puffed her cheeks in thought. "Long after the '*psst zing*.' That was around six, I guess."

"Pzz."

Annie leaned closer. "Psst."

"Pzz—"

"Ssss. With a T."

The officer nodded blankly. "Right." He scribbled more.

A firefighter rushed to her chief with an armload of burnt cables. "Found a doozie of a wiring job. Short circuited by something wet. Could have burnt the whole kit and caboodle down. Someone really did a cheap and terrible job. Could have been worse."

The fire chief turned to Annie and the police officer. "There's your power outage."

"Good thing he had to pee," Varsha said. "Put the smoldering right out."

Annie turned to her. "When did you get here?"

"Oh. Early. I didn't sleep very well. My girlfriend slept with one of those pap smear machines."

"My mother has one of those," the police officer inserted.

"You know, those things are loud."

He nodded. "Yes, they are."

Annie was certain they were related somehow.

"I just ended up heading back home around three," Varsha continued. "Then, Mom kept me up the rest of the night. She has allergies. Coughing and sneezing. The polyp count must be high. Anyway, I came in the back way here and heard a weird scratching. Thought it was a mouse in Mr. Tiddle's wall or something. So, I took this fat book and hammered it."

"Tolstoy's *War and Peace*," Annie observed.

"Well. Then it sounded like a big rat. But, because my mom taught me Morse code at age four, I just knew it was strange that a rat could be tapping the code for 'help.' That's when I called 911."

"Wow," the police officer exclaimed. "You knew Morse code at four?"

Annie commented, "Unless you have time for a thirty-minute dissertation, I wouldn't ask."

Annie was relieved to watch the rescue team leave with the police officer. She stood at the back door as Varsha brushed past.

"Headed next door for a caffeine something. I'm crashing. Want anything?"

"No. Thanks." Annie watched her leave and collapsed against the door frame and threw her head back. "I just got ran over by a flamboyance of flamingos."

* * *

Later that afternoon, Annie was locking up Yodel's when a text from Scott appeared on her phone.

Dad's back in the hospital. Asking for a ride home. Been there since 5:00 a.m.

"Oh, my freakin' God. You've got to be kidding me. This is not a good time, Dad. Dammit."

Oz looked over her shoulder to the phone. "Well, you do have options."

Annie released a heavy sigh. "Damn. I want to go to Catrin's dinner. Not deal with Dad's bellowing and vomiting of confusion and Mountain Dew melodrama."

"Pause a moment. Think about this. Think about what's on the other end of the stick."

Annie inhaled a fresh breath. "You're right. There's a solution here. Get out of the problem. I don't have to do it all. I don't have to be it all. I don't have to allow it to sink me into its spiral." She released a hardy breath and texted her brother back. "I'm going to ask Scott to do it. I need to take care of me. I want this to be a good evening for me."

"And the key?"

"To not feel guilty?"

"That's it."

"How do I do that?"

"By understanding that your guilt is from not pleasing other people who will never be pleased," Oz replied. "By understanding that, right now, if you do what feels good, you're on the better path. If assisting your father feels good, then do it. If going to dinner feels good, then do that. Feel the difference? No one forces you to do anything that you don't allow."

Annie clicked her car fob and headed for her car. Varsha's car pulled around the building and stopped short of Annie's.

Varsha rolled down her window. "Hey, you're not closing up yet, are you?"

"Yes, I am," Annie replied. "Since Mr. Tiddle isn't here to bark at me, and no customers want to be within fifty blocks of the place, I decided to make an executive decision and close up shop early. Besides, I have somewhere else to be."

"Oh. Can I just grab my phone? I forgot it."

"Varsha. You clocked out over two hours ago. You haven't fallen to ashes from cell phone withdrawal?"

Varsha's dark eyes rolled around, and she slipped past her. "Tanzy wanted a quickie. I didn't have need for my phone until now."

"A quickie. For two hours?"

"Hey, I'm a love bunny. A flopsy mopsy. Smooth operator. Not a jerk-off generic."

Annie walked her to the back door and slipped the key in the lock. "I knew not to ask."

"Wait," said Varsha. "You have somewhere else to be?"

"Yes. Is that so unusual?"

"Is it your dad?"

"Happily, no. It's Scott's turn."

"Then, your mom?"

Annie didn't wish to prolong this conversation. "No. It's a…a…dinner."

Varsha gasped and wiggled. She looked as if she'd explode into Technicolor. "A date? Is it a date?"

"No. Dinner, party-ish, something or other. With other friends of hers."

"Hers? As in Catrin's?" Varsha jumped into Annie's arms and hugged her tight. "Oh, my Annie's going out!"

"Okay. Calm down, Varsha."

"This is great!"

"I think it'll be good. Something new." Annie twisted about and took a few steps with Varsha still clinging onto her and petting her head. "Can you let go now?"

Varsha leapt off her with the enthusiasm of a kid ready to unwrap a Christmas present. "Tell me you're going to ask her out."

"No. I won't tell you that. I wouldn't even know where to start."

"A simple hello can lead to many other things, Annie."

"Like germs and viruses. Unwanted and awkward talk in front of other people who only want to gossip about stuff they have no business leaning into. Incessant talking about four hundred things that make you nervous, and inappropriate things you shouldn't share, but escape from your lips before you think. Then, there's the thought of who should ask who on a date. Then finding a restaurant you don't particularly want to eat in, and hoping you don't choke on your own spit as you try to say something cool. I'd probably pee my pants at that point."

"Geez'o Pete, Annie. Are we into self-sabotage or what? It's not a life-changing event. It's just talking to somebody."

"I project too much, don't I?"

"More like you projectile puke your watermelon of negativity with the velocity of a whiz bang before allowing the gravity of your imagination to drop it square on a fresh cow patty."

Annie looked up at her just as Varsha finished the thought with an interpretive dance move.

"Splaaaa."

* * *

Pork and Beans sat atop Annie's bed as she shambled out of her closet, weighed down by a load of clothing in every style, thanks to Pinky's divine guidance a month before. The boys slowly drew their eyes from the pile before them and met Annie's.

One outfit after the other she tried on and posed before a full-length mirror. Red button-up? No. Blue pinstripe suit? Too sharp for a simple dinner. Yellow, too springy. "Come as you are" T-shirt. Nope. Too suggestive. Red and navy plaid shirt, too obvious. White on white, ready for the Oscars. Finally, she felt comfortable in her old pair of brown oxfords, faded blue jeans, ivory flowered button-up, and tweed vest. She placed a matching brown, wool newsboy cap on her head and tilted it slightly, then glanced at her boys behind her, who had kept an eye on her the entire time. She twisted about and opened her arms with a confident smile to a less than enthusiastic crowd. At least Beans offered her a supportive nudge.

Walking up the sidewalk to Catrin's place, Annie was a ball of jitters. Maybe it was the balmy seventy-two-degree evening. Maybe it was her nerves. Whatever it was, she felt she could burst into flames at any moment. She took to the front steps and tripped onto the porch. She readjusted her vest and stood at the screen door with a glancing eye about to make certain no one saw her. The porch was a delicate mix of small potted plants and ferns. A pale gray paint went well with the white trim. It provided a nice backdrop to the white, wrought iron bench with multicolored cushions. So much about a person's personality is read from their taste in décor. Catrin was definitely a traditional gal with a flair for Pop Art. The house was full of joviality and various stories floating about. All of a sudden, Annie felt her legs weaken. She took an uneven breath. She turned for the steps just as the door swung open. An unfamiliar face beamed at her when she twisted back around.

"Come on in," he said.

Annie was greeted with smiles and welcomes from many folks. *Quite a diverse crowd*, she thought to herself. Excellent. The bottle of German white Riesling she white-knuckled grew heavier with each step she took. It was a hard road to kill off a long-practiced absurdity to believe everyone on earth was an alcoholic, or at least drank as much as she once did. She had recovered from that misconception with a true respect for anyone else who was capable of a casual drink. A thick fog deafened her, as her heart pounded louder. Thank goodness the rooms seemed quite small. Not much further to go.

"Looking for Catrin?" a woman asked.

"Yes, actually."

She pointed in the direction of the dining room beyond. Every inch was filled with plates of hors d'oeuvres and bowls of snacks. All manner of drinks occupied a side table, from alcohol to juices to flavored waters. Annie set the bottle down and turned to spy Catrin's figure in the kitchen. She immediately cast off her inhibitions and side-stepped a group of women incessantly chattering about the latest vacation faux pas they each had witnessed over the summer. Rounding the doorway into the kitchen, Annie halted before a sight that hardened her. Catrin was being cuddled by a rather tall, beautiful woman of athletic build. The woman didn't seem to be interested in engaging in any of the conversation between Catrin and her two friends. She was clingy, and nudged Catrin to respond in kind. Annie felt her stomach turn. The worst occurred when Catrin raised her head for a kiss.

Annie stepped back and was ready to leave, when Catrin noticed her.

"Annie," she said cheerfully, and met her at the doorway. "I'm so glad you made it."

"I can't stay," Annie heard herself say. "I just wanted to thank you for inviting me. Left you a bottle of Riesling."

Catrin's eyes followed Annie's thumb over her shoulder. She held up a bottle of flavored water. "Thank you. I stick to this nowadays. I'll open it for my guests, though. Would you like a glass?"

"No. Thank you."

"Won't you stay for a little bit?"

"I've had a lot going on at work. Both of them."

Catrin's eyes looked deep into Annie's. She hoped she wasn't giving herself away.

"Yeah. I heard about the owner of Yodel's, and how close the building was to burning," Catrin sympathized. "Must have been scary."

"It was. Thank you for your concern."

Annie couldn't stand before her any longer. Breathing in the sweet scent of Catrin's perfume and reveling in the warm gaze that could stop a clock. She envisioned this moment as one she would relish, with tingles and a surge of optimism and magic within. Yet, the moment desperately sank beneath the waves of foreboding shadows and drifted away on disenchantment. An unnourished melancholy overtook her, and a hot flush tingled the back of her head. She felt as if Catrin could read every inch of her distress. Annie turned away to leave, but a firm hand on her forearm and a softened voice stopped her.

"Annie. Stay a while. At least eat something. There's plenty of food."

Even though Catrin had attempted to lighten her mood with a wry smile, Annie knew she was burnt toast. "Really. I appreciate your wanting to include me. But I have to go." She dug her hands in her pockets and left.

Leaning against her car door, Annie exhaled and rolled her head to the heavens. Her whole body felt numb. Her eyes drifted to Catrin's house across the street, where she could see Catrin standing at the window. She had just been distracted from meeting Annie's eyes. Her lover embraced her and swept her away. Catrin's response appeared stiff and ill-interested in the attention. Annie held that impression in her mind the rest of the evening. Perhaps out of spite.

CHAPTER FOURTEEN

On the sidewalk before the Empire Café, Annie finished writing the specialty drinks on an A-frame chalkboard. Her hands were a smear of colorful powders. As she stood to wipe her hands on a rag, her eyes drifted to a figure slouched against a building not two blocks away. It was early morning. Not much traffic. In fact, downtown Cincinnati was eerily calm except for the merchants, delivery trucks, and customers scrambling to buy fresh products at Findley Market. So, to see a staggering individual in the shadows of a tall form of architecture was a chilling reminder that not all who visit came for the joy of experience. She recognized immediately the figure of Rita, her old drinking buddy. She was quite a mess. Yet, Rita stood up and embraced a commiserating male companion in shoddy clothing. The two walked on, within their own perspective of whatever the morning held for them.

Annie then caught Oz standing beside her.

"But for the grace, there go I," Annie said.

"Not today."

Annie turned to her in relief. "No. Not today." She picked up her box of chalk and headed back inside, welcoming a couple and holding the door open for them. "I'm beginning to find a lot of clarity in my life. And I sort of have a handle on why last night with Catrin happened the way it did."

Annie headed into the restroom and stood before the sink. She placed her phone on the counter and washed her hands.

"We know you did," Oz replied. "We were there."

Annie glanced up with the awkward realization that Oz didn't have a reflection. "I was nervous. Fearful. Doubtful. I called that in on myself, didn't I?"

"Yes. But long before you think. Not everyone is your dad, Annie. Not everyone is out to judge you, criticize you, or make fun of you. You created this habit of avoiding life years ago."

A text appeared on Annie's phone from Catrin.

Can we talk?

Annie picked up the phone and waved it at Oz. "See this? Even though I don't really blame her, I'm not responding to her right now. Am I avoiding? Or am I choosing a boundary?"

"You have to decide which one feels better. Sometimes feeling angry is better. Own it. Allow it."

Annie tucked the phone into her back pocket and snatched up a paper towel. "It's not her fault I assumed things were different between us. I should have known better. But something about her behavior still pisses me off."

Annie dried her hands and walked out with her box of chalk, shoving it in a drawer as she rounded the bar.

"I should have read the signs."

Oz continued to follow close behind. "What signs?"

Annie started creating a customer's coffee. "The fact that she didn't like me in the same way."

"Do you know that for sure?"

"Well, how could I tell with Ms. Octapussy climbing all over her like Catrin was her personal little clam bake?"

"All humans contradict themselves daily. She is no different than you are. That's why you exist. To mix it up a bit. Experience is the only teacher to get you to focus on what it is you really want in life."

"Maybe so. Maybe she just wanted friendship. I'm cool with that. As soon as I get over this."

"Maybe," Oz answered. "Listen to yourself and tell me how this is all feeling to you. Are you happy?"

"No, I'm not happy."

"Then, that's an indication you're off-base. Do you believe in the right timing of the universe?"

"Yeah. Until I get my hands into the mix and sabotage it."

"You can't sabotage the timing. But you can cut yourself off from your aspirations."

Annie felt the beady eyes of her hulking, Italian coworker, Harry Leto. She reached for the drink he made and slid to her, ignoring his ruffled stare.

"Rocket Man, and Hurling Girley," she called to the couple. "Thanks, folks. Enjoy your day." She turned back to her next drink and continued with Oz. "I know from my past that the residual belief in not feeling worthy, feeling less-than, taints my optimism in other aspects of my life. I happen to like my life today. Reasonably. Mostly. Somewhat. A little. Well, it's crap right now, I gotta tell ya. But, it's better than that life." Annie pointed toward the street. "I just need to practice it more. It's about replacing the old behaviors that no longer serve me, right? Being of service. Stay out of my head. Sometimes it's with great devotion. Sometimes it's an endangered species, to grimly persist without loathing too much, or actually allowing myself to wallow in the toxicity of negative thoughts a bit longer for the effect."

Oz laughed. "Oh, you really love the drama of it all, don't you? Ever ask yourself why you push against so much? Do you enjoy it? Or do you feel the need to be validated?"

"I really do believe in doing the next right thing. It's honorable. And I do believe in honoring my integrity today."

"There's no debating that. Just remember why you want to do it."

Annie met Harry's eyes briefly. Funny, she didn't care. "As soon as it stops being joyful, I should find another direction."

"And in what direction would you go, if you could go anywhere?"

Annie paused. "I have quite a bucket list." Annie allowed her imagination to float. "I'd love to play hooky in Italy and eat fresh honey drizzled over pecorino. Always wanted to do that."

Annie watched big Harry Leto tip his head and pucker his lips with a nod.

Oz rubbed her chin. "We can make that happen."

* * *

Annie called Mr. Tiddle from a Tuscan farm in Italy. She had to raise her voice above the breeze that traveled over the wide valley dales of deep green countrysides and long, windy roads. "I'm not going to make it in today, Mr. Tiddle. I'm out of town. Slightly."

"You're where?" Mr. Tiddle asked. "You're breaking up."

She smiled at the honeybees flying in and out of dozens of hives surrounding a large meadow. "Aww. Look at all the hives."

"Hives?"

"Yeah. They're everywhere." Annie waggled a finger at a honeybee. She really wanted to pet it.

"Aren't those highly contagious?"

"Oh, it is outrageous, Mr. Tiddle. Gives me goose bumps."

"What kind of lumps?"

"Bumps, Mr. Tiddle. Goose."

"Loose? Oh, now that's just TMI."

"Uh, yeah. Good." Annie shook her head to Oz. "So am I."

Static rose on the connection before Mr. Tiddle's voice hollered back. "Don't worry about it." "You stay right there. Keep it to yourself. But keep me posted."

Annie's phone beeped at her. "Mr. Tiddle? Huh. Guess I lost him."

A plate of pecorino cheese drizzled with fresh honey was presented to her with pleasant distraction. She wiggled with delight. Dreams do come true.

Annie rubbed her earlobe and rested in the evening comfort of Rome's city lights. She and Oz stood on a tiny rooftop balcony that overlooked the Vatican and streets beyond. "How lovely this is. All of it. Tuscany, Rome. I've always wanted to just get away from reality sometimes. In a healthy way, of course."

"It is healthy to rebel against reality, you know. Imagination is powerful juju. Things you want will come along much faster when you leave the end results to us."

"Your bibbity-bobbity-boo was much faster and cheaper than airline delays and ticket prices." Annie slumped in thought. "I wish Mrs. Winkle could have traveled to Rome. She had some dandy stories. I really miss her. I think she'd love Rome. Well, maybe not the fountains. All that running water. She'd have to pee. And all that cheese on pizzas and pasta. Gas. Hook her up to a scooter, and she'd power herself from Rome to Switzerland on one street pizza. Come to think of it, she hated crowds. And trains. And touristy stuff. She would have hated Rome, actually."

* * *

Mr. Tiddle plopped down an armful of books down on Annie's desk. "Mark these down, please, and have Varsha put them in the sidewalk racks."

Annie picked up the top book and read the title out loud. "*All That Is Necessary for a Happy Life. Lessons for how deeply you should drink in all that matters to you.*"

Mr. Tiddle stared out the window. "I suddenly feel the urge for a mai tai. Progress, not purity, Miss Freckle."

"Progress is an evolutionary process that's full of storms. Volcanos and hurricanes, tornados and taxes, bloating and gas."

"You forgot rush hour and overripe avocados."

Annie felt a challenge coming on. "Acid reflux and killer hornets."

"Fake spider eyelashes."

"Quote boards and patchouli incense."

"Speedo bathing suits and Cheeto fingers."

"Eww." Annie cringed. "You won."

The shop's little bell tingled when Varsha entered. Annie couldn't get her eyes past the gawdy, tiger-striped yoga pants.

"Tiger. Never thought of you with tiger stripes, Varsha. Never envisioned you at all, actually. Wearing tiger, that is."

"You like it? Tanzy picked it out."

"Not surprising. Very tiger."

"Boom diggity smackity whack attack. Never really thought of it, myself." Varsha spun around in a dance move. "She said I should expand my horizons. Try to be a little more—you know—cultured."

"Fleeting moments are precious moments."

"Right."

"Right up there with Minivans, '70s hair, and root canals."

Varsha's eyes drew to slits. "What's a minivan? Yeah. Wait. You, uh…You don't really think I look good in this, do you?"

"That's up to you, Varsha. If you're happy, I'm happy for you."

"Oh. Well. I don't know. Maybe a fresh Bengal's orange dye slice above the ear, huh?"

"It's just different. I'm not used to seeing you wear that sort of thing. It doesn't matter what I think. What matters is if you like it. It sucks, really."

Mr. Tiddle walked up to the front desk and winced at Varsha. "Oh, my. Cleaning out our mother's secret campy closets again?"

Varsha looked down at her striped leggings. "Nah, this is new."

"Oh. She has a new closet?"

Annie made a face at him. "Your accountant is on line two. Something about the purchase of security electric wiring in your office ceiling?"

He wiggled his nose at her and rolled his eyes with a huff. "It's not a big deal. I'm getting it installed Wednesday. You know they had a break-in next door. The sons of bitches came in through the ceiling tiles from a vent in the alley."

"I should think stealing thirty-six boxes of French macaroons is way more interesting than lifting old boxes of lapsed billing and tax records."

"Miss Freckle, all the records of authenticity of our first editions are also located in there."

"No, they're not."

"What do you mean they're not?"

"Remember? You moved them to a safe deposit box at the bank. They were having a discount on new accounts for old members. They felt sorry for you and removed a service fee just two weeks ago after you refused to pay because Danny, the teller, wouldn't go out with you."

He squirmed and mumbled under his breath before stomping a foot and marching away. "I'll take the call in my office. Get the electrician on the line for me."

Annie transferred the call.

"Hey," Varsha said. "Did you ever call Catrin back and talk about that party night that turned south?"

Annie frowned. "No."

"Dude. I thought she'd been trying to talk."

"She has." Annie kept her head down and acted like she was interested in her old Rolodex cards.

"Then, give her a chance."

"To do what? Play me again?"

Varsha expelled a long vowel. "Look. I know you really like her."

"Liked. Past tense. I've dismissed my curiosity."

Varsha held her phone up to Annie with a photo of Catrin.

"You're stalking her now?"

"She works the postal route near my campus."

Annie had to admit, seeing a picture of Catrin stirred her senses into a soft dance.

A gargled laugh drew Annie's attention to Varsha's wide-eyed grin. "See. That look was not a dismissal. That was something that resembled a sob. She still gets to you. Come on. You're my gnomie. I know you. When you do that thing that you do..."

Annie glared at her. "What thing?"

"You escape into your ancient collectables, classic books, 60's records, that old flippy address contraption."

"It's called a Rolodex." Annie withdrew a card and held it up to Varsha. "The electrician's number. I still use it."

"Yeah. I'm sure it's a riveting experience."

Annie sat back and met Varsha's silly face. "Okay. Yes. I can't stop thinking about her."

Varsha leapt and pressed hands on the desk, startling Annie to sit back. "Let's all go on a double date," Varsha declared.

"Varsha. No."

"Why not?"

"I'm not ready. I'm not too trusting right now."

"Dating is supposed to be playful," Varsha said. "You're taking this all too seriously, Annie. Lighten up. You remember what happened when I took it too seriously?"

"You were a mess."

"Exactly. You're a mess, and you haven't even been dating!" Varsha stared agog at her phone. "Whoa. Did you read this? A woman was shot by her lover in the foot. Thought her snake socks were a real snake. Who wears snake socks?"

"This, coming from a woman who wears tiger pants."

* * *

Pork and Beans pawed around Annie's black high-top Converse shoes, playing with a tossed, fluffy toy mouse. She stood before a full-length mirror and adjusted her black slacks, tucking in the white T-shirt that read, "Take Notes, Boys." The sun peered through her window from parted white, puffy clouds. She felt exceptionally joyful today and gave herself a thumbs-up after grappling with her hair. Pork batted at the clip on her suspenders before she stole it away.

"I need that," she said, reasoning with his adorable reaction. "I've got to go, baby boys. It's going to be a long day at the bookstore.

She slipped on a matching black blazer and walked past the tiny mirror above the umbrella stand, pulling at her long bangs again. The boys met her at the door as she turned to their attentive eyes.

"I'll be back. I promise. We'll have your favorite fish tonight. And stream your favorite show. I'm off tomorrow. All day. Won't that be fun?" Pork turned away and left Beans to eat her offering of treats all to himself. "Good boy. I love you."

Passing a little mirror by the front door, Annie stepped back to look at herself again.

"You." She pointed to herself. "You are...good. You are good." She took a breath. "In fact, you're brilliant. You are real. You are talented. And you...are loved. You are worth...everything. And I'm proud of you. You're doing very well. You deserve the best. Only the best." Again, she pointed at herself. "Don't forget that." She looked deeply into her eyes, and enjoyed the smile on her face.

Annie locked the door behind her and turned toward the steps.

A car door slammed, drawing Annie's attention to the street. Lo and behold, it was Dottie Winkle standing before a taxi cab.

"No, I'm not giving you a tip," Dottie spat at the driver. "I'm lucky you got me here in one piece."

Annie threw herself against the house and held her breath. "No, no, no, no. This isn't real. This can't be real." She launched herself down the stairs and ran out to the taxi.

"I tried telling you not to take Third Street," Mrs. Winkle continued. She marched past Annie in a huff. "I'm not at all impressed with Tuber drivers."

"Uber," Annie corrected the ghost, poking at it. She drew her hand back in a start. It was real flesh. She followed Mrs. Winkle to her door.

"Gosh, look at you." Mrs. Winkle beamed. "My, aren't we spiffy today."

"Holy crap. They said you were dead."

"Ha. That's what they thought!"

"According to custom, the belief is that you should then appear dead."

Mrs. Winkle patted her sides down. "I guess I've misplaced my keys, dear. Can you let me in?"

"Does Keith know?"

Mrs. Winkle stared at her. "Now, why would he care if I lost my keys?"

Annie closed her eyes and felt tears swimming in them. Her stomach was all in a knot and she didn't know if she wanted to laugh or cry. She collapsed into an uncontrollable blubber and swept Mrs. Winkle up in her arms.

"Oh, Mrs. Winkle!"

Mrs. Winkle's tiny limbs stiffened under Annie's clutch. "That's okay. We'll find them."

"Mrs. Winkle, you have no idea how much I appreciate you in my life. I am so happy you're alive. Here. Now. Oh, my God. I don't care what else happens. This, this is great. Oh, my God."

"Umm. Honey?"

"Yeah."

"I can't breathe."

Annie released her and stumbled back. "Oh. Oh. Gosh. Sorry." She dusted away the wrinkles in her shirt.

Mrs. Winkle placed hands on her hips. "You wouldn't believe the crap I had to put up with to get out of that hospital."

"Because they thought you were dead too?"

"Precisely. I'm an organ donor. I wake up after a two-day nap, believing I'm in Egypt, being carried like a queen on a lounge by slaves. Then, someone shined a spotlight in my face, and some masked man with a paring knife tried to carve my liver into an ice sculpture. I would have been back yesterday, but they insisted I stay another day. This, after five days of just sitting there, doing nothing."

"To make sure your heart was still ticking, I'm sure."

"I guess. Not like they could tell either way! The doctor said my heart runs as quiet as a jellyfish in a bath. They haven't gotten money outta me in over fifty years. Back then, it wasn't such a butt-load to birth a baby, but it still emptied the wallet. Keith was the first and only baby born with a birthmark that read, 'This too shall pass.' I should have bought stock in him." Mrs. Winkle turned around to Annie and lifted up her shirt. "And look at this." She pinched a thick piece of flesh at her side. "What did they give me in there? I'm bloated or something."

"Those are just love handles, Mrs. Winkle."

"These are not love handles. This is a roasting pan."

"You've always had those, Mrs. Winkle." Annie turned away from Mrs. Winkle's scowl and faced the wireless door lock on the front door, Annie proceeded to press a series of numbers. "No keys anymore, by the way. Keith had your locks replaced with this fancy new setup."

"Oh. That's a relief."

Annie followed Mrs. Winkle into the house and watched as she looked around her house. "Something's wrong here. Where are my babies?"

Annie rolled up the sleeves of her blazer. "Your asset had them hauled away by the dog warren a few days ago."

"He what?"

"Dottie, Keith's operating as if you're dead. We all thought you were dead. Oh, and I've been evicted." Annie pulled the paper from her pocket.

Mrs. Winkle pulled the paper from her hand and threw it aside. "Never mind that. Oh, I should have known better. He's not wasting any time, is he?" Mrs. Winkle whacked Annie on the arm. "Well, don't just stand there. We have to get my babies back!"

Annie's little yellow Smart two-seater puttered down the windy hill toward the highway, and she could feel the air of skepticism in Mrs. Winkle's glare.

"What kind of one-dimensional go-kart is this thing?" Dottie ranted. "More like a flowerpot on wheels. Back in my day, the littlest car was a VW Bug with a heater box the size of a spam sandwich. Both of which were crap."

"It was cheap. And it was all I really needed to get around town. And it reminds me why I need to stay single. It doesn't let me down like people do. At least cars are predictable. They don't lead you on. Sorry. I shouldn't air my resentments to you like you're some fairy godmother." Annie cocked her head. "You're not, are you?"

"What was that, dear?"

Annie waved it off. "Never mind. I'm just grateful you're back."

"That's awfully sweet of you. Well, the seat is comfortable. But where are we going to put Bones? Guess she'll just have to sit on my lap."

Annie felt herself slink down into her seat with unease. "I don't know that they'd really keep her this long, you know? It's almost been a week."

"Where would they put her?"

"Down, Mrs. Winkle. They would put her down. She's old. Needs meds. No one would want to bother with that."

"They better not have put her down. I say when she's goes."

"Yeah, but didn't you say if anything should happen to you to put Bones down?" Annie pulled her phone out and spoke into it. "Hamilton County Dog Pound."

"Why are you yelling at me?"

"Not you. I'm yelling into my phone."

"Okay," her phone replied. "I found a pound called Nut Ewe 526.3 miles from here. Would you like directions?"

Annie slapped her phone. "No, no, no. That's not what I said." A blaring semi horn jerked her back to the road, and she realized she was ten feet from getting run over. Annie swerved her tiny car aside and straightened herself back out. Annie drew back in her seat and huffed. "Did someone really call an animal shelter Nut Ewe? Never mind. Anyway, Mrs. Winkle, I did think about calling the pound, but I didn't. I was afraid of what they'd tell me. Tell you what, why don't we think positive thoughts, huh? I'm on a roll here, today. Maybe I've got the Midas touch. Wouldn't that be fun?"

"If you ask me, we were one hair's breath away from finding out how recently Midas lubed his nuts. And just for the record, Midas killed himself. I didn't sit in the hospital for a week just to get flattened like a cat sucked in on a pheromone trail running across the interstate!" Mrs. Winkle grabbed Annie's phone from her. "Just drive. This cat's got eight lives left, and I'd like to keep them."

Annie barely pulled into the pound parking lot before Mrs. Winkle climbed out and sprinted toward the door. Annie quickly caught up with her to open the door for her.

"For an old gal, you sure move quick. You know that?"

"Nothing gets in the way of me and my babies."

"Except cottage cheese and maple syrup."

"Oh, that sounds good."

A young woman from behind the counter stood to greet them. "Hi, I'm Mary. May I help you?"

Mrs. Winkle didn't let the height of the counter deter her. She raised her nose above it and slid her ID across to the woman. "My name is Dottie Winkle, and I've come to get my two dogs back. They were taken from my home this week."

Mary squinted at the computer screen. "I see that a Keith Winkle signed the form on the day of pickup."

"That's my son. He was acting out of misinformation. It's not his fault he's a moron. He works for a bank run by social media moguls; he's used to believing misinformation."

"Her two dogs have tags and microchips," Annie interjected. "Their names are Saqi and Bones."

The large lobby was unusually quiet—Annie had figured a dog pound would ring with dog barks and whines. The walls were filled with surreal images of half-human, half-animal figures in black and white photographs that bordered on the macabre. A stately, yet severe woman with dark hair and thin lips approached the counter, and she sneered down her slender nose at them.

"I'm afraid once the release form is signed by the responsible party, the dog becomes our property," she said with a harsh, Swiss-German accent. "We are not concerned about chips or names." She sighed out the last word like it the name of a haunting ex-lover she detested.

"Well, Mrs. Winkle is the responsible party and owner," Annie spat. "If you could just let us know what she needs to sign, we'll leave you to your unsettling, sterile lobby."

Mary spoke up, albeit with hesitation toward her supervisor. "Ms. Fluckinger, I can put a call out to our client's veterinarian. That would determine her rightful ownership, wouldn't it?"

Mrs. Winkle slid a business card atop the counter. "There's the place and number. Dr. Sarah has taken care of all my sweeties for a couple decades, now. She's really very good at her job, and she's one of the best in Cincinnati, I'd say. Lovely woman."

Ms. Fluckinger drew her lips in a sour pucker. She plucked a clean wipe from its container and with it, slid Mrs. Winkle's ID and card closer. It seemed to take quite an effort to politely form the words, "Very well."

Mary looked up and over the counter to Mrs. Winkle's expecting grin. "If you'd like to take a seat, Mrs. Winkle, I'll let you know as soon as we hear back from Dr. Sarah."

Mrs. Winkle met Annie's eyes before turning back to Mary. "Uh…Can't I just see Saqi and Bones now, while you call? I miss them so much. I never thought I'd see them again."

Mary shifted her weight and traced a line on the floor with her eyes. "Well, I suppose we can get a tech to escort you to a private room."

"Oh, thank you, dear."

Ms. Fluckinger's lengthy finger thrust straight at Annie. "Not you. You sit. Over there."

The only seating available was a space on a small shabby sofa with shredded arms. Two gentlemen sat quietly beside each other, leaving little room for anyone else. One was more fashionable, wearing pink plaid pants and loafers, where the other favored a Hawaiian shirt and flip-flops. She turned away and leaned against the wall, her eyes to her phone.

"Have a seat, please," Ms. Fluckinger announced.

"Thank you. I'll stand."

"I said sit."

Her tone was not one to question. The two men on the sofa scooched to the opposite arms and patted the space between them. Did she have a choice? Her only comfort was the pinging on her gaydar. She returned the smile of Pink Plaid and nestled next to him.

"Dominatrix," Khaki murmured.

Pink Plaid replied, "I'm sure poodles in pantaloons think she's very sexy."

Annie rolled her lips in. "Hmm."

"Well, this is cozy," Pink Plaid purred.

Khaki turned to her. "Is it good?"

"Yes," Annie said. "Fine. It's good. Thanks."

Pink Plaid leaned across. "I feel good too."

"Good." Khaki nodded.

The large wall clock across from them droned on and on, ticking away every second with a *doink, doink, doink*. It was quite annoying. There was a television, but its cord lay frayed and disemboweled on the floor.

"You'd think this joint would be hopping with dogs howling or something," Annie mused.

"Oh, not with Medusa at the helm," Khaki quipped. "One look from her and they all turn to petrified yard art."

"Years ago, gossip round town was that she would dip them into cement and return them to their owners as gifts," Pink Plaid said.

"Eww," Annie said. "How horrible."

"Shhh," Ms. Fluckinger said. "You are to remain quiet until your name is called."

Annie hoped Mrs. Winkle would make it back out soon. Visions of Bones, Saqi, and Dottie as yard art haunted her. "This isn't exactly a library."

Pink Plaid flipped through his magazine with an upturned lip. "The least they could do is offer us some sensible reading materials newer than *Good Housekeeping* from 1984," he whispered to her. "This is atrocious. Yet, I do love these curtains."

Khaki laid a hand on her knee and leaned over to them both. "Remember the 1980 *Cosmopolitan* quiz from last week, and the article on sexy words to make a woman fall into the arms of her husband's best friend?"

Annie looked at him. "Come here often, do you?"

Pink Plaid said, "We were here looking to adopt a darling Chihuahua, but we had to wait a week. In case the owner showed up."

"Saqi?" Annie blurted. "That's Mrs. Winkle's dog."

"Shoot. Guess we'll have to go with the poodle-derringer mix."

Khaki leaned next to her. "Swallowed a miniature pistol."

"That way," Pink Plaid said, "he can bark and fire at an intruder at the same time."

"Well, we can't afford to put the good china out then, can we?"

Ms. Fluckinger stood and slammed a hand upon the counter, startling them.

Doink, *doink*, *doink*, ticked away the clock.

"The air is too cold in here," Pink Plaid announced moments later. "If I knew I needed a sweater in August, I would have worn my turtleneck."

"It's delightful," Khaki said. "Feels good."

Pink Plaid shrugged. "Cold enough to harden the next victims of cement castings. But somehow, *he* feels good."

Khaki closed his eyes and smiled. "I feel good."

A woman's voice resounded close to Annie. "Do you feel good?"

Annie was so humored with eyeing Khaki's tickled smile she hadn't noticed Ms. Fluckinger looming close by. She practically jumped into Khaki's lap when she let out a frightened, "Aah!"

"Do you?"

Annie felt her head bob uncontrollably. "Good. Fine. Yes. I'm fine. Good. Yes. Thank you."

Ms. Fluckinger raised herself and drew a long fingernail through the air toward the counter. "Your grandmother is preparing her leave. You may wait by the door."

Annie followed her to the counter as another assistant approached Ms. Fluckinger with a paper.

"Ma'am, the new line-up of perps has arrived."

Ms. Fluckinger kept her eyes to the document before her and said, "Isolate. Clip. Clean their filthy hides, and place them in detention until my inspection tomorrow."

"Yes, ma'am. What about food?" the assistant said, cocking her head.

Eyes squinted and stared down the girl. "You must be new. Was there any mention of food in my sentence?"

"No. But—"

"No food. None. Not until my inspection."

Mary jumped to her feet and held the girl's arm. "This is her first day, Ms. Fluckinger. I'll make sure she understands our procedures."

"Make it happen." Ms. Fluckinger raised a lip to their leave and turned away. "Disgusting, the level of intelligence in young adults today."

Mrs. Winkle appeared from an opened door, escorted by a tech, with neither Saqi nor Bones in hand. Annie felt the worst for her.

"They looked so sad," Mrs. Winkle said. "I hated to leave them."

"Dr. Sarah is out for the day," Mary said. "We'll try again in the morning, Mrs. Winkle.".

"It'll be too late." Mrs. Winkle shot a pointed finger at Ms. Fluckinger. "She's got my Bonesy girl scheduled to be terminated come dawn."

"You've had plenty of time to make your claim to that dog," the woman argued. "The only reason she's still alive is because we didn't have enough pentobarbital on hand." She turned to Mary, who shrunk away. "Seems someone forgot to order it."

"She's been in the hospital," Annie said. "All week."

"I was dead," Mrs. Winkle said.

"Dead," Ms. Fluckinger repeated. A wide grin and doubting demeanor crept upon her with a twitch of the eye. "Well, what an interesting recovery we've made. I still must keep my schedule."

Annie approached her. "She's old. Older, if you count dog years. Although, now she's gathering some cat lives to hear her tell it." She caught herself being the only one humored. "Don't you have a heart to allow a beloved companion its last months with her owner?" Annie quickly withdrew her hand from the woman's counter when Ms. Fluckinger flared her nostrils like a wild animal.

Mary swiftly pulled a wet wipe from a container and polished down the countertop.

Ms. Fluckinger drew back and clasped her hands. "As I've already stated, I will not change the schedule."

"Come on, Annie," Mrs. Winkle said. "Let's leave the wicked witch to her cult of desensitized dippies."

Mary dashed to meet them at the door, opening it for them. "We should hear back from the vet by 8:00 a.m. We'll keep you posted. Thanks for coming." She shoved a wad of paper at Annie's torso before closing the door behind them.

Annie knew Mrs. Winkle all too well to believe she would allow this defeat. She was already plotting something on the way to the car. She could see it in the old gal's pace. Annie's mind was awhirl. All she could think about was poor Bones. She pulled her keys out of her pocket, unlocked the car door, and raised her eyes to the street in time to notice a truck's side panel printed with the word, "Grace." A tingle raced through her veins as it sped by. The wad of paper was still in her hand. Annie slid into the seat and unraveled the note.

"We've got things to do," Mrs. Winkle said. "This is no time to read a love letter."

"This isn't a love letter, Mrs. Winkle. This is our saving grace."

"What?"

"It's from Mary." Annie read the tiny handwriting. "I purposely hid all the pentobarbital in hopes someone would adopt Bones. Come back ten minutes past closing and I'll help you get both your dogs back."

Mrs. Winkle slapped her hands on her legs and shouted, "Hot-ass coyote, we're in business!"

CHAPTER FIFTEEN

Promptly at 6:00 p.m., the door to the dog pound was locked and lights turned out. Moments later, Ms. Fluckinger followed the last of her employees out of the parking lot in her silver Maserati.

Annie and Mrs. Winkle hid across the street, behind a sidewalk hedge. Annie followed the Maserati with her tiny binoculars and caught herself drooling. "Wow wee. Too bad Ms. Fluckinger is a rotten apple. I'd just bet she'd look sexy in a man's white tank top. And to see her in that tank top driving this 1953 Berlinetta just puts the whipped cream fantasy in a big bowl with the whole jar of cherries, baby." She felt Mrs. Winkle's eyes upon her and lowered the binoculars. "Not that she's my type, or anything."

"Well, I hate to smear a bugger on your titties, honey, but could you focus on the task at hand? We've got a break-out to do."

Annie grabbed Mrs. Winkle's arm and tugged her back behind the bush. "Wait. No. We're not breaking them out.

Mary's helping us. Remember?" Annie's phone dinged. It was Mary's text telling her she was headed back. "She's on her way back. She stopped at UDF. I'm telling her the coast is clear."

"Is she bringing us a cappuccino? I do love those."

"No. She left her number on the note. I just thought it was smart to stay in contact, so we're not guessing."

"Very wise choice. Have you done this before?"

"No. And I hope never to do this again."

Mrs. Winkle sat next to her. "I'm sorry to drag you into this, Annie. We could really get into some trouble doing this. Mary is so sweet. But she could lose her job. This isn't the sort of thing nice, wholesome people do."

Annie watched Mary's sedan pull into the parking lot. "Mrs. Winkle, when was the last time you were wholesome?"

"You're right. Let's go."

Annie slipped her binoculars into a backpack and followed Mrs. Winkle across the street. Her mind reeled with all the possibilities—all the things that could possibly go wrong. She halted beside the corner of the building just as Oz appeared before her. Her back was against the wall, with a foot cocked up behind her.

"Remember how you always focus on the best outcome when visiting your dad?" Oz asked.

Annie caught her breath and nodded. "Yeah."

"I would do that."

"You're right. Good. Thanks."

"Click your heels, Dorothy, and repeat after me," Oz coaxed. "Everything always works out for me."

Annie nodded and waved back to Mary's urging gesture. "Everything always works out for me. Everything always works out for me. It does. I know it works out. This will be smooth sailing. Everything's going to be okay. It'll be okay. It'll be okay."

Annie slipped inside the building and shut the door behind her. Mary reached around her and pulled on the knob until she heard a click.

"You have to force it," Mary said.

"Sounds like the going theme here," Annie replied.

They followed Mary down a long, ill-lit corridor. Not even a ruffled mumble from any of the kennels. So many dogs behind the glass, most of them still awake, but not one yipped or barked at them.

"I have to say, Mary, you've done a marvelous job at training them to stay quiet," Mrs. Winkle said.

Annie watched Mary's composure sink a bit.

"Most of them are sedated," Mary commented. "Not my idea. Ms. Fluckinger doesn't have the patience for anything… unruly."

"Yes, quite the regimented governess," Annie murmured.

"You have no idea." She halted them before a door and inserted a key.

"Mary, you don't seem the type to work for a kill shelter. You have this—oh, I don't know—humanitarian spirit about you, that's all."

Mrs. Winkle inserted, "Yes. Aren't you worried about being fired?"

Mary looked to them both. "She can't fire me. I'm her niece. I'm worth a boatload."

"How wonderful. Keeping it in the family, eh?"

They followed Mary inside and down an aisle as she continued, "After her husband, my uncle, died in Zermatt from an—uh—mysterious skiing accident, she's taken up a hobby of selling her crafts on eBay."

Annie frowned. "One helluva lot of crafts to afford a Maserati. Don'tcha think?"

"Her part of the inheritance, I suppose. I just work here at the front desk to get a bit on my resume before I finish college. I've already been accepted at my father's financial firm in Zurich."

Annie nodded, keenly impressed. "A banker in Switzerland. Good for you."

Mary tugged at her earlobe. "Thanks."

"What happened to the husband?" Mrs. Winkle asked.

"Apparently, he had a stomach full of poisoned ginger ale. Whatever it was, it blinded him, and he smacked square into the trunk of a tree. Dead as a doornail. Made his arms considerably longer. You know how hard it was finding a shirt from the big and tall department to fit a short torso?"

"No autopsy?" interjected Annie.

"Sure. But they couldn't do a tox screen, cause his body had already been embalmed when the forensic team found him."

"Embalmed. At the tree?" Mrs. Winkle exclaimed.

"No," Mary answered. "In the coroner's lab. Someone had slipped his body in the wrong fridge."

"Don't you just hate it when you think you've put the celery in one dehydrator bin, to find it in the other, with the rutabagas?" Mrs. Winkle said.

Once they reached the kennel where Bones was trapped, Annie turned Mrs. Winkle about. "Ms. Bones is awaiting your hugs."

Mrs. Winkle held out her arms and dropped to her knees as Mary opened the kennel door. Bones's tail wagged happily as she made her way into Mrs. Winkle's embrace. "My little girl. You're so precious! What a darling. How could I ever wish to put you down before your time? Will you forgive me?"

Annie rested her back on the wall next to the door and crossed her arms with a small smile. All was well.

"Oh, careful," Mary chirped. "Don't hit that red button."

Annie stood away from the wall and looked over her shoulder.

"That opens up all the kennels at once. In case of an emergency. Fire, or something."

"Geez. We don't want them all. Just our two." Annie's curiosity drifted to a mini spray bottle on the table beside her marked "Chicken." She held it up to her eyes. "Uh—chicken? What's this for?"

"That's to spray on their food. A flavoring to enhance a sagging appetite. Works on anything."

"Huh."

Mary escorted Annie across the way to release Saqi. He was more than ready to hightail it out of that place. Annie laughed at all his excited licks to her face. "You're safe, little man. I've gotcha. We're getting out of here together."

Mary put a stern hand on Annie's arm. "We have to leave. Now." She showed Annie her phone. "I slipped a tracker on Ms. Fluckinger's car. She's coming back."

Annie shoved Saqi in her opened daypack and zipped him close to her chest. The women gathered up Bones and Mrs. Winkle and rushed down the hall. After a turn, Annie found herself alone, having headed down the wrong hall.

"This is like a house of mirrors," Annie said.

Mary grabbed Annie's arm and pulled her back, shoving her toward the way out.

Once at the back door, Mary halted and turned to them. "Out this door, take a right, and you'll come out the other side of the building."

"We'll give her the slip." Mrs. Winkle winked.

"Right."

The door opened to Ms. Fluckinger, with a scowl that would frighten Genghis Khan. Two technicians stood on either side, blocking any chance of a quick escape. Ms. Fluckinger held her phone up to Mary.

"I have a tracker on your car."

Mrs. Winkle pointed to Mary's phone. "Well, isn't that something? She does too."

Ms. Fluckinger's face peeled in utter disgust. "I knew you were a weak replacement for your sister. She would never have disappointed me like this."

Mrs. Winkle turned to Mary. "You should have kicked her ass to the curb long before now, sweetie."

"This…" Annie added, gesturing a finger to all present. "This wasn't at all in my expectations on how I wanted this to turn out. So, can we speed this up a bit?"

"My sentiments, exactly," Ms. Fluckinger crooned.

Annie jumped to close the door. Mary pressed her back into it as well. Yet, neither had the strength to hold back the force of two muscular technicians.

"Go, Mrs. Winkle!" Annie hollered, wincing against the tug of war. "We can't hold them back much longer." When Annie finally opened her eyes, Mrs. Winkle had disappeared, leaving

Bones staring at her from the corner of her eye. "Where'd she go?"

An axe suddenly pierced the door between Annie and Mary. Annie heard Mary yell in chorus to her own terrorized bewilderment. Mrs. Winkle then appeared from around the corner with a fire extinguisher pointed at them.

"Stand down, girls," Mrs. Winkle demanded. "Let's dance, bitches."

Annie released the door and flung herself out of the way of the white powdery foam, tripping onto the floor.

With the door wide open, a tsunami of spray spackled the three women with a pounding force, their limbs flailing like salmon up a river. Within seconds, a misted poof was all that was left of Mrs. Winkle's onslaught attack.

"Uh-oh," she said.

Bones was ready to lead, barking at them to follow.

"Come on, girl," Mrs. Winkle replied. "Better get a head start."

Annie picked herself up from the floor. Ms. Fluckinger and her techs slid, stumbled, and fell from the slick ooze around them. Annie decided to cut down a familiar corridor with a not-so-brilliant idea.

"This is crazy, this is crazy, this is crazy." As she ran, she pulled out her phone and voice-texted her brother. "I've got an exclusive for your girlfriend and Channel 5 news. Hamilton County Dog Pound. And please call the police. There are a few citizens here who need backup. Bat signal, bat signal!"

Around the corner, she stopped and ducked into a door. She hit the red button, sending off red lights and sirens as every kennel door opened. After the first few alarms went off, the loudspeakers suddenly switched to playing The Doors's "Break On Through." Dogs awoke, startled from their quiet interludes.

"Come on out. Come on," she coaxed. "Wanna play? Come on. Let's go play."

Annie grabbed the mini bottle of chicken spray and dodged back into the corridor in time to find Ms. Fluckinger and a tech fighting back the freed dogs.

"Get back!" Ms. Fluckinger screeched. "Get back—stop her!"

Annie's heart leapt, and her legs suddenly felt like overcooked pasta. She unzipped her daypack and peeked in on Saqi. "We're okay, right? Good?"

Saqi raised his head out and peered toward the host of barking, fleeing dogs before shrinking back down into the pack. Annie sprinted down the corridor, away from the mess she created, only to stop at a cross hall where more dogs were escaping.

"This place is worse than IKEA."

Annie followed the hoard a bit before being distracted by a long-windowed laboratory. She took a quick look around before stepping in. Two examination tables with bulging sheets loomed ominously before her, and she couldn't help herself. Curiosity got the better of her.

"What the hell kind of giant dogs are these?" She crept up on the sheet like it was going to be startled before she lifted the corner.

The glimpse wasn't enough of a surprise. She threw off the sheet to expose a thick pile of hides. Dog hides.

"Holy black market mod. Don't look, Saqi."

She turned around and yanked the other sheet off its table to uncover another pile of hides. Cat hides.

"Oh, my God. I see Maserati money."

A door slammed behind her. Annie spun around to face Ms. Fluckinger, her eyes ablaze with fury. Saqi returned to the pack with a whimper. Annie would have laughed at the woman's features and clothes, all slathered and dripping with extinguisher residue, had she not been so frightened. It did make the moment a bit lighter to bear, however.

"You might need to blot that with vinegar. I hear it helps."

Ms. Fluckinger tightened a fist. "You have put yourself in a very unfortunate circumstance."

"Kinda had a feeling."

Ms. Fluckinger gestured to the cat hides. "The Swiss value cat hide to cure rheumatism."

"And the dogs?"

"Russia. The meat is great in stir-fry."

"Eww." Annie cringed.

"It is a pleasure to rid the streets of disease-filled filth."

"Why not rats?"

"The other lab," she said, drawing a long fingernail over her shoulder. "There is such a market for Vienna sausages in your country."

Annie repressed a gag. She lifted Saqi out of the pack and held him up to her eyes. "I got your back."

Ms. Fluckinger smirked. "Chihuahua hides are useless to me. But the meats are good food for the boa's breakfast when they tire of rats."

Annie followed her gaze to the corner tank where an albino boa lingered. She felt a hard gulp catch in her throat, and she tucked Saqi under her arm like a football. "I knew that one season of rugby would come in handy someday. The only reason I wasn't very good at it, besides the long-ass runs up and down the field, was that I never remembered to toss the ball behind me."

She tossed Saqi's little body at Ms. Fluckinger with a launch that would have impressed NASA. With Ms. Fluckinger's flailing, Annie was at the ready with the chicken spray and dowsed her in the eyes. Saqi fell to the ground with a growl. Annie tried to grab Saqi up and run, but Saqi looked like he had a better idea. He turned his head aside at the woman's wide stance and looked back at Annie with hooded eyes. Leaping straight for the woman's crotch, he bit down with all the gusto his little passion could afford.

"Whoa," Annie said, drawing back with a fright. She watched Ms. Fluckinger yelp and fall into a fetal clump. Annie swiped up Saqi, sprayed Ms. Fluckinger a few times for good measure and added, "Aren't you glad you don't have balls? Now, if you'll excuse me. I have a newscaster just outside waiting for a really good story."

Annie's hands shook. She shuffled her way down the corridor and followed the signs to the lobby, kissing Saqi on his little head.

"I am so proud of you, little man. Let's go see your mama."

A loud gunshot pierced the glass lab window beside her, making her stumble against a wall with fright. Medusa stood awkwardly behind her, with one hand to her crotch and the another grasping a small pistol, pointed straight at Annie.

"No one will hear your story," she seethed.

Annie couldn't feel her legs. "Is that what you told your husband before you poisoned his ginger ale?"

"He was in the way. So are you."

Shouts and barks drowned out the fearful musings in Annie's head. She looked over her shoulder to see a hoard of dogs turning the corner and halting beside her.

"Oh, God," Annie puled.

Their snouts were wet, and their teeth were bared, dripping with enough saliva that Dr. Pavlov would find quite gratifying. Panting breaths approached so close she could feel the heat through her slacks. The pack leader sniffed at her. Annie felt paralyzed. A small bleat escaped her lips. She turned to view the snout as it searched the air for something else, which caught its attention. The large, muscular mastiff mix began to growl in Ms. Fluckinger's direction. Wads of drool dripped off its exposed teeth.

Medusa looked puzzled and lowered her pistol. She lifted her shirt and sniffed it.

"Chicken," she moaned.

Annie suddenly felt relieved. "Hmm."

At once, the pack leader sped off in Ms. Fluckinger's direction with his pack propelling themselves close behind. Annie held her hands overtop her glasses and closed her eyes as the woman screamed. When Annie opened them again, she wondered how it was Ms. Fluckinger had scaled the wall and clung onto the exit sign with such finesse.

"Get them away," she shouted. "Call them down! Go. Get. Down!"

Annie fell to the floor. Her body couldn't take the stress of watching her life flash before her. She rubbed her face and watched, almost entertained, at the sight of a hungry bunch of dogs jumping with vengeance at such a detestable figure.

"I think this is what they call morbid curiosity. Better hang on if I were you," she yelled. "Maybe you should have fed them earlier."

Footfalls quickly rounded the corner. Mary's voice echoed with Scott's.

"Annie," Scott cried. He fell beside her and embraced her. "Oh, my God. Are you hurt? Shot? Stabbed? Dismembered? Hungry?"

"Scott. Other than a little acid reflux, I'm good. Really. Let go, will ya? You're squashing Saqi." She pulled Saqi out of the pack.

"Oh. Hi, Saqi. What a brave little fella."

Annie looked at Saqi. "Boy, have we got a story for him, don't we?"

Two police officers ran past them and stopped. One held up his phone and started a video. "Oh, this is great," he cackled.

Mary met Annie as Scott pulled her on her feet.

"Are you okay?" Mary asked.

Annie nodded. "Mrs. Winkle?"

"She's safe. And so is Bones."

Annie released her tense shoulders and felt as if she'd burst into tears. "Thank you."

"The techs didn't have a chance. Mrs. Winkle clocked them both with trash cans and hog-tied them with leashes and collars. She completed it in record time."

"That's our Dottie." Annie raised her chin to Scott. "Get me out of here, please."

Mary puffed her cheeks out and blew a sigh. "You know how hard it is to corral a pack of wild dogs?"

Annie handed her the chicken spray. Mary turned to leave, hiding a laugh behind her hand. She and Scott met the news anchor, Vanessa Young, and her cameraman.

Scott nudged her and asked, "Lunch tomorrow?"

Vanessa flashed a very pretty white smile. "Yeah. Let's do."

Annie allowed Scott to keep a hand on her arm and escort her out the building. "She your girlfriend now?" She hadn't seen him grin like this since he was a kid with his first bike.

"Not yet. But I'm working on it."

The parking lot, lawn, and street were filled with a healthy amount of mayhem, with police and rescuers chasing dogs and cats scattering in every which direction.

"The only thing I want to work on is getting into a hot bath with a lot of candles and my very own Pork and Beans singing along to Dad's hand-me-down album of Hawaiian music."

"I'm sorry it was such a sucky day for you and Mrs. Winkle, Annie."

Annie received a wink from Oz as she passed the fire truck.

It felt good, despite all that happened. "You know, brother, this was a good experience. A little stressful. But, a lot of stuff fell into place with perfect timing. It might look like a jumble of confusing and stressful decisions to us. But I've a feeling the universe can sum them up with some pretty damn good calculations on its own."

Saqi barked after spotting Bones and Mrs. Winkle across the street. Annie lowered him down and watched as he happily ran over to them and dashed in circles. Annie stopped when her feet hit the sidewalk and imitated Bones with her usual corner-of-the-eye stare-down.

"Come here, big girl."

Bones's tail wagged. "Roool, roool, roool, roool!" she remarked with dimples showing.

"I agree."

Bones leaned into Annie's hug. "I do love those dimples, Bonesy Girl."

CHAPTER SIXTEEN

September started out dry, with one of Annie's favorite wildflowers, chicory, drifting along roadsides and highways, surviving the dwindling summer heat. The dainty, pale blue flowers mixed well with strands of purple ironweed and dying thistle heads. The day was bright, beautiful, and full of opportunity. Annie decided it was a perfect day.

She was enjoying the bright white clouds drifting by when her phone rang. It was Varsha.

"Hi, Varsha," Annie said.

"Annie. Did you leave the coffee shop yet?"

"Yeah. I have a quick stop. Then I'm on my way to Yodel's. Why, what's up?"

"Dang. I was going to ask you to bring me a choca mocha berry latte with oat milk."

"Sorry," replied Annie. "I left a few minutes early so I can stop and uh…"

"What? You cut out on me. Where are you going?"

Annie was hesitant to explain. "I'm stopping off at Cindy's family restaurant. To apologize to her for my behavior the day of the big accident."

Annie had to pull the phone away from her ear. Varsha screamed a series of unintelligible half words. "Why, Annie? For cripe's sakes. She's a nutty multigrain twiglet. You don't owe her an apology. She brought that consequence upon herself with that weed brain behavior of hers. You had every right to say what you did."

Annie turned the volume down on the car radio.

"Varsha, I'm not excusing her behavior. But I'm not about to make it a crutch for mine. That day, I just snapped. It hasn't sat right in my gut since. Resentments don't drown anyone but the person doing all the paddling. Apologizing doesn't mean that I have accepted her behavior. It means I don't accept mine. There's no room to play victim when you're busy being empowered by your integrity."

"Dude. You are my guru."

* * *

The Quad was a popular five-star family joint in the heart of a shopping labyrinth Annie never knew how to manage without the guidance of stellar charts. She arrived early enough that the lunch crowds hadn't yet hit the parking lot.

With no one to greet her at the gold-trimmed podium, Annie made her way around the corner and into the large dining room toward the bar. Crystal chandeliers, starched linen tablecloths, and fancy bread plates made in Italy added grace to the ambiance.

Cindy appeared from behind the kitchen doors and met her halfway. "Annie."

Her greeting was more like a reported misfortune. Annie expected no less.

"Hi. Cindy. Wow, you're looking good. Happy?"

Cindy's eyes drew to tiny slits. "You're not here to make a scene, are you?"

"What? No. No. I just wanted to talk a minute."

"You know, Annie. This is not really appropriate behavior for someone like yourself who doesn't want a relationship. This is not a talent, by definition, that you can build on like stickers on a skateboard. I got that from the *Lez Manners* textbook you sold me. Page one ninety-four."

Annie shook off what felt like a detached mental thread that drifted from nowhere to nowhere like a gnat. "Cindy, on my firstborn kitten's life, if I had known that *Lez Manners* was going to haunt me for the next twelve years, I would have sold you *Wendy Gets Wet in Paris* instead. In a heartbeat. Look, I just wanted to apologize for my behavior toward you, that's all."

"Which part?"

Annie puffed out her cheeks. "How much time have you got?"

Cindy took an about-face and marched back to the bar with Annie following.

"Come on. I'm really trying here."

"Look, I've got a girlfriend."

"Great. Wonderful. I'm proud of her courage." Annie reeled. "To be vulnerable. Both of you. In therapy. Can't quite imagine that leap of faith. I still suck at friendships."

"Goes without saying." Cindy grabbed liquor bottles and turned away from her, arranging them on the back bar.

"Touché. All right. I deserved that."

Cindy's father strolled out from the kitchen doors.

Annie greeted him. "Hi, Mr. Russo. *I tuoi piatti sono sottaceto in bei calzini!*"

Cindy remarked over her shoulder, "You just told him his dinner plates are pickled in nice socks."

"Oh. Crap." She winced. "Sorry. Guess I need more practice."

He stared at Cindy as he said something with a gesture Annie was certain to be a repressed spit. He swiped up a water pitcher and departed back into the kitchen.

"See, I'm being given lessons in Italian from a coworker at the coffee shop. Hard to wrap my head around some phrases and words. I'm trying something new. You know, branching out.

I even tried my hand at *Cacio e Pepe*. Such an easy dish. But, you've got to be quick, right?"

Cindy twisted about and leaned against the counter with an impatient stare.

"I've overstayed my welcome, haven't I?" Annie stood back from the bar. "Look, Cindy. I just wanted to tell you how sorry I am for treating you like an object. You are weird," she laughed. "Yet, you are a human being, with feelings, and sensitivities, and ambitions, and desires. And I couldn't see that in you. Didn't... want to see that. I didn't respect you the way you deserved. Yeah, you are one screwy gal. And maybe you'll get better at being appropriate. Being human, it's a full-time job. Take it from me. Anyway. It was rude of me to allow you to get me all riled up. Bottom line, I'm letting you off the hook. I'm not asking you to change so that I can feel better about my life. Feeling better is my job. I hope you and your girlfriend are truly happy, that your family's happy, that your dog or cat is happy."

Cindy relaxed her stance and let her gaze fall. "I have a gecko."

"Gecko. Awesome. I wish your gecko a great day." Annie started backpedaling. "I gotta go. Sorry to take up your time." She raised her voice and waved to the kitchen door. "Love your sauce, Mr. Russo."

Annie returned to her car, settled into her seat and rubbed her face. She felt a presence and turned to Oz in the passenger seat, returning her smile.

"Felt good, did it?"

Annie stared at her steering wheel. "God, yeah. I felt like I just took an evolutionary bounce. Did I?"

Oz fist-bumped Annie.

* * *

Varsha struggled to carry rolls of vintage maps from one spot to another. Then a giant box of books from one aisle to the other.

"Varsha, you know you can do just one thing at a time, right?" Annie said.

"That's okay. Half of one, six dozen of the other."

Annie watched as Varsha picked the box back up and walked it over to the desk. She opened her mouth to speak just as Mr. Tiddle waved her down.

"But—"

"Shhh. Let her do her calisthenics."

"Varsha."

Varsha stood up and met Annie's eyes. "Yo."

"I didn't see your car out back."

She bent back down to lift another box near the counter. "Still in the shop," she grunted.

"Oh. You rode the bus," Annie said.

"Nope. Misplaced the card."

"How'd you get here?"

Varsha popped her head up over the counter and swooned. "From Afar."

"Afar."

"Yeah. That was my taxi driver's name. And, you know, it occurred to me I hadn't been in a taxi since the day I was born."

Varsha described in length her mother's uterine yoga and meals, including details of the nutritional supplement cream for her vagina she took during her pregnancy.

"That explains a lot." Annie said.

"Hey, placenta girl," Mr. Tiddle hollered. "Think you can give me a hand here?" He waved a list of new arrivals. "Just check-mark the ones we're missing, and I'll work on backorders."

"Gotcha."

"Working out for another hot date with Miss Vegas?" Annie asked.

Varsha sat the paper down. "Didn't I tell you? We broke up."

"No."

"Well. She left me, actually."

Annie tilted her head. "How do you know she didn't right you?"

"Hey. I like that. I have no sense of direction. Golly, this is suddenly the best week of my life."

Mr. Tiddle dug into his burger bag and pulled out a box of fries. "I could tell once your fashion sense returned to the usual drabness."

Annie furrowed her forehead at him. "What happened?"

"She wanted me to drop her off at Love's Truck Stop. Damn car barely made it. She was hitching back to Vegas with a trucker she had met through Instalips."

"Your car?"

"No. It was Tanzy's car. Told her I'd drive it back to her mom's house for her. It wouldn't have made it past Terre Haute, Illinois. That thing saw more sex than the bathroom floor at Shirley's Bar."

"Some stories, huh?"

"Dandies. But I couldn't even start the dang thing. She never bothered to tell me the blow-and-go only turned the car on if you played "Irish Eyes" into it."

Mr. Tiddle balked. "Well, that's pretty low."

"Tell me about it. I didn't even know she was Irish." Varsha snatched a fry from Mr. Tiddle's bag. "What's the word with you and Catrin?"

Annie shuffled a few papers, attempting to hide her recoil. "It was achingly transparent to me that I read her all wrong. I'm just not good at this stuff. And before you ask, yes. Yes, I texted her back."

"There's other stuff you're not good at?" Mr. Tiddle asked.

Annie shot him a glare. "People. I'm much better at keeping relationships with cats and books and coffee."

"You have me," Varsha said. "Like cream-filled donuts, I'll always be here for you."

"Yes. Thank you for reinforcing my conclusions of single and sugar."

"I thought she was into you, dude. Sorry. I guess it was just a false alarm."

"Never defecate more than you can eat," Mr. Tiddle said before stuffing his mouth with fries.

Annie winced. "Profound advice."

"Chilian proverb."

Annie reached for her coffee and clumsily dumped it in her lap. She vaulted out of her chair with growling curses. "These are new pants." She wiped and dabbed at the wet stains on her pants and shirt.

"Don't worry. It builds character," Mr. Tiddle blurted, his mouth full of burger.

Annie twisted about, nettled at his comment. "I suppose letting your nose hairs get in the way of eating that freshly killed deer-burger has built your character, huh?"

"I refuse to expound on that very natural, very snappy comeback of yours, young lady."

"Should I use a swear word to imply a better retort?"

"That won't be necessary. Just take pride in your mediocrity."

Varsha interjected, "Personally, I don't like to chase my food while it's scared and running. Tacos are made from couch-potato cows that enjoyed the sweet meadow grasses of Indiana in sunshine and spring rains."

Annie knew this interaction would take a moment. "Uh, Varsha."

"Yeah."

"Where on God's green earth did you hear that?"

"My parents told me."

"Your taco cows actually have a stressful life, never knowing a blade of grass or a warm morning sun. I suggest you Google it and watch a video on it."

Varsha stood disenchanted and tearful. "They lied to me?"

"Yes," Mr. Tiddle renounced with a fresh mouthful of burger. "Terribly."

Annie spotted Varsha later in the day tying a calf borrowed from Young's Dairy Farm to the bike stand in front of the shop, holding up a sign of mercy, shouting, "Have you hugged a cow today?"

* * *

The morning sun drew Annie to her living room window. Beans had been laying upon the rug with the dash of light upon his belly.

"Did you find Mama Sun, Beanie?" Annie bent down and rubbed his warmed little belly. A happy purring ensued as he curled around her hand. "Good for you. Where's your brother?"

She opened the thin veil of drapes to expose Pork on the ledge.

"Oh, there you are, silly Gus. Hiding on me, huh?" She followed his nod back to the window. "Whatcha looking at? A pretty dove?"

Down below, Annie spotted a man and Mrs. Winkle's son, Keith, planting a For Sale sign in the front yard.

"What the hell?"

She descended the stairs and rounded the house to Mrs. Winkle's porch, catching Keith's eye.

"Aren't you out of here yet?" he spat.

"Obviously, you haven't heard from your mother."

Keith made a squishy face. "I haven't yet made it a habit of sitting in séances, asking to speak to my dead mother."

Annie rolled her lips tightly and held up a finger. "Hold that thought." Annie proceeded to unlock the front door.

"Hey, you can't go in there!"

"It's all right. I have something I want to show you."

Annie poked her head around the living room doorway and found Mrs. Winkle on her couch, cleaning her rifle. *Oh, this will be good.* "Psst, Mrs. Winkle." Seeing no response, she whistled. "Dottie."

Mrs. Winkle raised her head with a start. "Oh. Hello, dear."

Annie motioned her to come closer with a wiggling finger. She held Dottie's shoulders and gently pressed her to walk out on the porch. The real estate agent stood aghast at the old lady with a rifle in her grip.

Even though she was behind her, Annie was certain the look on Mrs. Winkle's face just enriched the experience for him.

"What in tarnation are you doing with that sign in my yard, Keith?" she stormed.

Keith's head turned over his shoulder with the expression of a paralyzed gazelle before a charging lion. He collapsed, fainting beside the agent with a thump on the ground. The agent began whimpering and held up a white handkerchief.

"Now, now," he pleaded. "Easy does it."

Dottie pulled the rifle up on her shoulder. "Get."

"Yes, ma'am." He no sooner dashed off in the direction of the street than a shot was fired at his feet to halt him with a flailing scream.

As he turned back, Dottie politely added, "You forgot your sign."

The agent tippy-toed back and over Keith's shaken form, pulling his sign from the yard. Once at his car, he turned to her and shouted, "You're crazy. You know that?"

Annie drew an arm around Dottie and snuggled her with a kiss to her head. "You should stop by sometime for a coffee," she hollered to him. "She makes a killer Reuben."

* * *

Bones was on watch, from a distance. She kept a look askance on Keith as Saqi chewed on his shoelace and Annie replaced the icepack on his head. He barely acknowledged her in reply, sitting on the couch as he did, slouched over his knees.

"How was I supposed to know you were alive?" he grumbled. He sneezed before pushing Saqi away from him.

Mrs. Winkle drew fists to her hips. "Did you even call to claim the body? No."

"Bad move, dude," Annie added.

A sour grimace turned her way.

"Didn't even have the decency to contact a funeral home," Mrs. Winkle said.

"I thought that was standard procedure of the hospital administration," Keith retorted.

"I really should have let you dangle off that Grand Canyon cliff a while longer when you were five, you know that? Maybe then, you'd have more appreciation for life."

"Wow," Annie marveled. "Haven't heard that story before."

Mrs. Winkle picked up a folder from the little corner desk and walked it over to the couch. She slapped Keith over the head with it, saying, "Well, I'm glad you're here, at any rate. We've got some business to discuss."

Annie was grateful, actually. A clear indication she could dismiss herself. "I'll just leave you two to it. See you later."

"Annie, get your butt back here."

"Why?" Keith and Annie asked in unison.

Mrs. Winkle pulled her shoulders back and faced Annie. "Because this includes you." She handed paperclipped stacks of papers to Keith and Annie and continued, "Met with my attorney the other day."

"Uncle Tolman?" Keith asked.

"Yes. He fast-tracked me to a speedy conclusion, with signatures and all. Sometimes it's who you know, not what you know."

Keith grimaced at the papers then to his mom. "What's this?"

With hands folded before her, Mrs. Winkle replied with a calm voice. "I'm releasing you from any responsibility concerning this house. I'm selling it to a very responsible person that I can trust to care for it."

"You have a buyer? Who?"

"I'm selling it to Annie."

Annie's legs wobbled. "What?" She read her name on the paper. Good thing there was a wall to catch her fall back. "I don't know what to say. I…I love this house. But, Mrs. Winkle. I really can't afford to buy a house."

"For one dollar."

Annie was speechless.

"Suits me." Keith's reply was a huff followed by the toss of his papers onto the coffee table. "Didn't want the headache anyway," he mumbled.

Mrs. Winkle nodded to him. "Didn't think so."

"But," Annie spurted. "I don't understand. Why me?"

Mrs. Winkle walked over to her. "Sweetie, it's practically yours anyway. You do all the work. I'm getting on in years now, just like ole Bones. This way, I can feel at peace knowing you'll never have to fear of ever being kicked out by anyone ever again." With her last word, she jeered at Keith. "You've been such a great help to me. I just wanted to return the favors."

"I—um." Annie's face felt warm as tears streaked down her cheeks.

"Oh, you'll have to pay for all the maintenance, utilities, and such. I'll still help while I'm able. But I see you moving up in the world. I think you'll do just fine. That is, if you don't mind me staying around."

Annie's papers crumpled in her shaking hands as Mrs. Winkle embraced her. "Oh, of course, I don't mind." Annie returned the loving hug.

"You're the closest thing to a granddaughter I've ever had." Mrs. Winkle held her at arm's length. "I couldn't be prouder."

"Oh, God." Keith sneered. "All this affection is making me sick."

* * *

No matter where Annie was, thoughts of Catrin dovetailed into her everyday duties. Annie turned her head to every auburn-haired woman with similar features at the park while walking Saqi and Bones. Every postal carrier's vehicle she passed along the sidewalks would trigger a bleak spirit. Even when Flapjack delivered the mail at Yodel's, she couldn't help feeling dampened just looking at the mail, wondering if Catrin had touched it.

She sniffed the envelopes, hoping to recall the perfume Catrin had worn the night of the party. She caught sight of Mr. Tiddle gaping at her overtop his reading glasses. Several times, she thought about phoning Catrin up; each time, she abandoned the idea. Varsha texted her from several aisles away, inviting her out for the night. Annie met her sad, puppy-dog eyes as she poked her head out from around a corner. Annie shook her head.

Varsha plopped her forearms on Annie's desk. "I'm trying this new thing."

"Making decisions based on common sense?"

"Thought I'd give it a shot."

"How's that working for you?"

Varsha cried in a sloppy slump, "I miss my omens and voices. They were my best friends. That's why I dress frumpy, like you used to. Hoping it'll soothe my pain. Ex vogue."

"No one bears sorrow better than one who has been frumped."

Varsha sat on the corner of the desk, disheveling papers and files to fall on the floor. "Oh, geez."

Annie let out an exasperated huff and began helping her pick it all up.

"Let me just tell you, Annie. Love is a tantalizing liaison. It loves to hunt us and kill us for sport."

Annie grimaced. "I'm usually questioning whether English is your first language. Now, I'm wondering how it is you're too smart for your own good. Would you please choose a level of intelligence? You're creeping me out. Besides, I wasn't in love."

"Yes, you were."

"No. I wasn't."

"Uh-huh."

Annie frowned. "Ah, yes. The sibling rivalry I never knew I wanted."

"Speaking of Scott," Varsha said. "How's he and that news gal doing?"

"Oh, hit it off marvelously after the dog pound incident." Annie slapped a few files and loose papers on her desk. "She even got a work bonus. Now, they're investigating the lifespan of sea salt in crotches for a week in the Virgin Islands together."

The two turned their attention to Mr. Tiddle and a couple of customers near the Classics shelves.

"Oh, I revel in the adulation," Mr. Tiddle cooed before approaching the drooling patrons.

"What an attractive specimen you have there," the patron said.

"A real attention-grabber, that one," the other mused, with sheepish intent.

"Indeed," Mr. Tiddle squealed. "Thank you. Tends to take up a rather large amount of space, so plan accordingly."

Varsha leaned over to Annie. "Are they flirting over books or body parts?"

Annie shrugged her off. "As long as he's given a fair amount of money to pay his overdue bills, I frankly don't care what he sells."

Varsha craned her neck over Annie's paper. "Whatcha writing?"

"Um. A poem." Annie ripped the paper off the notepad and wadded it up.

"What'd you do that for?"

"Silly crap."

Varsha leaned her elbows on the desk. "Annie. You're still thinking about her, aren't you?"

"No. Not at all. Yeah, well, maybe a little."

"Maybe a lot."

"Rarely. Mostly." Annie tipped her head into a hand and began scribbling again. "Can't help it."

"Women who write feel too much."

Annie's phone rang.

Varsha picked up the trash can at her feet. "I'll take the trash out."

"Yodel's Bookstore," Annie announced into the phone.

"Yes," a gravelly voice on the phone said. "My name is Charlie Thatch. I emailed you about my interest in the P.T. Barnum papers."

"Yes, Mr. Thatch." Annie began sorting through the files atop her desk, to no avail. "I have them right here." She searched and searched.

"Good. I'll accept your offer. I'm in town and I'd like to come and pick them up in about fifteen minutes, if that's suitable."

Annie's blood raced and she broke out into a sweat. No sign of the file. "Sure thing, Mr. Thatch. I'll have them ready for your viewing pleasure promptly."

"Thank you."

"Yes, sir."

Annie hung up the phone and fell to the floor in a whimper, feeling her worst nightmare had come true. "No, no, no, no, no. Where'd it go? Jesus, Mary, Joseph and the damn donkey!"

"Miss Freckle," Mr. Tiddle's shoes said. "Not going back to the old habits of crack hunting, are we?"

She really wanted to spit at him.

"We do have a vacuum in the back."

Annie felt full panic set into her toes. Her ears were ringing. Her breathing accelerated as she searched under the desk.

"What in the queen's crackers are you doing?"

Annie bounced back up and shuffled, pushed, flipped, shrieked, and hid her head in her arms. "Crap—where is it?"

"Did I just hear you on the phone with Mr. Thatch?"

"Yes." She stood to him.

Mr. Tiddle winced and tilted his head. "And?"

Annie paced her words and tried to breathe normally. "He's coming in fifteen minutes. He took the bait. Um, price."

Mr. Tiddle's eyes widened. "No."

"Yes."

"But?"

"But..." Annie had a sinking hunch and grabbed up her trash can with a squelching, "Varsha!"

Mr. Tiddle's voice cracked. "No way did you throw them out."

"It was a mistake!"

Annie took off in a run through the shop, dodging customers and hurdling over stepstools to burst out the back door. Varsha was midway through tossing bags into the dumpster when Annie dove in after them with a wailing, "Nooo!"

She found herself tilting half-in and half-out of the dumpster door.

"Damn. I'm stuck here." Annie struggled at the awkward angle of her stomach precariously balanced on the painful rim of the metal doorway. "My buttons must be caught. Varsha."

"What in the world are you doing, Annie? There aren't any raccoons in there to save."

"I'm not trying to save raccoons, Varsha. I'm trying to get the P.T. Barnum file you threw out from my trash can."

"Why would you throw that out?"

Annie allowed her body to slouch in deflation. "It must have fallen in there when you dumped all my papers onto the floor."

"Oh, no. Dude, I really dropped the gun, didn't I?"

"Ball, Varsha. You dropped the ball. If you dropped the gun, you'd better be running from someone."

Mr. Tiddle's voice echoed in vague overtones within the dumpster.

"I've got your Barnum file, Mr. Tiddle," Annie responded. "As soon as Varsha gets me a stepstool."

"Oh. Good idea," Varsha said. "Be right back."

Annie felt the blood rush to her head.

"You're fired," Mr. Tiddle said.

"What? You can't fire me," Annie sparred.

"Oh, yes I can."

"Oh, no you can't. I know things. This place will wilt faster than a titty sprayed with ice water. One call to the IRS. That's all I need."

Mr. Tiddle seethed. "Why do you always threaten me with that?"

"Because you always fall for it. And you know I can."

He mumbled a variety of flubs, flusters, and fidgeting verbalizations. "Just…get your ass in here and finish your job, will ya? And hurry it up."

"Wait. Mr. Tiddle? Can you pull me out?" Silence. "A little help here! Hello? Anybody?"

Annie reached into her back pocket for her phone. "OMG. OMG."

"Here we are," a husky voice behind her announced. "Patience with impatience at your cervix."

"Ahh!" she screeched.

Annie strained to look over her shoulder. A tall woman with pink lipstick and a long ponytail smiled at her. She wore a pink, blue, and white pride pin on the lapel of her leather jacket.

"Sorry. I thought you knew I was here."

"Fluff a duck. You look just like Eddie Izzard. That's pretty amazing, actually. How do you do that?"

Eddie flipped her long, blond hair over her shoulder. "So, we all met. No, wait. We hung out! Well, we just kinda stood near each other in a Tesco once, waiting for an avocado to ripen. There it goes. No. Not yet. Now. No, wait...ah. Ah. No. So, there we were. Collectively. As we are all part of a collective consciousness. In this roomy space. Not bumping into one another, just kind of enjoying our unique genius, admiring one another's brilliance. Oh, you look very nice today. Yes, thank you. You are glowing. Let's call it radiant. Yes. Fabulous idea. We became, like mold on bread. Beneficial universal breath. Not bad breath. Colorful. Like gas. Fun idea, we wanted to place ourselves in this form we mushed together called Humanity. A clump of meaningful expansion. Like spandex—in a relaxed, easy way, you see. But a vastly stretchier version. Like a turtleneck on a giraffe. Only bigger. A sieve of diversity."

"I—uh...cool?" Annie decided it was best to reach for the nearest bag and begin digging through it.

"And compost," Eddie continued. "Poo. Like grass and trees, and the creatures of the earth, and Aunt Selma's pot roast. Hula chairs, and spam email. Only, we didn't want to make it too easy to always get everything we wanted, exactly when we wanted it. Because that would be disastrous. Trust that. Oh, you. I really wanted a sheep with a beard to sing, 'The hills are alive with the sound of—' And be my chauffeur. I'll make millions on bottled diet water and Ford Pintos. Definitely something lost in translation there in that one. To get what you want before you croak? Delightful idea! Doesn't matter what you can imagine, we'll bring it. Humans really do look a little wilty after a hundred years. Nothing should last forever, we said. Except cockroaches. Yes. Let's make it a guessing game. Now, why did we want them? Ha. Yes, we forgot. Yet, humans, beautifully ripened, humans and plants and animals. Humans croak and compost. We thought, yes, this is it. This is great. We come and poo, and we turn to poo. You think humans will get it? Um—no. We actually answered ourselves before we could finish the question. No. So, here we are, answering questions about similar features."

Annie nodded blankly. "I'm glad I asked. Remind me later, okay?" She wiggled painfully. "Right now, I need you."

Eddie appeared inside the dumpster, up to her breasts with bags and boxes. "Results. Easy. Yes. Need help, dear?"

"Please," she squeaked.

In a blink, Annie was standing on her feet, outside the dumpster, with the file in her hand. "Oh. Golly. Shoo." She started flinging off brown residue from her shirt. "Thanks."

Eddie reached over and, with a deep pink fingernail, plucked a colorful blob off a button on Annie's shirt. She tasted it. "Mmm. Strawberry cream pie."

* * *

Annie slammed the door behind her as she bolted toward the front of the store. In the distance, near the counter, Annie spotted Mr. Tiddle with a customer she assumed was Mr. Thatch. Mr. Tiddle twisted his torso and glared at her with much insistence. His hand drew out behind him like a spy waiting for a delivery on a busy street corner.

A patron then entered the main aisle with a toddler, right in front of Annie as she charged forward. Annie came to a complete stop, faltering inches from the toddler, sweeping the file over the toddler and to Varsha's outstretched hand.

Varsha accomplished a perfect hand-off relay with nimble fingers, agile legs, and a most impressive and skillful slip into Mr. Tiddle's ready hand. Annie twirled around and walked her Olympic dash off in circles, hands to her hips. She was out of breath. She high-fived her new fairy godmother, finally understanding how those track and field folks felt winning the gold.

"Gold medal, Annie," Varsha said excitedly.

"That's what I was thinking."

They watched as Mr. Tiddle shook hands with Mr. Thatch and handed him a shop bag with the file.

"Hope he brushed the coffee grounds off them," Varsha said.

"Eh. Adds to the vintage look," Annie said. "Now, we just need six more purchases like that, and we'll be out of the red. Might even pay the store rent this month."

"How is he paying us?"

Annie shook her head. "Not our problem. As long as I get a paycheck, it's a happy day."

"Yeah. I suppose."

Mr. Tiddle danced his way down the aisle with wiggles and giggles. "Time to celebrate, ladies."

Annie turned and eyed his sashay and poor, nerdy disco moves before he twirled and dipped into his office.

"Does that mean I can leave early?" she asked.

He poked his head back out with a definitive, "No."

CHAPTER SEVENTEEN

It had been a strange, yet satisfying season. The summer had certainly created a stockpile of fragmented spiritual growth, like a squirrel headlong into its gathering of nuts. Even the times when she felt she was in the middle of the road in heavy traffic, it all seemed to work out to her favor. It always felt good to know life was unfolding, and all she had to do was appreciate the moment. There was, however, still that longing, a groping for something on the fringes of desire she couldn't quite let go of.

Catrin. Maybe it was her smile. Her eyes. The way she shied away from disclosing her pent-up secrets that Annie would have treasured and kept safe. Vulnerabilities. Insecurities. Fears. Everybody has them. Not everyone wants to trust they'd be safe in someone else's hands. Such fundamental aspects were certainly not foreign to Annie. *Maybe it's not about Catrin at all. Maybe it's more about trusting the universe has her back, and not worrying about the end results. Just focus on her desires and be happy things are always working out. Even when she's not seeing it.*

Annie looked across the counter at the Empire Café to watch Jimmie and Harry both dazzling customers with their artistry of frothy cappuccino creations. Harry was shaking his butt and humming along to a jazzy tune while in his zone of flowery swirls.

Annie glanced outside to see her brother, Scott, performing a street show with a couple friends. They were bringing in quite a few bystanders; including Annie's ole drinking buddy, Rita.

Scott was playing keyboard along to an electric bass player and drummer, with an elaborate tin can set up. The jazz was smooth and exciting and Rita was in her element.

Annie approached her. Rita was looking cleaned up and joyful.

"You're glowing, Rita," Annie praised.

Rita held a hand up to the heavens. "Clean and sober two months, six days, and twenty-two hours. Thank you, Jesus!"

Annie howled, picked her up, and twirled her about. "Damn! Oh, I'm so proud of you!"

Rita cackled with a richness Annie had never witnessed. So clear her eyes, beset with tears of happiness. Annie too wiped a wetness from her eyes.

"You inspired me, Annie," Rita admitted. "You really did."

The crowd applauded the band with cheers. When the band started to play "Blue Skies," Rita instantly started singing along. Scott nodded to Annie, handing her a microphone. At first, Rita waved her off with embarrassment. Annie pleaded, and won.

Eddie, Annie's fairy godmother, danced alongside her, as both swooned emotionally over Rita's smooth as butter vocals. Ella Fitzgerald, herself, would be pleased.

* * *

Two large bags of brewed coffee were awaiting delivery when Annie returned to the café.

Annie pulled on her jacket. "Hey, fellas, I'm going to take this delivery down. Be right back."

Annie enjoyed her walk past the colorful murals that covered the sides of buildings. Features, large and beautiful. Over forty such murals in the downtown area. A real treat for anyone wanting to embrace the extensive Cincinnati art community. A block down from the café was a political campaign office. The bustle of volunteers in full swing of their duties was quite a buzz. Almost as lively as the café on Saturday mornings. She hadn't taken two steps into the place before a host of drooling faces lurched in on her.

Annie stepped back with hands in the air to allow the swarm their prey. "Bonnie and Clydesdale?" she said.

"Here," a voice answered.

"There's two in there for you with a cake pop. Happy Birthday."

"Aww, cool. Thanks."

The crowd burst into various versions of congratulations and began singing "Happy Birthday," toasting with their respective cups of brews.

A beautiful red-headed woman gestured to Annie from an office doorway. Annie couldn't take her eyes off her gorgeous legs.

"Yowzah," Annie said as she made her way to her.

The woman smiled. "How much do I owe you for that?"

"Nothing. It's on us. He's a regular customer on our birthday list."

A hand grasped hold of Annie's jacket and forcefully pulled her within the office as the door closed behind her.

Fingers wrestled with Annie's bowtie as lips pressed against hers. As soon as she could come up for air, she blurted, "Wow. Are you sure you haven't mistaken me for someone else? Not that it matters at this point."

Hands groped down her slacks. "I just love tomboys. And tailored tweed. Good lord, you've got me wet already."

Annie's blood began to rush in every which direction as the whispers tingled her ear. She could feel her face flush with the next kiss. Her black frames tilted off one ear, and her toes seemed like they'd pop right out of their shoes.

"Gracious," Annie squeaked, sliding away from this delightfully possessive creature. "What, what do you guys do here?" One hand searched for the edge of the desk as she attempted to replace her glasses with the other.

Heels came off her seductress in a natural step, and the woman's insistent charm pushed Annie back over the desk as she stroked Annie's face and hair. Annie hadn't recalled such a limber pose since she attempted to limbo under the bamboo stick at Varsha's twenty-first birthday party.

"Well," the beauty breathed, "there's the campaign manager. Day-to-day operations. The finance director. The press secretary. Interactions with the media."

"I see. Is that you?"

She pursed her lips in a breathy, "No."

"No." Annie's vagina had never been so enlivened by the word no in her life.

"I'm the field director."

"Oh."

She slithered against Annie, arms on either side, her knee forcing Annie's legs apart. "I get the message out through direct…voter…contact."

Annie gulped as a hand grabbed hold of her crotch. "You, you must be very good at it." She then had a crazy idea. "Say. Would you like to go out to lunch?"

Just then, the woman's phone pinged. Her distraction was such that she stood and paced away from Annie with a huff, dashing her phone back down on the desk.

"Sorry. That was my partner. We've got plans."

"Okay, wait. What?"

The woman jutted out a hip. "That was a no."

Annie began to feel her legs again and stood. "Did I miss something? You were acting like you were single."

"I am."

"No. You just pointed out that you're with somebody."

"Oh, that."

"Yes, that."

"Never mind about that. Why not do Saturday?"

"Look," Annie said. "I'm sure for you, this is common behavior. But, I'd rather not. This is kind of a maladroit moment for me."

"Wait a minute. I thought we were having a thing here! I thought this was going to be meaningful or something."

Annie paused zipping her jacket. "You're with somebody."

"Not right now."

"Are you single?"

"No."

"Then, I can't do this."

The woman called after Annie as she left the office, "Wait. What about lunch?"

Once out on the sidewalk, Annie sucked in a big mouthful of air and bent over. "Oh, my God. My privates have never throbbed so much—ever!" She stood with hands on her hips. "Walk it off, Annie. Walk it off."

She hoped people didn't notice her waddling oddly back to the café.

* * *

Annie spent the next morning dancing with her fairy godmother and playing string games with Pork and Beans through the long hall.

Dressed for her café job, Annie shoved keys in her pocket and opened the front door. Mrs. Winkle stood before her, smiling sweetly.

Annie jumped back. "Geez'o, Mrs. Winkle. You startled me." She looked over her shoulder to see if Eddie was still there. Eddie sat on the floor playing with the cats. She still couldn't grasp the idea that her fairy godmothers were only visible to her and animals.

"Oh, I'm so sorry, dear." She looked down to a pie in her hands. "It's still warm. Your mother wanted the recipe. I thought I'd send you off with that and the pie."

Annie graciously accepted it from her. "Gosh, Mrs. Winkle. Thank you so much. Mom loves your blackberry pie. I do, too."

"Steal a piece for yourself, then." She winked.

"I'm so glad you're feeling better."

Mrs. Winkle nodded and led Annie down the steps to the driveway. "I'm allowing myself more pleasures. Nothing like a good near-death experience to jolt your old bones into living a bit more generously."

"I bet. I've recently had a few myself."

"I eat raw cookie dough now. And I put extra pickles on my chicken sandwich."

"Didn't I see you running through the sprinkler with Saqi and Bones yesterday?"

"Yep. And I didn't have a panty liner on, either."

"That's pretty bold."

Mrs. Winkle propped fists atop her hips. "It's a new chapter in my life, Annie. I can't wait for my skydiving lessons next week."

"Skydiving?"

"Why not?"

"Hey. Sure." Annie was impressed. "You can have anything your heart desires, Mrs. Winkle. I've learned that, too."

Mrs. Winkle waved her goodbye and headed for a beige sedan that pulled up. "See ya later. I've got a hot date for breakfast with the father of the fireman who rescued me." As she climbed in the car, Annie heard her say to him, "Come on, toots. Let's get high."

* * *

Annie spent a few minutes at the bar in the café learning more Italian phrases from her coworker Harry Leto. He was eating a piece of blackberry pie she gifted him.

"*Noi non po…*"

"*Potemo*," he said in between chews.

"*Noi non potemo avere perfetta vita senza amici*. We cannot have a perfect life without friends."

"Mmm," Harry muttered with a wink and a raised fork.

She toasted his fork with a cup of espresso, then sipped and held onto a thought. "Harry?"

His reply was a grunt as he scraped up the last of the berry off his plate.

"If you owned a café with a bookstore, what would you name it?"

"Coffee and books."

Annie sniffed. "As in, Caffè e Libri. I like your style, Harry. Simple and to the point."

* * *

Mr. Tiddle looked appalled at the fingerprints and smears on the store's door window. Annie entered the shop as he withdrew a handkerchief from his pocket and removed a book off a table by its cover like it was a used pair of dirty underwear. He slinked up to the front desk, looking like he was about to spit out a hairball before plopping it atop Annie's basket, labeled, "INtrude."

"When you have time, Miss Freckle, I'd appreciate if you or Varsha would do a little dusting and cleaning around here. And oh, what is that nasty smell? You aren't burning your candles around my books again, are you?"

"Might be leftover singed hair," Annie mumbled. She had better things to concentrate on.

"Miss Freckle. Did you hear me?"

He stirred uneasily behind her raised finger. "Let me finish this one sentence. I'm replying to someone's email. I've been dictating on my phone while driving."

"What do you want, a star?"

She tapped the send button. "I certainly thought you'd find an importance in this patron's interest. Hopefully, we'll get a sale from this."

He reached down and picked up the slip of paper she wrote her notes on. "Wilma Jekyll."

"Pronounced Jeekle. Like the British horticulturist and famed garden designer of the Victorian era."

"Who?"

"Aisle three, on your left. Just past Ponds and Roses. We have a generous selection, if you wish to study up."

"Never mind." Mr. Tiddle took a step toward his office. "As long as she buys something."

"It's the Darwin notebooks collection."

Mr. Tiddle choked on his sip of coffee and twisted about. A tremendous vein arose on his forehead before his face melted into something that was akin to baked custard. "What did you say?" Before Annie could spit the words out again, he nodded. "Yes, yes. But, when? When is she coming?"

"I only now sent her an acknowledgement about them. Saying, indeed we do still have them."

He pressed his chest against the counter. "Well, see if she has responded." His nose raised and his eyes squinted. "Strange smell. Don't you smell that? Is something burning?"

"It's probably the oils worn by the patrons back at the Retro Fiction/Sci Fi section."

"Oh, my God. You're kidding. We need to remove those… undesirables."

Annie began cleaning the book with a wet wipe he insistently waved at her. "Those undesirables are helping to pay your electric bill—not to mention the new box and wiring you so creatively destroyed recently. These clients are really cool. They just purchased a tiny, off-grid home in Adams County, and they want to fill an entire wall with dark academia books. You really should get to know your patrons better."

The two clients passed by the desk, and Annie observed the artistic, disheveled fashion of dreadlocks, drab and torn pants, and heaps of bracelets.

"They stink."

"They're wearing essence of eucalyptus and patchouli oil. The latter has an aroma that acts like an aphrodisiac."

"What could be so attractive about a distilled mushroom ninny eating legumes, grass seeds, and bird poop, while smelling like pond mucus?"

"Not everyone wants to smell like a Lysol swab dipped in nut rub and old socks." Annie made a face at him. "Your accountant is on line two. Something about the recent purchase of security wiring and camera in your office ceiling that you're attempting to get a refund on?"

He dodged her questioning eye through a few verbal expletives. "It's not a big deal."

"You had a fire, Tim. You blew the entire block. Thank God we were on generators."

"Thank God he had to pee," Varsha added with a repressed laugh.

Mr. Tiddle marched off. "I'll be in the back. No calls."

Varsha waited until he was out of whisper range. "I wouldn't be surprised if his conspiracy theories have leaked from the fire department to the FBI. Maybe they'll come by and check out his vacuum-sealed glass case."

"What vacuum-sealed glass case?"

"It's on top of his mini fridge. He has a grilled cheese sandwich, purchased on eBay, with images of Vladimir Putin and Pope Francis eating pickles together. There might be questions I have to answer. Like, why in the hell do I even work with this nut ball? And where does this kind of crap come from?"

Annie's eyes followed Varsha's gaze.

"Hey, Annie. Would you look at that pair of Americans, huh?" Varsha's head hit the window as she got closer to a passerby with cleavage as wide as the Ohio River. "Ow."

"I would follow only the low branches, hon. The higher ones would consume the eye too much for one not educated on their distractions."

"Distractions from what?"

"The lower ones, when they fall after forty years."

Varsha turned to Annie. "You think her perkies would give her a black eye when she runs?"

"Why don't you chase her and find out?"

Varsha dashed toward the front door before turning to Annie. "Eh, not on duty."

Varsha then pounced on Annie's desk, snatched a veggie chip from her bag, and leaned into her to peer at the computer screen.

"Whatcha doing?"

"I'm posting a pic of us and the book scarecrow on Yodel's social media page."

"What's his name?"

Annie leaned away from Varsha's chip breath. "He doesn't have a name."

"You should name him."

"I'll let you name him."

"Weedbutt."

"You had one job."

Annie hadn't paid much attention to her further joking. She was distracted by a fax that came through from Mr. Tiddle's attorney. She sat agog at the report.

Mr. Tiddle appeared from around an aisle. "Miss Freckle. Can you please bring a canister of clean wipes to the children's aisle? Those little bastards can't seem to keep their sticky-ass hands off the shelving. I swear, I'm going to have to restrict parents from bringing in food and drink."

"So says the penniless Philistine."

"I beg your pardon?"

She held up the paper. "It's official. You're a broke bunny."

A gentleman in a sleek suit and tie whisked into the shop and headed straight for Mr. Tiddle. "I'm sorry, Tim. I tried to hold the final paperwork off until next week when the bank manager went on vacation to Dollywood. But he wanted it finalized before the next batch of salt water taffy hit the streets."

"Oh, I love the root beer flavor," Varsha swooned.

"Shhh," said Annie. "Use your inside voice."

Mr. Tiddle's expression was not unlike one who had just lost their pet.

Annie's heart went out to him. "I'm sorry, Mr. Tiddle."

He stumbled after reading the papers of bankruptcy and eviction from his lawyer. "Give me a few moments to get used to this."

Annie whispered to Varsha, "He's looking very feral right now. What comes next could be very unpredictable."

"Should we put some treats out and leave him alone for a while?"

Annie nodded in agreement and handed her a snack bag of Goldfish.

The attorney departed, leaving Mr. Tiddle to drift aimlessly toward the window, fingers tasseling his hair.

"Oh, look at that. He's being drawn to the light. Just like your mother's rubber plant."

"Better water him."

They watched him as he plopped down on the window seat. Varsha sat a bottle of water and the Goldfish next to him and backed away slowly.

Annie crossed her arms in front of her. "I guess this is a bad time to mention to him our paychecks bounced too, huh?"

"Aw, man!" whined Varsha. "I was looking forward to climbing Adventure Dude's Slim Rock Wall."

* * *

Bones loved sticking her head out the car window and biting at the air. Saqi sat in Annie's unzipped daypack and hung out the other window with his goggles on. She took them to a nature preserve and let Saqi chase a few minnows in the creek while she and Bones reflected on the quiet bird songs together.

Annie held her phone up and took a selfie of her and Bones just as a text from her brother popped up.

Don't forget, the hospital social worker wants us to meet her in an hour and a half.

"Come on, kids. Looks like our fun is over."

* * *

Stomach groans and murmurs reminded Annie that the bowl of shredded wheat she ate three hours earlier didn't quite do the trick of keeping her appetite at bay. She pulled out her steampunk pocket watch from her olive vest just as her brother and the social worker walked in the office.

"Have a seat next to your sister, Scott," the social worker said, "and we'll get started."

"Look at you," Scott cooed. "You're dashing."

"Thanks," Annie said as she wiped dirt off her wingtip cognac oxfords. "Had time to change from trail gear into something more appropriate for the meeting with Mr. Tiddle's accountant today."

"Is that my tie?"

"Ex-tie. It was in your donation box."

"Looks better on you than it does on me."

Annie felt quite pleased with herself. "Starting a new trend. What do you think?"

"Suits you very well, actually."

The social worker sat before them with fingers entwined, waiting with silent, patient features.

Scott glanced to her. "Annie's job is closing shop after sixteen years."

"Oh," the woman said. "What sort of work do you do?"

"Accounts payable/receivable, inventory."

"Well, you might want to check out the hospital. We're always in need of such services. Could branch out into something else. You never know." The woman slid her a business card. "Just call the main number there."

Annie took the card and smiled politely. "Miss Dinklefrank. Thank you."

"Frunk," she corrected Annie. "It's Dinklefrunk."

"Oh. Sorry. Actually, I'm not too worried. I don't know why—I just feel good about the next chapter of my life."

"Well, that's a great way to be. Until the bills pile up. Unless, of course, you're interested in cosplay retail."

Her demeanor and tiny pursed lips reminded Annie of a teacher she once had in elementary school who visited her parents once a week, explaining how her lapse into 'boyhood' and scuffling with other kids was disturbing the natural order of society. The social worker even flipped through her clipboard with the same frail and distinct motion, like she was afraid she'd rip the pages if she moved too quickly. She scrutinized the documents carefully, slowly, as if she was determined to find the hidden language of the dissection of worms.

"Your father, on the other hand," Miss Dinklefrunk went on to explain, "is another story. Which is why we're all here today. Quite a handful, I see."

Scott leaned into her. "We paid for the broken cart. You saw that, right?"

Annie turned to him. "What broken cart?"

"I didn't want to bother you about that. When they brought him in last night, he was a little upset that no one was paying attention to him."

"Upset enough to break a cart."

Miss Dinklefrunk eyed the pages and raised her voice above the large lawn mower noise outside the large bay window. "Patient picked up a room chair and proceeded to slam it several times upon a nearby medical car, destroying the monitor and keyboard. Scattered three fully stocked drawers of medications and supplies, valued at one thousand three hundred and twenty-two dollars and fifty-six cents."

Annie had slid down in her chair, embarrassed.

"Not to mention ripping up bedsheets and blankets with a pocketknife."

Annie turned to her brother. "Was it his Army knife, the one with the crossed canons?"

"No," Scott replied. "It was from Grandpa's collection."

"Oh. The one with the thin blade?"

"The smaller one, I think."

A landscaper with a weed whacker distracted them from Miss Dinklefrunk's attention, as he stepped into the bush under the window and got stuck. The blurring noise was intense enough to make Miss Dinklefrunk press her fingers together and stare blankly into space.

The landscaper ducked something from a low hanging tree branch then jerked this way and that before leaping out and away from the shrub. He had stirred up a nest of hornets, swatting at them like he was practicing a new dance move.

Scott burst into laughter, smacking Annie's arm. "Did you see that? Oh, my God."

Now and again, the landscaper, along with a couple others, sped and flailed past the window, darting about the yard until finally dashing through the Doctors Only parking lot.

Miss Dinklefrunk had twisted about slightly to eye the incident before picking up the phone. "Yes," she said into the receiver. "This is Miss Dinklefrunk, in Social Services. Expect a visit from Ted in a few minutes. He found another hive. Yes. Better get the epinephrine ready. Thank you. You too."

Scott slumped in his chair and began to swallow his laughs. The more Annie suppressed hers, the more tears she had to wipe away.

"That was great," Scott sighed, wiping his tears. "I needed that."

Silence returned after a moment. Miss Dinklefrunk tipped her head and cleared her throat. "Good? Are we good?"

Annie and her brother nodded in unison.

Adjusting her readers, Miss Dinklefrunk pulled a tea bag out of her cup and sipped the tea without taking her eyes off the pages. "Mr. Freckle then continued—"

"Colonel," Scott corrected her.

The woman removed her readers and, with a daft stare, rested an elbow on the desk.

Annie nodded. "He really likes being called Colonel. Since he served."

"Yeah. He earned it," Scott added.

The woman paused before waving her hand in acknowledgment. "Yeah. Sure."

She reached for an elaborately decorated wooden box on the side of her desk, and dug around for a pencil of her liking, even though they all were No. 2 pencils. Placing the pencil in a sharpener with one hand, she took a sip of tea with the other. After a length of time of listening to the grinding, she pulled the pencil out and wrote the word "Colonel" in teeny, precise print above the name. She then looked to Annie and Scott. "Good? Are we good?"

Annie and Scott nodded in unison.

The woman took a slow, deep breath and placed hands on either side of the documents. "Okay. Colonel Freckle. Colonel?"

Annie nodded. "Yes."

"Good. Colonel Freckle then continued," she read, "in a wheelchair, threatening staff and visitors in several halls, two elevators, and one closet."

"A closet?" Annie asked.

"A nurse and staff member, whose names will remain undisclosed. Separate issue," the woman hissed, and sipped her tea."

Scott added, "Apparently, by the time hospital security found Dad, he was enjoying a Coke and hot dog in the cafeteria with another war veteran, bonding over memories of wearing snowshoes while having sex with Korean hotties in army pup tents."

"Go, Dad," Annie exclaimed.

Miss Dinklefrunk sat wide-eyed and tittered in reply. "Okay. Which brings us to why we must insist on his transfer to a facility with 'round-the-clock care. Papers here, signed by his physician."

Annie balked. "Good luck convincing him of that."

"We didn't have to."

Scott jumped in. "Yeah. Apparently, the other veteran convinced Dad the facility where his wife was in had several ladies delightful to gawk at on third shift who could resurrect any mummified male package. Even if it hasn't seen the light of day since 1984."

"If I had known a chat about sex would've tugged his interest, I would have long ago placed boobs and butts all the way to the facility like breadcrumbs," Annie said.

Miss Dinklefrunk stood, and Annie followed suit. "Because of your father's slight behavioral issues, we can suggest a few different facilities, if you both are open to the idea."

"Didn't you do a psychological screening on him?"

"Yes."

"He clearly has dementia."

Miss Dinklefrunk tipped her head and frowned. “No. He doesn’t.”

“After six times, maybe more, he’s been here acting out. You just told us of his most recent escapade. You can’t tell me there isn’t something very wrong with him. He’s not the Dad we know.”

“There was nothing in my test to suggest he wasn’t sound of mind. He answered all my questions promptly. He really has a great memory of names and years, doesn’t he?”

“You caught him on a good day,” Annie grumbled. “The other day, he thought I was his sister.”

“He’s losing it,” Scott inserted.

Miss Dinklefrunk shifted her weight. “See, here’s the thing. We don’t really have a way of pinpointing the moment someone actually has Alzheimer’s or dementia until the patterns are consistent. I’m afraid your father is in, quite possibly, the early stages. But I can’t sign off on that.” She walked them to the door. “Good luck with all this. I do hope, with time, you’ll help him come to the right decision.”

* * *

In the hospital parking lot, Scott walked Annie to her car. “I appreciate you coming,” he said.

“Hey. Dad has desperately needed help. I really can’t believe no one would sign off on how crazy he’s become. Of all folks, the medical community should know better. I just hope that Dad stays on course and doesn’t back out.”

“Dad did ask me to find a home for Gunny.”

“You’re kidding?”

“No. Look.” He held his phone up to her. “I found a farmer with six kids happy to take him in.” Scott showed Annie a five second video sent to him from the farmer, with the kids yelling and jumping.

“Hopefully, he’s still trainable.”

Scott exaggerated a whole-body sigh. “I hope so. All he needs is love and tons of play.”

Annie halted in thought. "I think dad deserves a big Bob Evans breakfast plate with a sausage gravy and biscuit to go."

Scott drew an arm before her. "Operation Butter-Up to commence."

"We'd better stop off and buy him more porn magazines and Diet Mountain Dew. Just for added ammunition."

"Oh, great idea. Vanessa and I are in need of a few more sex toys, anyway."

Annie squelched and slapped him in the arm.

"Don't knock it till you try it," he laughed.

Annie plugged her ears and sang, "Oh, what a beautiful morning. Oh, what a beautiful day."

"I've got a beautiful feeling," they sang in unison. "Everything's going my way."

* * *

The Szechuan chicken in Annie's take-out bag smelled really good. She could hardly wait to get to Yodel's and dig in. The early autumn breeze kicked leaves from the street about her feet in tiny tornadoes. She was so enamored by their dances she almost walked right by Eddie, her fairy godmother.

"Hi. What are you doing here?"

"I'm here delivering your rightly timed manifestation." Eddie waved a hand toward a postal carrier's vehicle in front of Yodel's.

Annie stepped back. "No. Tell me that's Flapjack, back from his Puerto Rico vacation."

"Why would Catrin be Jack? That's silly. You weren't thinking of Jack all this time, were you?" Eddie held up her phone and plugged away at a few searches. "No. No, you were definitely thinking of Catrin."

"No. No. I was trying not to think about Catrin."

"Ah, well. You see, thinking about not thinking about her tossed her into the stream. Ah, look. There she goes. Into the stream. No, wait. Out of the stream. No, there she goes, back into the stream. Check this out," she said, holding her phone up. "I've got a live feed of your mind. Heh. Look, there she is! Don't want this, don't want this, don't want this. Not wanting to think about this, and aaaahhhh—there's a bombshell redhead, sex goddess. Similar. Yeah, not so. But maybe we wanted similar. Go for it baby. Noooo. Screech. Halt. Yeah, no. Good timing about Daddy, feeling good now. Oh, what a beautiful feeling. Oh, what a beautiful day," Eddie sang. "But look. There's more. Look. Life stream is flowing, flowing. Szechuan. Yum. Stream flowing. Feeling great. Pretty dead leaves. Not wanna think about her—now you're thinking about her. Not wanting to. Wanting to. It's great. Flowing, flowing. Happy day. And here we are."

Annie deflated. "Sorry I asked."

Eddie jumped at her excitedly. "No, no, no, no. Trust me. This'll be good. Excellent! You've been wanting this, right? Well, ta-dah!"

It took a moment to admit it. It took seeing Catrin depart Yodel's and climb into her vehicle. She sat there, filing through a tote. Annie could feel blood rush to her cheeks. She looked back at Eddie and steeled herself, flapping away her prodding. But her confidence faded the closer she walked toward Catrin. Just as she redirected her steps toward the bookstore, she heard Catrin's voice call out to her.

"Annie."

Annie pivoted to face her. "Hey."

Catrin climbed out of the vehicle and approached her, almost hesitantly. "Hey."

They both stood there, staring at each other for what felt like a long time.

"How are you?" Catrin asked.

Annie dropped her eye contact and nodded. "Doing well, actually."

"Yeah? Good. Me too."

"Good to know." Annie turned back to Yodel's door. "Was there any mail for you? I'll check."

A hand reached out and stopped her.

"Annie. Please. We need to talk."

Annie spun around to Catrin slowly and backed up against the brick wall. Her gut became a jumble of undescriptive agitations.

"I owe you an apology."

Annie shook her head. "Catrin."

"No. Really, I do. A really big amend."

Annie looked at her. "Amend."

"Yeah. See, I live an honest program today. And that night at the party…with you—and my stupid head. I wasn't acting in the most respecting of ways. I wasn't being honest with you. And I wasn't being honest with myself. Trying to be someone I wasn't."

After such verbiage, it suddenly dawned on Annie. "You're in Recovery."

Catrin's shoulders dropped. "Y-yes." She settled into an awkward stance.

"Hey," she said, trying to get Catrin to look at her again. "It's okay. I am too."

Catrin's grimace eased. "Really?"

Annie smiled. "Seven years, now."

"Wow. Good for you. Five." Catrin then held herself taller. "Look. That night, I don't know what I was thinking. I really wanted you to come. But I didn't want to you to feel like it pit you and Sabrina…"

"I get it. You played me. Consciously or subconsciously, you kind of used me to gauge your feelings. Am I right?"

"You're absolutely right. Stupid."

"Yes. It was. And hurtful."

Catrin waited for a couple to pass them before continuing, "I never wanted that to happen."

Annie shifted her weight. "What did you think would happen?"

"I don't know. I never expected to feel…to watch my heart walk away with you."

Annie felt her defensiveness begin to melt. The look in Catrin's eyes was complete sincerity. "I'm sorry. What?"

"You looked so damned cute in that hat and outfit. You make me smile every time I see you. And this, now. Look at you, so dapper. Annie, you've been the most wonderful person to hang out with. You have such a kind heart; you care about animals and elders. You're funny. Respectful."

Varsha popped her head out the door and interjected, "She's all that and fries too. I can put her on a bun for you, to make it a complete meal."

Annie turned to her. "Do you mind?"

"Can I have my sweet and sour soup?" Varsha said.

Annie thrust the bag at her and closed the door.

"I was a jerk," Catrin said. "Dating a jerk—she barely ever talked to me, and I barely ever felt like we were even a couple, but I didn't know how to break up with her, so I just...didn't."

"Catrin, you're so much better than that."

Catrin raised her eyes to the sky. "What I'm trying to say is that I really screwed up. I've been feeling it for days. Feeling like I may have lost the one good person in my life that really liked me for me."

Annie wrinkled her brow. "I've never seen anyone in you, but you. A beautiful, perfectly imperfect human being. Catrin, I'm a normal, everyday, white-bread human being too, with a crap ton of quirks and falterings just like you. Fears. Angst. Judgements. And a whole basket of insecurities. I have fairy godmothers starting a union all because of me, for God's sake. I'm a handful."

"But she can cook a mean meatloaf and sing and play the ukulele," Varsha added.

"Go. Shoo." Annie pushed her back inside and closed the door again.

Catrin grinned.

"I'm a mess," Annie admitted. "Don't let this fashion fool you. I know. I may look pretty studly right now. Witty. Brilliant. A genius in embryo, really." Annie grinned. "Underneath it all, I'm still—a messy, sloppy, chicken pot pie."

"So am I," admitted Catrin. "Annie. Please. I'd really love to start over."

Annie shoved her hands in her pockets. "Depends. Are you still with Whatsername?"

Catrin sucked her lips in and shook her head. "I'm officially single. And available."

Annie straightened up and ran her fingers through her hair. Not so long ago, she wouldn't have taken the risk. And, there was no denying that lately, she had to admit, passions had driven her down an unknown road. Choices like this either limit the person or redefine them.

"You know," Annie said. "I have to be honest. It's been really hard not to think of you. And yet, I often found myself thinking about not wanting to think about you. Not notting like I've never not notted before. So, maybe it was a good thing that we caught up. You know, to air things out. It was good seeing you."

Varsha popped her head out the door again. "Psst. Annie. You're kinda needed in here. Sorry, Catrin."

Catrin's eyes deepened.

"Gotta go." Annie turned away from her and grabbed hold of the opened door. She stopped. "Dammit, Catrin. I don't know."

Annie turned around, right into Catrin's kiss. Catrin held Annie's face between her warm hands and lingered for what seemed a dreamy length of time. Annie's senses went aflutter, swimming in the basking of limitless space. Afterward, Annie opened her eyes to see Catrin before her.

"Can you say that again?" Annie murmured. "I didn't quite hear you."

An extended kiss drew Annie to embrace Catrin with a longing she had never experienced.

"That was very nice of you." Annie didn't know where that came from.

Catrin brushed a hand on her tweed vest. "You should go. I've taken up quite a lot of your time."

"Oh, I don't know." Annie tugged at Catrin's pinky. "I might need a little more convincing."

Catrin's smile lit up. "How about a picnic? Say, Friday?"

"Sounds fun."

Catrin stepped away. "I'll text you."

Annie nodded and watched her climb back into her truck. Varsha skipped alongside Annie as she floated into Yodel's.

"Oh, my God, Annie. This is so sweet," she squeaked. "Now, take it easy. This is where breathing starts."

"Uh-huh." Annie felt a numbing bliss. Nothing mattered. Nothing could replace the high she was on. Her fingers danced willy-nilly above her like sparkles. "Smooth jazz."

Varsha assisted Annie to her desk. "Here. You'd better sit down. I'll get you some water."

"Uh-huh."

"Are you with me?"

"Uh-huh."

"Whoa, dude," Varsha said. "She nailed you good."

Annie tried to focus on Varsha's face. "Hmm."

Varsha dug around her backpack and pulled out a bottle of water. She wrapped Annie's fingers around it and helped bring it to her lips. "This is so crazy. I have never seen you like this before."

A cluster of people started chattering indistinctly down the main aisle, and Annie couldn't quite make out what they said. Varsha was rubbing her back.

"Come on. Take another drink. Quick. Mrs. Proust is coming. Shake it off. Shake it off."

Annie suddenly awoke from her state of inebriated inertia. "Proust. Did you say Proust?"

"Yeah, dude. That's what I've trying to tell you. This is big news! Mrs. Proust and her legal team have been in a meeting with Mr. Tiddle and his accountant. I think she wants to buy Yodel's."

Annie shot out of her seat, buttoning up her vest and straightening up her hair. "Crap. Tell me you're not making this up, Varsha."

"Scout's honor."

She made a face to Varsha's Spock hand salute and refashioned her fingers into a three finger sign. Annie straightened her vest. And ran a hand over her hair. "How do I look?"

"Like a winner." Varsha dashed around to Annie's side. "You think Mr. Tiddle kept his shop?"

"Just the thought of that hideous notion gives me PTSD."

Men and women in sharp suits and pencil skirts flocked past Annie so quickly, she couldn't tell who was wearing what. She greeted Mrs. Proust's approach to the counter with what she hoped wasn't too fake of a smile.

Mrs. Proust laid a firm hand atop the counter. "Mr. Piddle tells me you have a prospective buyer for my husband's Darwin notebooks collection."

Annie's mind was still reeling from Catrin. "Uh. Yeah. Yes. Yes, we do. Very interested, you'll be glad to know, Mrs. Proust."

"Tell you what. Why don't you and Varsha split the money? As a sort of bonus."

"Excuse me?"

"Sweet." Varsha beamed.

Mrs. Proust raised her head and looked down her nose at Annie with the pride of a mother bear. "You, my dear, are looking at the new owner of Yodel's. I've had my team keeping a watchful eye out on this treasure for quite some time now. We were just waiting for the right moment."

Mr. Tiddle waggled a finger to everyone as he stood at the door with his attorney. "When the smoke clears from this Pompeiian eruption, I just want to make it clear that my offer and opinion was rejected. So screw y'all. Next time you're out in the open air and you see bubbles, that was me. I'm now following my bliss."

"He wouldn't be caught dead in the open air," Varsha said, "without his inhaler, pack of antacids, snake boots, and a bulletproof vest with pockets stuffed with Viennese sausages."

"You wanna know what's in those things?"

"No, dude. Really." Varsha waved to Mr. Tiddle as he passed the window. "Good luck, Timmy!"

Annie felt a little abandoned. She turned back to Mrs. Proust, spiritually deflated. "I'm not sure to feel relief or sadness. At any rate, congratulations are in order for you, ma'am. Just give me the word, and I'll start packing up." She began looking around for an empty box. "Only a few candles, hand sanitizer, pens." She waved a rainbow flag. "And such. It won't take me long."

"Wait." Mrs. Proust had guided herself around the counter with a cane in one hand, laying the other on Annie's to halt her. "I'll need a store manager. I've been watching you."

"That's creepy."

"Nothing to be offended by. But a person in my standing can't be too careful."

"I see. Yes, of course."

Mrs. Proust lowered herself into a seat next to Annie's and gestured she sit. "Generations of woman have launched themselves into this world with dreams and desires of success, and I am very impressed to see that you are no less ambitious. And many have strived in vain to find a substitute worthy of self-value. I'm saying we women owe ourselves the right to independence. Don't ever suffer yourself less than you are worth, my dear. You are a career woman, yes?"

"I believe so. Yes."

"You will learn that there are weaknesses men have, still, within their preconceived ideals of what a woman should do and how she should perform in society. All are completely unknown to even themselves. Such behaviors are trained into their brains. They are a privileged lot. Not their fault. Each generation is better than the last, of course. Yet, we've a long way to go, I think. At any rate, all I'm saying is that you should never lower your standards to who you strive to be."

"I have a lot of sheroes I look up to," Annie announced "Many courageous women."

"Schopenhauer once said that courage is merely the virtue of a second lieutenant." Mrs. Proust stood. "It is not courage that will help women excel, Annie. It is being true to our own dreams. I can see you've never doubted that power."

Annie stuck her bottom lip out. "Appearances can be deceiving, Mrs. Proust. But…I am learning to trust myself." Annie leaned a hand on her desk and another on her hip. "Forgive me. I'm confused that all this is coming from a woman who sold Mr. Tiddle the Darwin notebooks collection with tears and stories."

Mrs. Proust rolled her shoulders and tilted a head with a wry smile.

"Wait." Annie looked at her askance. "That was all made up?"

The woman returned with a giggle and wiggle akin to a teenager.

"Mrs. Proust," Varsha yawled. "A stellar Oscar performance, that was."

"I was a very young stage actress back in the day when Mr. Proust's eye caught mine. I always wanted to play a role fit for the big screen. And, by God, I gave it my best, didn't I?"

They laughed together.

"Wow," Annie said. "And the handkerchief thing?"

Mrs. Proust leaned closer and whispered, "Sixty-nine cents at the St. Vincent's thrift store." She began to drift away from the counter.

Annie followed her toward the door.

"I've never forgotten my roots," Mrs. Proust added. "I tend to appreciate women like yourself who are trying to make a difference in people's lives, as well as your own. Now, it's my turn." She faced Annie. "My offer to you is fifty thousand, to start. With incentives, of course."

Annie was glad she had a hand on the doorknob when her body drew limp. "Fifty?"

"Oh, all right. Sixty. You have me in a generous mood. That should also cover any politician's legislation in the wonkery workings of being self-insured."

When she was able to speak, Annie burbled, "Mrs. Proust. I don't know what to say."

"You say yes, dear."

"Yes. Yes. I would like that very much."

"Good. I'll have my team draft up a contract. Oh," she chirped with a spin. "And I do like that vintage fashion you're wearing. I'll send you and Varsha to my tailor. What do you think of knickers?"

Annie beamed. "Oh, I've been wanting those!"

"Good. Then, we'll have all the employees wearing Edwardian era fashions as our code of dress. Won't that be fun?"

Annie's head spun with new and delicious ideas and visions.

Mrs. Proust drifted around the place, eyeing the old, plain bookshelves. "This place will get a whole new look. Yes. Thick walnut stained shelving with dandy molding. A fireplace over there with several distressed leather chairs. Paintings by local artists. What do you think of making this a coffee bar and bookstore?"

Annie couldn't help but feel giddy inside. "Oh, my God, Mrs. Proust. I've had that vision for such a long time. I really think it would bring an added boost to Hyde Park."

"Agreed. Any ideas what we should call it?"

"As a matter of fact, I do have a suggestion. And I have the perfect person to operate the coffee bar."

Mrs. Proust smiled. "Good. Send that to me, and any other ideas you've had in that creative brain of yours."

Annie followed Mrs. Proust's glance to Varsha.

"And you, young lady," she said.

"Me?" Varsha said.

"I'm certain Mr. Piddle has you on some lowly bent-penny amount. We'll put you on salary too."

"She's very good, actually, at inventory and aisle design," Annie interjected. "I've seen her artwork. She can do murals, if you wish, here and there on sandwich boards."

"Excellent. Assistant Manager's wages for you. Thirty thousand? And I'll hire a few assistants for each of you. Oh, this is so exciting, isn't it? Okay, ladies. There's much to do. Save your energy. I'm going to make you earn those paychecks."

Varsha slid up to Annie's side with enthusiasm. "We are going to make you so proud, Mrs. Proust."

"You already have."

With a wink, she was gone. Annie quietly closed the door behind her leave, then joined Varsha in her screaming and dancing in jiggles, shimmies, and twists.

* * *

Mid-December was full of construction workers, bustling directives, and gently falling snow. Varsha looked impressive with gentlemen following her about as she pointed to her sketches from a clipboard, while Harry Leto grumbled to plumbers and electricians to bring his design of the coffee bar up to vision. Annie couldn't have been more pleased to see her own dream unfold. She had always loved the bookstore. Any bookstore, for that matter. Now, she had a more defined reason to enjoy its comforts. The Classics section was a much larger design, wrapping around a cozy limestone fireplace. The whole place was more spacious, as Mrs. Proust had purchased the two stories above the shop to extend its treasures and to lease out office space.

Annie ducked under the heavy, half-installed Art Deco doorway, brushing the drift of sawdust off her colorful fair isle sweater. She wanted to watch as they raised the new sign into place. Caffè e Libri was already being advertised as a hot spot, with folks all over Cincinnati touting it as the next popular beat on the rhythmic trail of the Queen City's heartbeat. No doubt because Mrs. Proust owned one of the largest advertising agencies in the Tristate. Annie knew that, with her at the helm, Caffè e Libri was going to be around for a very long time.

Catrin appeared from around the corner with a four pack of coffee.

"Yay," Annie cheered. "Thank you."

Catrin handed her a coffee and kissed her. "Mmm. You smell good."

Annie placed the cup to her lips. "Cashmere and snowflakes."

They entered the store together, dodging the carpenters and greeting the happy faces of Harry and Varsha.

"Got a postcard from Mr. Tiddle," Varsha said, handing Annie the card.

Annie stared at a colorful scene of a beach. "Mexico. Imagine that."

Catrin eased her head closer. "What does he say?"

Annie flipped the card over. "'Enjoy your cold toes.'"

"Very sweet of him. Don'tcha think?" Varsha said.

"Considering it all, he wasn't that bad of a boss, you know," Annie mused. "He just didn't manage himself very well." She handed Varsha a tiny brass bell. “Here. Tell the fellas to hang Mr. Tiddle’s bell back up above the door, will you? So that I can be reminded when I’m not managing myself very well.”

Annie’s office was spacious enough to feel important. Yet, small enough to keep all her essentials in their vital places. Annie led Catrin in and posed with arms wide. Antique desk with brass lamp, vintage wallpaper and drapes, and a large vintage map of Cincinnati decorated the space.

“Mom helped me shop with the bonus I received.”

“Very Churchill chic. And perfectly you.”

Annie pinned the postcard to the board by her desk. “You’re biased.”

“Maybe.”

Annie took a sip of coffee and felt a drip run down her jaw, then wiped it off with a flustered gulp. “If I only had a brain.”

Catrin stepped up closer to assist, then started fiddling with a button on Annie’s shirt. “Your straw is showing, scarecrow.”

Annie loved the scent of Catrin. “What do you see in me, anyway?”

“Hmm. A different part of myself that I haven’t been in touch with, I suppose.”

“Like food poisoning, or cavities. I bet I was a dare.”

Catrin slapped her in the arm. “No one had to dare me. You’ve been a delicious continuance of something I must have tasted once in a previous lifetime.”

Annie picked up a tiny pink tutu left hanging on her doorknob and grinned to herself. She turned to Catrin and dangled it. “Possible. Maybe it’s a kind of magic.” She tacked it up on her board.

“I like the little promise you made. Not forever, not always. Not even next week.”

“Just today,” Annie added. “No remorse of the past. Forward thinking. Makes it easier, and a lot more fun. And if one of us decides one day someone else suits our fancy, or no one, I’m totally cool with that.”

“So am I.”

Catrin had that twinkle in her eye that Annie knew harbored a bit of orneriness. Annie allowed herself to be pulled by her tie and met Catrin's lips for a welcome start to the day.

"And yet, I can't imagine myself behaving in any other way around you," Annie admitted.

A soft kiss replied.

Catrin pulled away with a murmur. "Is that such a bad thing?"

"Hmm." Annie shook her head slowly. "Self will run riot, if only towards you at full gallop through a meadow. Promise to pick me up if I fall face-first with a twisted ankle?"

Catrin held Annie's face and kissed her again. "Let's cause a disturbance."

"It's a task that might take an absorbent amount of time, I'm afraid."

"Do it for your country, woman."

Annie caught the lineup of fairy godmothers outside the office window, all looking joyous in her delight. She smiled back and rolled the blinds down as Catrin started to pull her toward the floor.

"Oh, I love being patriotic."

Bella Books, Inc.

Women. Books. Even Better Together.

P.O. Box 10543
Tallahassee, FL 32302

Phone: 800-729-4992
www.bellabooks.com

CPSIA information can be obtained
at www.ICGtesting.com
Printed in the USA
JSHW032236290622
27466JS00001B/2

9 781642 473957